THE USBORNE BOOK OF CLASSIC HORROR

Frankenstein   3

Dracula   145

Jekyll & Hyde   289

First published in 2003 by Usborne Publishing Ltd,
Usborne House, 83-85 Saffron Hill, London
EC1N 8RT, England.
www.usborne.com

U.E. First published in America 2003

A catalogue record for this title is available from
the British Library

ISBN 07460 5846 2

Printed in Great Britain

Edited by Felicity Brooks & Anthony Marks
Designed by Glen Bird and Brian Voakes
Cover designed by Glen Bird
Cover image by Barry Jones
Series editors: Jane Chisholm & Rosie Dickins
Series designer: Mary Cartwright

FRANKENSTEIN

FROM THE STORY BY MARY SHELLEY

Retold by John Grant
With an introduction and notes by Anthony Marks
Illustrations by Barry Jones

CONTENTS

About Frankenstein   7

Icebound   10

To Create Life   17

Fever   39

Death in Geneva   51

On Montanvert   67

The Monster's Tale   79

The Bride   101

Wedding Night   119

Among the Snows   134

Other Versions of the
Frankenstein Story   141

About Frankenstein

The author of *Frankenstein*, Mary Wollstonecraft Godwin (later Mary Shelley), was the daughter of two English writers. In 1814, at the age of 16, she eloped with the poet Percy Bysshe Shelley, whom she later married. They journeyed through France and Italy, and in 1816 settled near Geneva, Switzerland. Her step-sister Claire also lived with them, and the poet Byron lived nearby. Mary Shelley later described that period as "a wet, ungenial summer" and wrote that because of the endless rain, they were often unable to leave the house for several days. To amuse themselves, they read to each other from books of French and German ghost stories until, one day, Byron suggested that they each write a ghost story instead. While the others quickly gave up, Mary Shelley persisted. She later developed her story into the novel *Frankenstein*, which was published in 1818 when she was just 21 years old. It was an instant success, and is now one of the most famous novels ever written in the English language.

In her introduction to a new edition of the novel in 1831, Mary Shelley described how the idea for the story came to her one night as she lay in bed. She had spent the evening discussing current developments in science and philosophy with Shelley and Byron. (This was an age of rapid scientific discovery, and they were well aware of, for example, Volta's and Galvani's experiments with electricity, as well as the work of Humphry Davy on oxygen.) They were considering how electricity could be used to reanimate a corpse, or the possibility of creating a living being out of dead body parts. These ideas took hold in her imagination in the form of Victor Frankenstein.

In the original publication, *Frankenstein* has a subtitle: "The Modern Prometheus". This refers to an ancient Greek myth about Prometheus, a man who brought fire from the realm of the gods to humans on earth. A lesser-known version of the myth refers to Prometheus creating human life out of a clay model. This myth is also referred to in poetry written by Shelley and Byron written around this time. Mary Shelley's creation is a modern fusion of these two myths, for Victor Frankenstein uses electricity to animate human flesh. And like the ancient Prometheus, who was punished by the gods for his arrogance, Frankenstein lived to regret his deeds.

Frankenstein has fascinated readers for nearly two centuries. There are several reasons for this. Firstly, while it is horrific, it is not just a horror story. It also asks questions about the purpose of science and the responsibilities of scientists. The author seems to find the power to create life exciting and terrifying at the same time: Victor is both fascinated and repelled by what he has done. Secondly, the book asks whether people are born good, evil or neutral. (This was a popular philosophical question at the time the book was written and it continues to provoke discussion today.) Frankenstein's monster cannot tell good from evil, but he learns to become evil because he is badly treated, first by Frankenstein himself, then by other people in society. But as his understanding grows, the monster learns that evil is wrong. This is a third strand of the book, which deals with the power of learning and education.

Frankenstein provoked very strong reactions. For example William Beckford, himself a writer of horror and fantasy books, called it "the foulest Toadstool that has yet sprung up from the reeking dunghill of the present times". But these reactions only contributed to the book's fame. Mary Shelley was also surprised and slightly scared by the success of her book. She likened her "creation" to Frankenstein's monster, but unlike Victor, she was happy to wish it well. In her introduction to the 1931 edition she wrote, "I bid my hideous progeny go forth and prosper". Her inspiration ensured that people would keep returning to her work again and again, to be both frightened and fascinated.

Icebound

High above the Arctic Circle, in the Land of the Midnight Sun, Captain Walton, polar explorer, peered through the steam of his breath at the thin channel of black water ahead of him. Shivering, he pulled the thick hood of his fur overcoat closer around his head and stamped his feet on the deck. Then he squinted for the thousandth time at the orange sun, low in the sky. He looked back to the channel: narrow as it was, it seemed to get even narrower in the distance. Then another gust of fog swept across his gaze, and behind it came billows of snow. What had been a sort of twilight deepened into a misty darkness.

Reluctantly, he turned to his first mate, Rostop.

"We'll have to lay anchor," he said. "Give the command to the men. We can't continue in these conditions." The huge man looked equally reluctant, but after a moment shrugged philosophically.

"Yes, Cap'n," he said.

For many weeks now Walton's little ship, the *Margaret Saville*, had been working its way through the unexplored polar wastes, heading for the North Pole. Much of the time had been spent in perpetual dusk, but in another few weeks a six-month darkness would fall.

Walton shivered again. Perhaps they had enough food and fuel aboard to survive the winter months should they be caught in the ice, but he was uncertain. Though his every instinct cried out against it, he knew that if the weather got worse he would have to turn the *Margaret Saville* around and head south. Maybe he could mount another expedition next year, but he doubted whether he had the funds to finance it. He crossed his fingers and stared out into the fog and swirling snow, praying that they would disappear as quickly as they had descended on the little vessel.

Rostop turned away, then paused.

"Hear that, Cap'n?" he said.

"Hear what?" Rostop gestured vaguely at the

white blankness surrounding them.

"Out there," he said. "Bells. Dogs."

Walton listened carefully. At first he could detect nothing, but after a while a muffled sound began to reach his ears. Just at that moment an eddy of the whistling wind cleared the mist and snow away, and far in the distance he could see a black shape moving swiftly against the white plains of ice.

"Quick, Rostop!" he snapped. "Pass me the telescope!"

With the telescope to his eye he could make out a sled being pulled rapidly across the ice by a team of huskies. As the driver raised his whip to encourage the dogs to go even faster, Walton's attention was drawn to him.

"A giant," he breathed. "Even bigger than you are, Rostop. Here, take a look." He passed over the telescope and wiped the back of his glove across his beard, trying to clear it of ice. After a moment the first mate hissed, but made no further comment.

"Let's hope there aren't too many more of those roaming the polar wastes," said Walton, trying to sound nonchalant. "We'll be in for a fine time if there are, eh, Rostop?"

"He'd have us for dinner," said the mate.

The fog and the blizzard returned and, after the ship had been firmly secured to the ice, Walton ordered rum to be brought out to go with their supper. When he and the crew had eaten, they retired to their bunks, hearing the creaking of the ice all around as they tried to sleep.

Walton awoke to the sound of shouting voices. While groping around for his clothes, he tried to make sense of what was being said. But it was only when he came up on deck that he could make out some of the words. Two or three of his crew were leaning over the rails, calling. He hurried forward to join them. At last the storm had abated, and the ice had broken away from around the *Margaret Saville*. The ship, still moored to the ice, was bobbing in the water. As Walton had slept, the ice had ripped itself apart. The far shore seemed distant.

Between the ship and the shore, however, there was a floating island of ice. On it there was a man with a dog sled, looking in the direction of the ship and waving his hands above his head. Around him lay the stiffened bodies of the dogs of his team; only one still seemed to be alive. For a moment the captain thought this must be the giant he had seen through the telescope the night before, but then he realized it was merely a normal man. He was shouting in a language Walton did not understand.

"What's he saying?" Walton asked the crewman next to him. "Do you know?"

"He wants to know whether we are bound north or south."

"With the weather like this," said Walton, "I hardly care to guess. But I want to continue heading north. Tell him that."

The crewman cupped his hands to his mouth and bellowed out some staccato syllables which Walton vaguely recognized as German. But he understood the distant figure's reply pefectly. For this time he spoke in English, though with a curious inflection.

"Your captain," the stranger shouted across the ice, "he is English?"

"Yes," Walton yelled back. "I'm English."

A whim of the current brought the island of ice closer to the *Margaret Saville*.

"If you're indeed heading north," shouted the stranger, "then for God's sake let me come aboard!"

With difficulty the crew managed to haul the man

over the rail and onto the deck. Rostop rescued the dog as well, and it whimpered appreciatively alongside his knee as he scraped his gloved fingers over its forehead and tugged its ears.

"Quick!" said Walton sharply. "Get this poor man below! Put him in my bunk. Heat up some soup."

The stranger, on his hands and knees, looked up at Walton from the deck. The captain thought he had never seen a pair of eyes so weary, and yet there was a fire of fury burning in them.

"You are kind," said the man in his slightly stilted English. He was wearing furs much like those of Walton and the rest of the crew. "I have not eaten for days. When the dogs died I almost. . ." He paused, and Walton thought he heard the beginning of a sob.

"You have earned the thanks of Victor Frankenstein," concluded the man after a while, allowing Rostop to put a blanket around him and then pick him up bodily.

"Of Victor Frankenstein," repeated the stranger as Rostop carried him to Walton's cabin, the husky trotting along behind. Walton stared after him. Unnoticed, the rift between the shores of ice began to narrow once more.

"I have a story to tell." began Frankenstein as Rostop tucked the blankets around him. "I must tell it before I die."

15

"I'm sure it's a fine story," said Rostop, trying to make his gruff voice sound soothing, "but it can wait until morning."

The stranger grabbed his arm. "No! You don't understand! It's a story I have to tell!"

Rostop raised a bushy eyebrow.

"There are stories I could tell you," he said, "but you'd probably not want to hear them. In Riga, for example, there was this-"

"Please," begged Frankenstein. "Sit down beside me and listen."

"Let the man speak," said Walton quietly from the cabin door. The first mate grunted.

"All of you! I must tell all of you!"

Walton shrugged. There wasn't much else for the crew to do at the moment. Perhaps it would even be a good story. He turned and called over his shoulder for the other men to come below.

Once they were all in the cabin there was little room left for comfort, but after the first few minutes of the stranger's story none of them noticed that.

"I was leaving home to attend the university in Ingolstadt," he began. "Elizabeth was there, telling me to be careful. . ."

Hours later, when he fell asleep, his story only part-told, they left his bedside to discover that the *Margaret Saville* was locked fast in the ice.

To Create Life

"You will be careful, won't you?" said Elizabeth plaintively, staring up at Victor. He had never seen her look so pretty, although there were tears in her eyes. In the background Victor's father was openly weeping at the prospect of his son's departure. William, Victor's younger brother by seven years, was striving manfully to keep his eyes dry as he clung to the waist of his nanny, Justine Moritz.

Beside him in the carriage, Victor's best friend Henry Clerval stirred restlessly, eager that the two of them should be on their way to Ingolstadt, but too courteous to say so. One of the horses whinnied. Victor reached down through the window and tousled Elizabeth's fair hair. The wind was catching her curls and making them flutter around her face.

"Of course I'll be careful," he said, forcing his voice to stay light. "The university is a safe enough place. Besides, I'll have Henry here" – he nudged his friend in the ribs – "to look after me and keep me in line!"

Henry laughed. Like Victor he was seventeen. The two had been friends since boyhood. Elizabeth was a year younger. As children the three of them had played together in the fields surrounding the Frankenstein estate on the outskirts of Geneva, where the tall Swiss mountains looked down austerely on their games.

Then, a few years ago, Victor's father – whom Elizabeth also called 'father', though in fact the girl was adopted – had decreed that from now on Elizabeth must be groomed for ladyhood. And it was then Henry had begun to realize, from the way Victor and Elizabeth occasionally looked at each other, that there was a special bond between his two friends, a bond which had grown ever stronger as they reached adulthood.

Elizabeth made a strained attempt at a smile, her eyes still locked on Victor's.

"But it will be many years before we see you again," she said.

Justine, a few yards away, let out a wail. William buried his face in her dress. Although, as a nanny, Justine was officially a servant, she had become more like an elder sister to the boy. She had come from a poor family and had been employed by Baron Frankenstein almost as an act of charity, but now it was difficult for any of the Frankensteins to imagine their family without her.

"Not so many years," said Victor quietly to Elizabeth. "The time will pass more quickly than a long, tearful farewell." Elizabeth nodded, understanding. She took his hand and brushed a kiss across the back of his fingers.

"I'll be thinking about you every minute of every day of every one of those years," she murmured.

Victor lowered his eyes.

"And I'll be thinking of you too," he said slowly. "I wish . . ." He paused, glancing at the impatient horses. He cleared his throat.

"I'll come home for holidays whenever I can."

She took a couple of paces away, and Henry shouted to the coachman to drive on. Within moments, when Victor looked back as the carriage rounded a curve in the long driveway, Elizabeth was a mere dash of blue in front of the gaunt stone façade of Castle Frankenstein, but through the tears in his eyes he could see that she was still waving.

As they neared Ingolstadt, ten days later, the two young men leaned forward intently in their seats, hoping to catch their first glimpse of the German university town in which they were to spend the next few years. Henry planned to study the classical languages, but Victor was intent on the sciences – in particular, the biological and medical sciences. He couldn't remember when he'd first had the ambition to help the sick and suffering in the world; it had been a part of him for so long that he'd forgotten it not being there.

Now the excitement of reaching the university – where he would be allowed to continue his fumbling schoolboy experiments – was so great that he felt he could hardly breathe.

"There!" said Henry, pointing.

Victor followed the direction of Henry's finger, and sure enough could see a church spire.

"At last," he said, pulling at his friend's shoulder so he could get a better view. He wanted to shout at the coachman to make the horses go faster, but realized it would be useless. The road they were on was rutted and irregular, and he and Henry were being bounced from side to side.

They came around the shoulder of a gently sloping hill and there, laid out in the valley below them, was the town of Ingolstadt. Henry let out an enthusiastic whoop of joy.

The university town looked beautiful in the early evening light. Already there were lamps burning at some of the windows. As they drew nearer, the carriage speeding down the long, well-surfaced road that led to Ingolstadt, Victor could see the many churches as well as the buildings that housed the university. Huddled around these larger edifices were countless smaller ones: houses with roofs of stone or thatch, gabled inns, schools, a place that looked like a kindergarten, and brightly-lit shops with bowed windows made of dozens of hand-sized panes of glass. It all seemed so terribly different from Geneva – so much more sophisticated.

Victor smiled to himself. In fact Ingolstadt was not really unlike Geneva at all. It was simply that the town held the university – the goal he'd been striving to reach since he first became intrigued by, and then obsessed by, the sciences.

It took the coachman almost an hour to find the lodgings that had been booked for Henry. After searching among the higgledy-piggledy streets, they finally drew up in front of a rather forbidding ramshackle house. Henry was first to climb down, and Victor and the coachman helped him struggle with his luggage up some narrow, crooked stairs to a cramped little room. Henry's landlady, a dour widow in black clothing, looked on morosely as Henry threw himself down on the bed.

"I'll see you in the morning, Victor," he said cheerfully, "assuming I wake up before the afternoon."

"Not tomorrow," replied Victor, pausing in the doorway. He patted his pocket. His father had given him letters of introduction to some of the leading professors at the university. To Victor they were more valuable than gold. "I don't want to wait a day before I find someone who will let me study under him."

"You take life so seriously," laughed Henry.

"How very true," mumbled Victor to himself as he followed the coachman back down the rickety stairs. "But not, dear friend, quite in the way you think."

Professor Krempe was the first scholar Victor called on the next morning, and within minutes he wished that he hadn't. The professor was a squat man, yet somehow seemed much larger despite the fact that his shoulders slumped habitually forward so that his eyes appeared always to be staring at and despising everything they saw. He had long, greasy black hair, but not quite enough of it, so his white scalp showed through in unexpected places.

"So, my fine young man from Geneva," he said with a sneer. "What have you learned of the sciences so far that you think it would be worth my while trying to teach you more?"

"Albertus Magnus," said Victor, trying not to quail under Professor Krempe's stare. "And Paracelsus." He waved a hand. "All the greatest scientists."

"Alchemists!" barked the Professor. He slammed his fist on his desk so that the inkwells rattled. "Buffoons! Fools who thought they could turn iron into gold!"

"But –" Victor began.

"Silence!"

Then Professor Krempe's mood changed. "I suppose it's only to be expected," he said, a bit more gently. "In Geneva there'd be no one to tell you any better." He twisted in his chair and glared out through the window at the Cathedral of San Sebastian on the far side of the square. "It's to your credit, young man, that you were interested enough in science to force yourself to read such twaddle."

"I didn't force myself," said Victor. "I was fascinated –"

"Silence!" Professor Krempe suddenly shouted again. He hit the desk even harder than before, but this time he didn't look around at Victor. "I'm not interested in your delusions. What intrigues me more is your enthusiasm. Hmm . . ."

He spun his chair around, then rested his chin on his knuckles for a while. Victor fidgeted nervously.

"Yes," said Professor Krempe at last, "I feel you may have something of what I require in my students. You've been exploring a blind alley in your studies so far, young –" Professor Krempe scrabbled on his desk for the letter of introduction "– young Frankenstein, but you have the thirst for discovery which every true scientist needs. I think I will take you on."

Abruptly he smiled. It was not a pretty sight.

"Consider yourself lucky, Master Frankenstein," he said. "Forty-nine out of every fifty would-be students who come to me are turned away, because all they want me to do is give them the knowledge that I have. You, though – you, I suspect, will not be satisfied until you know more than I do."

Victor made a noncommittal noise. Professor Krempe continued to stare at him.

"It's true,"Victor managed to say at last."I want – I need – to find out things that no one else knows."

"Well, young man," said Professor Krempe decisively, "that's settled, then. You will study physics with me each morning on Mondays, Wednesdays and Fridays, and on Tuesdays, Thursdays and Saturdays your tutor shall be Professor Waldman, who will educate you in chemistry. The Sabbath you will of course reserve for your devotions."

"But I wanted to study medi-" said Victor hopelessly.

"Medicine and biology are nothing more than physics and chemistry," said Professor Krempe with a derisive snort.

He was scribbling on a sheet of paper. Once finished, he blew on the ink and passed the paper over to Victor. "I ask one more promise of you. Tonight you will make a bonfire of all your books by Cornelius Agrippa and Albertus Magnus and every other fraud who claimed they would discover the impossible. If nothing else, the flames will keep you warm. And tomorrow you'll buy yourself the books I've listed here. You do have enough money, don't you?" He looked across at Victor with a cocked eyebrow.

Victor nodded.

"Good," said Professor Krempe, dismissing him

with a flick of his hand. "So many of your fellow students have no money at all, and I get tired of buying books for them."

Over the next two years Victor threw himself into his studies with an enthusiasm that astonished both his fellow students and Professor Waldman, the mild-mannered man who gently encouraged Victor's experiments in chemistry. Victor saw Henry occasionally, but less and less as their different interests drew them apart.

Professor Krempe watched everything with a sarcastic grin, and was generally abrupt and rude to Victor, often reminding him of the days when he had believed that the works of Paracelsus were the last word in science. Yet it was Professor Krempe to whom Victor more often turned when baffled by a problem, and sometimes they would talk over scientific matters far into the night, sitting comfortably across from each other at Professor Krempe's fireside and sipping Professor Krempe's brandy.

It was on one of these nights that Victor plucked up the courage to broach something that had been worrying him.

"Cornelius Agrippa and the other alchemists were not totally wrong about everything," he said nervously, aware that he had had just a little too much brandy. It was a grim winter's night and rain pelted the windows. "You and Professor Waldman have taught me that the body is nothing but a machine. You say that it's just a collection of levers and chemical reactions. But surely it's much more than that. Without something extra it would be just dead matter . . . or" – Victor was warming to his theme – "even if it could move around, it wouldn't be able to think. It wouldn't be able to talk things over the way we're talking things over now."

Professor Krempe grunted. In the light from the hearth his probing eyes glowed red.

"And what would you say this 'something extra' might be?" he said, as if ready either to laugh at Victor or throw him out into the night. "The soul?"

"No," said Victor firmly. "I can't believe there's any such thing as the soul. We're modern men of science" – Professor Krempe's lips, unnoticed by his young companion, curled into a smile – "and we're used to finding things, and measuring them. But no one has yet detected even the faintest whiff of a soul."

"No one has ever tracked down the home of the mind," said Professor Krempe softly, "but I'm sure you'll agree that each of us has a mind."

The windows suddenly lit up, and a few instants later there was a crash of thunder from outside.

"That's . . . that's different," said Victor irritably. "Each Sunday I go to San Sebastian to pray for the good of my soul, but I really don't know what I'm praying for."

Professor Krempe said nothing.

"It's not that I don't believe in God . . ." started Victor, but then he stopped. Did he really believe in God, or had he lost his faith over the past two years? The brandy made him shy away from the question.

"I believe in God," said Professor Krempe after a long pause. Lightning flashed again, and Victor leaned forward to hear the professor's words over the loud thunder. "But I believe, too," he continued, "that God gave us free will. If you can find the secret of the soul, my proud young baron-to-be, you will have found the secret of life. And, if you can find the secret of life and discover that it is not the soul . . ."

He let the words hang in the air.

A seam of resin in the firewood suddenly popped, distracting them both. Professor Krempe stretched out a leg and stamped out a spark that had landed on the hearthrug. "A final brandy?" he said.

"No," said Victor, looking out of the window. "The weather looks as if it's getting worse. I'd better go. Anyway, I think I've had enough already."

As he walked back to his lodgings through the thunderstorm, his shoulders hunched against the driving rain, he watched the lightning and thought more about the mysterious force that turned the machine that was the body into a thinking being. He had heard from Professor Waldman about the experiments the Italian scientist Luigi Galvani had carried out not long ago, making a dead frog twitch by applying an electric current. "Animal electricity" was what Galvani had called the force responsible for the twitch. A further flash of lightning seemed to split the heavens wide open.

If a small jolt of current could make a frog twitch, what might the power of a bolt of lightning do to a human corpse? Could the electricity animate not just the body but the mind? No, of course not – that was a crazy idea. Surely. He had had too much of Krempe's brandy. But if one could grow a person from living tissue . . .

The body was made from cells, and the brain was a part of the body. It, too, was made up of cells. Were all the secrets of the brain's cells locked up in those of the muscles or the heart or . . . ?

He trudged on through the rain.

He had planned to go back to Geneva the next summer, but somehow there just never seemed to be time. On one of the rare occasions he saw Henry he asked his friend to give his regards to Elizabeth – " I would, anyway," said Henry. Victor also gave Henry a sealed packet containing a long and effusive love letter to her. During the times when he wasn't working – and these were becoming increasingly rare – Victor missed Elizabeth more than he could have imagined.

"Are you all right?" said Henry, staring at Victor's pale face, red-rimmed eyes and unshaven chin as they stood in the street outside Victor's lodgings. Horses clacked slowly along the cobblestones all around them.

"Of course I am," said Victor irritably. "But I have so much work to do . . ."

The months went by, and Victor stopped attending lectures almost entirely. Neither of his two professors objected to his absences, even though he declined to tell them the nature of the research he was engaged in. What had started off as a sort of brandy-induced dream had become an obsession. He had found himself more spacious lodgings – the upper two floors of one of Ingolstadt's large town houses – and in the attic there he had constructed an extensive laboratory. In the very middle of the room stood a glass-sided tank.

Working over twenty hours each day, remembering only once or twice a week that he should eat, and sleeping on a filthy mat on the laboratory floor, he spent as much of his time as possible working out complicated chemical equations and experimenting with them at the crude bench he had built along one of the attic's sloping walls. He had started out by believing that through the mighty power of electricity he could bring a corpse back to life and, perhaps, give it a mind: now he was determined to do better than that – to create a thinking human being from scratch.

No! This creature would be better than any human being. Victor had grown to have a sour view of those around him. On the few occasions when he left the house, they laughed at his ragged clothes, his spindly frame and his unkempt hair. They – the rest of humanity – were lesser beings than he was because they were incapable of recognizing his genius. The creature he would bring into existence would be even better than he was. It would be untainted by the pettiness, the narrow-mindedness, of the world.

Very infrequently he saw the faces of people he knew he had once loved – whom he still did love, whenever he had the time. William and his father and his dead mother and Henry Clerval and, more than any of them, Elizabeth. Even less often did it occur to him that the power of his urge to create the next race of humankind might be driving him into insanity.

He had had the idea that every single part of the human body contained the seed of every other part: that from a toe or even a fingernail all of the rest could be grown – the face, the eyes, the stomach, the bones, the heart and even the brain. Where the idea had come from he did not know: perhaps Professor Krempe had made some remark that had set Victor off along this train of thought, but it was more likely that he'd come across it in one of those much-read books on alchemy that he'd brought from Geneva and which he'd dutifully, on Professor Krempe's instructions, burned.

But if he were to grow a body, perhaps from some of his own flesh, he needed to find the chemicals that would nurture the growth. He followed one sequence of theory and experiment after another until, in late October of that year, inspiration blossomed in his fevered mind. For forty-three hours nonstop he sat at his desk, scribbling so intensely that often his pencil tore through the paper. He ate nothing – hunger was a trivial sensation in comparison with the excitement he felt when he saw each of his chemical equations unfold into the next, developing his initial idea into something vastly more complex yet which contained a simple beauty of its own.

"Yes!" he shouted. At last the correct formula lay on the page in front of him. The diagram of what he needed looked so obvious, and the chemicals required to create the compound so easily available, that he was surprised it had never occurred to anyone before.

"Yes!" he yelled again. "Yes! I have it!"

It was three o'clock in the morning. The tenants on the lower floors started shouting, telling the mad scientist above them to keep quiet. Victor Frankenstein collapsed onto his mattress with a knowing smile on his face. He slept more than twice around the clock.

The tank that Victor had built in the middle of his laboratory was taller than a man and required a huge volume of chemicals and nutrients to fill it. Money was no problem for him – his father had established a more than ample allowance for him at one of Ingolstadt's many banks – but the sheer physical problem of getting the liquid chemicals up to his attic laboratory was more difficult to solve. In the end, he employed odd-job men to go to different apothecary shops and return with five-gallon jars of the various substances he needed.

The powders and nutrients required to complete the mixture, he drew from the university's stocks. He explained to an inquisitive Professor Krempe that he needed them in order to prove that Paracelsus had lied when he'd claimed that a particular formulation had enabled him to create silver. The professor seemed to relish this explanation and inquired no further.It was a full week before everything was ready. Now all Victor had to do was wait for the next thunderstorm.

Then, one evening, it happened. He stood in the doorway and gazed around his laboratory. There were jars everywhere, each bearing a label in his spidery handwriting. He'd left a narrow path among them from the door to the great tank in the middle of the room. Outside, the night sky was riven yet again by a dart of lightning. The large roof windows of the attic shook in their frames as the gale beat at them. He took a deep breath and raised his lamp higher. This was going to be very dangerous.

First he needed light. Picking his way around and over the jars, he lit the various lamps that hung on the walls and finally a cluster of candles on his bench.

Then he went into a frenzy of movement. It was important that the chemicals be added to the tank in the correct order. Each of the jars was very heavy – and seemed much heavier because of his poor state of health. By the time the tank was full he was staggering and clutching at his aching chest as he took painful gasps, struggling to breathe. He allowed himself to rest for half an hour, listening to the thunder roar and thump in the heavens above and praying that it would continue long enough for him to finish his experiment. At last, pulling himself together with a conscious effort, he forced himself to his feet. Although the most dangerous part of the experiment would come later, next was the part he was least looking forward to.

Shrugging, he picked up a scalpel from his bench. The flickering light of the lamps made the steel blade seem almost as if it were malevolently alive. To test its sharpness he drew the edge hesitantly across his thumb; he felt no pain, but a line of blood droplets appeared immediately.

It was certainly sharp enough for what he had to do. In a way, he wished that it wasn't. He gashed the left leg of his trousers with the scalpel and pulled the cloth apart. Through the rip he could see his thigh.

"The side of the thigh has fewer pain sensors than any other part of the body," he said out loud, trying to reassure himself. "You'll hardly feel a thing,"

The words were only a slight comfort, because a voice inside him was saying, "Yes, but the thigh still has some pain sensors."

If he waited any longer he'd be unable to go through with this. Gulping, he closed his eyes and plunged the scalpel into the flesh of his thigh and, before he could think any more about it, gouged away a strip of flesh.

The pain was excruciating. He thought he was going to throw up or faint, or both, but somehow he managed to keep control of himself. Opening his eyes again, he grabbed some clean cotton from the bench and crammed it into the wound.

Another thunderbolt crashed across the heavens, and at last he was able to allow himself a scream of agony. As the echoes of his scream died away, he leaned forward in his chair, watching pain-induced shapes floating in front of his eyes. When at last his vision cleared he saw the scalpel lying in the dust of the laboratory floor and the strip of bleeding flesh in his left hand.

He put the flesh – his own flesh – carefully on a clean dish on the bench and seized a roll of gauze. It took him only a minute to bind up his wound and then, at first clutching the edge of the bench for support, he was able to stand. Swaying, he released the bench. He should have added a strong dose of morphine to the list of requisitions, he thought ruefully. But there was no time to waste. The thunderstorm could end at any moment.

Hobbling, kicking aside empty jars with his left leg, he hurled the strip of flesh into the chemicals in the tank and then threw open one of the attic's huge skylights. At once he was battered in the face by the ferocious, wind-whipped rain. He put up an arm to shield himself and stumbled back to the bench. Underneath it was a kite he had made while waiting for all the chemicals to arrive.

The kite had two cords. One was of ordinary string, and this was the reel that he would hold. The other was metal. He attached it to a heavy lump of steel which he then dropped into the tank where the piece of his thigh floated gorily, tendrils of blood forming on the surface before slowly sinking.

He was going to pass out from the pain unless he hurried. "That's it!" he thought to himself. "Concentrate on the pain. It'll take your mind off the recklessness of what you're just about to do."

Somehow he got himself back up to the skylight. The wind and the rain lashed at him so hard that he had to close his eyes. He lifted the kite out into the gale, and almost at once it was snatched from his hand. When he dared to open his eyes again, he could see the kite swooping briefly over the roof of the building opposite, and then climbing up to the heavy, lightning-lit thunder-clouds. The reel in his hands thrummed as if it were a wild beast seeking freedom. Behind him he could hear the wire rattling angrily against the side of the tank. For a minute, maybe two, the storm seemed to abate, causing Victor to cry out once more, this time in frustration. Then a colossal crash of thunder shook the entire building.

Victor Frankenstein shut his eyes again, expecting to die. The metal cord brushed his sleeve. If the powerful electricity of the lightning . . .

But no. The tossing of the kite, far above in the sky, tugged the wire away from him just in time to prevent him from being electrocuted. And then the lightning struck. The entire sky was illuminated. Even through his closed eyelids Victor was almost dazzled by the glare.

He felt a sudden heat near him, and then heard the chemicals in the tank churning furiously.

It had worked!

Groggily opening his eyes, he saw a charred line running across the floor of the laboratory. The bolt of electricity had melted the wire as it had passed through it, and the hot gobbets of metal had fallen down onto the wooden boards. Nevertheless, he realized as the chemicals in the tank still churned, enough electricity had survived. Enough to initiate the generation of life.

Unless his calculations had been wrong.

Forcing himself not to think about that, he let his numb fingers drop the reel of string. He took a few clumsy steps in the direction of the tank, and fell headlong among the empty jars. He felt the pain of a hundred jagged edges of glass biting into his body, but then darkness filled him.

Fever

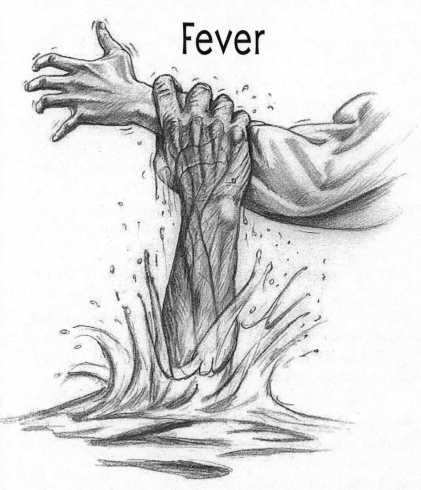

He came to his senses an unknown time later to find himself in a brightly lit, clean-smelling room. Someone was wiping his forehead with a damp cloth. For a few minutes Victor simply enjoyed the sensation, not even thinking about where he might be, but then the memories flooded back. He moaned.

"Take it easy, old chap," said a voice.

"Wh- Where am I?"

"You're in my lodgings."

Now Victor recognized the voice.

"Henry!" he said. "But how did I . . . ?"

"I found you," said Henry. "I hadn't seen you for weeks, and was worried about you, so the day after the great storm I skipped my lectures and came across to your place. You were lying in a mass of blood and broken glass and rainwater. I . . ." Henry paused momentarily, clearly still upset from the experience – "I thought you were dead."

Victor reached up a hand to his face. He could feel the scabs that had formed there. As if this were a signal, all the other parts of his body then began to register pain, complaining about the lacerations they had received. The deep wound in his thigh was a more ponderous ache.

"What else did you see?" he said wearily, turning over onto his side.

"Equipment. Jars. Some big thing in the middle of the room." Henry had recovered himself, and he spoke cheerfully. "I wasn't really looking, dear chap. I was more concerned about you than about your scientific paraphernalia."

"How long have I been here?" said Victor desperately.

"Only three days."

Three days? Only three days? Three days that he should have spent watching his creation grow. What might have happened to it by now?

"I must get back there!" Victor cried.

40

"No, you mustn't, Victor." Now Henry's voice was firm, almost strict. "What you must do is stay here a few more days until your fever lets up. You're not fit to go out. You're not fit even to climb out of bed. Now be quiet. I'm going to try you with some thin soup and see if you can keep it down."

A little later Victor felt a warm spoon against his lips and instinctively opened his mouth to let a little of the soup dribble in.

"But I must go back there," he protested weakly. "My experiment —"

"— is safely under lock and key," said Henry. "It can wait a week or so until you're well enough to continue with it."

"You don't understand," began Victor, and then realized he couldn't tell even his best friend about the experiment. Henry was not profoundly religious, but even he would be appalled by what Victor was trying to do. He would keep silent about it, of course, but if anyone else should ever learn . . . And if the Church authorities should somehow hear that Victor had been attempting to create life — to usurp the role of God — he would surely be arrested and perhaps hanged.

"All I understand," said Henry, "is that you have a fever and need to rest — and that's the end of it."

Under Henry's care, Victor slowly regained his health, but it was another ten days before he was well enough to make his way back across Ingolstadt to his

41

own lodgings. He could see that he hurt his old friend's feelings when he refused to allow Henry to accompany him, but there was no way that he could risk Henry seeing whatever the tank might now contain. In the end he mumbled something meaningless, embraced Henry while showering him with thanks, and climbed aboard the hired carriage alone.

When he reached his lodgings and paid the coachman, he paused in the street for a moment and looked up at the front of the building. From here there was no sign that anything at all unusual had taken place thirteen nights ago. He clenched his fists. What might be waiting for him in the laboratory? He had to find out. Sucking in air through pursed lips, he pushed open the door of the building and began to climb the stairs, feeling in his pocket for the key.

At the door of his laboratory, he forced himself to calm down, taking several deep, measured breaths before putting the key in the lock. With any luck, his experiment had been a failure. Otherwise . . .

The door swung open with a creak. Sunlight shafted in through the roof windows to reveal a scene of absolute devastation. Shards of glass lay scattered all over the floor, as if a bomb had been detonated. There was a rank smell in the air.

He took a nervous step into the laboratory, and stared at the tank. Its contents were the murky brown of dried blood. Treading cautiously, glass crunching

beneath his boots, he made his way to the tank and peeped over the rim. There was only the smooth, undisturbed surface of the liquid. He didn't know whether to laugh out loud with relief or to cry with disappointment. Confused thoughts and troubled emotions ran through his mind. He had failed, it was true, but maybe that was for the best. He sighed and relaxed slightly. Then, from the liquid, a huge hand shot out to grab him.

Henry Clerval watched the back of the carriage Victor had hired retreating down the busy Ingolstadt street, and frowned. Victor had fought against his confinement all the time he had been staying with Henry, and was obviously still in a state of high turmoil and anxiety when he left. It was true that his physical fever had cleared up entirely – although the scabs on his face and body had not completely disappeared – but that was obviously only half the story. Now that he was gone, Henry began to fret that his friend might still be suffering from some kind of mental fever.

He should have insisted on accompanying Victor back to his lodgings. He didn't care what the experiment was that Victor had been so obsessively secretive about. It was probably important to other scientists, who might steal the idea, but it was certainly of no concern to Henry, who didn't know the first thing about science.

"I should have gone with him," Henry thought again. "I should have clung to him like a limpet, and made him take me with him."

He put his hand in his pocket, looking for coins. He found a little small change, but certainly not enough to hire another carriage and go after Victor. He waited a few seconds longer in the street trying to decide what to do, then, his mind made up, dashed inside to lock up his room. It would take him the best part of half an hour to walk to his friend's lodgings, but he knew that the only way to quell his fears was to see Victor safely confined once more. Minutes later he was dodging the traffic of the Ingolstadt streets as he trudged determinedly toward the far side of the town.

The creature that Victor had grown from the shred of his own thigh sat up in its bath of chemicals and nutrients. Its hand still gripped his arm. Victor tried to pull himself away. The thing's body looked as if it had been flayed. Its eyes were closed. He had never seen a face so hideous. And the creature was huge – upright, it would be half as tall again as any mortal man.

The being refused to release his arm, however much Victor wriggled and squirmed. Yes, it was of human form – more or less. Perhaps it would have been less horrific had it not been a cruel mimicry of the human shape: then it could have been merely an unknown creature of gargantuan size. But, because it had vague traces of humanity about it, it chilled his heart.

"Let – go – of – me," Victor grunted, with each word trying to haul himself out of the monster's clutch. "Let – go." He knew the command was useless even as he spoke. How could the creature understand words? Still he tried to yank himself away, shouting at the thing.

The creature's blank face bore no malevolence, and yet it revolted him. This was an abomination! In trying to play the game of God he had been guilty of committing a crime against all humanity – that same humanity which he had been hoping to aid! He had created a grossly terrifying caricature of a human being. What if its mind were as hideously disfigured as that repellent face . . . if in fact the thing had a mind . . .

He reached behind him, searching for a scalpel – if need be he would hack this creature's vast hand off at the wrist – but his bench was out of reach. Stooping, he snatched up a piece of broken glass and with all his might plunged its sharp edge into the creature's forearm. The monster let out a howl of distress and released its grip just long enough for Victor to stagger back, coughing and spluttering, until he crashed against the back wall of the laboratory. He couldn't take his eyes off the creature, even though he desperately wanted to.

Its flesh was changing now that it was exposed to the air. The flayed appearance faded as traceries of leathery-looking skin formed across the surface then joined up, making, piece by piece, a tough, almost shiny hide. Even as Victor watched, the gash he had inflicted on the monster's forearm knitted itself together and slowly vanished under an advancing layer of skin that looked like parchment. The creature roared again, and clamped its two huge hands on the edge of the tank.

Spreadeagled against the laboratory wall, Victor watched as his creation, moving with apparent difficulty, hauled itself upright. It was having to learn

everything for the first time, Victor realized. Waves of
dirty brown liquid washed out of the tank to splatter
on the floor. As the colossal parody of the human
form rose to its feet, the transformation of its skin
proceeded ever more quickly.

"Oh, God," Victor said out loud. "I wish I'd never
left Geneva."

Had he only been able to shake off Henry Clerval
a few days ago the creature might have been man-
sized but, lying here in the tank, it had continued to
grow until he had disturbed it. If he had been delayed
another few days . . . He shuddered at the thought.

Victor had no weapons in the laboratory, apart from his set of scalpels – and these would be useless against something as enormous and monstrous as the creature had become. Part of him, the part that was a scientist, recognized that his emotions were just a throwback – if someone is sufficiently different from the rest of the tribe he must die – but the inner voice of the scientist was drowned out by the tide of sheer revulsion that swept through him.

Yet again the monster roared wordlessly. The windows shook. Its eyes opened, and turned to stare at him. They were a hideous, dirty yellow.

"If I could only kill it, no one need know," thought Victor. Then he heard footsteps on the stairs far below. He ran for the door.

"Well met, Henry," said Victor, almost bumping into his friend.

"What's going on, Victor?" Henry grasped the banister. "You look dreadful. Has your fever returned?"

"No." Victor drew the back of his sleeve across his sweating forehead. "But" – he sought desperately for some kind of excuse as he took Henry firmly by the elbow and turned him around – "but the shock of seeing my laboratory again may have been a little too much for me. The damage! You told me of the devastation, but I didn't believe you – not really. I don't want to look at it again – not for a while – not at the destruction of everything I've been working on these past months. It's too much to bear, my friend."

"Victor," said Henry, barely able to conceal the frustration in his voice as he was hurried down the stairs. "Victor, just what is it that you've been doing up there?"

"It would be impossible to explain to someone not trained in the sciences," said Victor, trying to control his breathlessness. "It was an experiment. It failed. There's nothing more you need to know."

He had to get out of here. He had to leave Ingolstadt. If anyone connected him with the monstrosity he had created he would surely be put to death. Let the authorities deal with the . . . the thing. Weren't they paid to cope with emergencies?

He had no clear thought in his head but flight.

"But –"

"There aren't any 'buts', Henry. I just want to leave this terrible place behind me for a few days. If you can miss your lectures, let's find ourselves an inn in the country somewhere, far from Ingolstadt, where I can recuperate from the shock I've just had and at the same time repay you for your goodness in nursing me through my fever. I can buy some new clothes for us both as we go."

They were at the front door. Suddenly there was a huge bellow from the top of the house.

"What on earth was that?" exclaimed Henry, shaking off Victor's hand.

"A dog. Just a dog. It's not important. Let's get out of here. I need to get to the countryside. Will you come with me, old friend?"

Victor reached out for Henry's arms and was only just able to stop himself from shaking the man. "Will you?"

Henry squinted at him suspiciously, and then his face cleared.

"Of course, old man. Anything you say. It's about time I took a break from my studies."

"And will you promise me you'll say nothing about anything you've seen and heard here?"

Henry forced a laugh. "You scientists," he said. "You think that I would understand anything about what I've seen?"

"Then let's go. Now. Let's go. Please, Henry. If I delay any longer I'll . . ."

Henry shrugged.

"Let's go," he echoed.

Death in Geneva

They spent two weeks away from Ingolstadt, wandering through the foothills of the Bavarian Alps, and staying the nights in the first welcoming inn they came across each evening. Although the end of the year was approaching fast, the weather was surprisingly mild. Only on one day did the snow fall heavily, and then they remained in their inn, surrounded by countryfolk who, like themselves, believed that the best way to endure a blizzard is by sipping a tankard of beer beside a warm log fire.

Sometimes Henry pressed Victor to talk about the nature of his experiments, but Victor refused to tell him anything. After being glowered at often enough, Henry stopped asking. Victor himself was trying to forget what he had done – and what might be happening as a result, even at that moment, in Ingolstadt. He imagined a different past for himself, a past in which he had never left Geneva. Perhaps he and Elizabeth might have been married by now.

At last Henry insisted that he must return to the university and his studies of ancient languages. He had abandoned the classics some while before in order to concentrate on ancient Persian and Sanskrit, and he was eager to pick up where he had left off.

After tending Victor through his fever and then taking this trip, he had missed nearly a month of lectures. If he didn't return soon he feared his professor would refuse to have him back

"That's the difference between the sciences and the arts, Victor," he explained. "Professor Krempe will assume you have been busy with research. My Professor Mannheim will assume I've been idling – which is exactly what I have been doing. We must go back. I must."

Sadly, Victor agreed. At every inn they'd visited, he had kept his ears open for any reports of a monster in the town of Ingolstadt, but had heard nothing. He turned away so Henry wouldn't see the wave of revulsion that passed across his face. Perhaps the hideous being he had created hadn't escaped from the laboratory but had died, unlamented, in the tank in which it had been grown. He wasn't sure what to think, but felt certain he would have heard something if the monster was on the loose in the town. They hired horses from a staging post and headed back to Ingolstadt, arriving the next day.

There were several letters waiting for Victor at his lodgings. Tucking them under his arm, he trudged up the stairs, remembering the last time he had climbed them and the horror he had discovered at the top.

But this time he didn't hesitate. The time away with Henry had improved his spirits immensely. He felt as if nothing could dishearten him now – not even the discovery of a vast dead body that he would have to dispose of somehow. Brimming with confidence, he climbed the last flight. What he saw at the top made his confidence drain away.

The door to his rooms had been flattened out on the landing, blasted from its frame by a mighty blow from inside. Splinters of wood dangled around the opening. The monster had not died. Victor had been deluding himself during these past two weeks. Surely such a vile creature could not survive for more than an hour, he had told himself every night. And surely he would have heard if it had escaped. But it had escaped – unless it was still here, waiting for him.

Victor tiptoed into the room, stepping on the door. The wood groaned under his weight and he flinched, putting his arms up as if he expected to be attacked. Controlling his fear, he took another pace. As soon as he was inside he relaxed. All his senses told him that he was alone. Wherever the creature might have gone, it was not here. He looked through the dusky light at the wooden stairway that led up to the laboratory, and plucked up a little more courage. He had to see. He had to know.

He found the laboratory much as he'd left it. There was still the litter of broken glass: tomorrow he

would have to start sweeping it away. There was a smell of blood in the air, and he realized almost immediately that it came from the tank. He crept forward and peered through the glass. The tank contained only liquid. The monster had gone – or perhaps it had dissolved back into the chemicals. Victor let out a deep breath. It seemed to him that he was free.

Much later that night he discovered that most of his bedding was gone. For a moment, slightly fuddled by the brandy that he had drunk with his supper, he thought that he had been robbed, but then he realized what must have really happened. The ghastly monster he had created had seized the bedding to wrap around itself. Victor sobered up instantly. Wherever the monster had gone, he was sure it was no longer in Ingolstadt – he would certainly have been told about it in the grocery shop where he had bought the food for his dinner. He imagined the creature roaming through the forests that surrounded the town on three sides, catching small creatures for its own meal. He remembered its horrible roar, and wondered if other people – forest folk – were now hearing it under the pale moonlight.

He shook his head. The monster had taken itself out of his life, and that was good enough for him. Tomorrow he would get rid of everything in his laboratory and start the long, slow process of forgetting all about his insane, foolhardy experiment. Tomorrow, too, he would have to face up to Professor Krempe, who would undoubtedly want to know what the brightest of his students had been doing these past few months with nothing to show for it. But that was tomorrow. Tonight was tonight, and Victor was exhausted. Not bothering to remove his clothes, he threw himself down on the bare mattress, dragged a pillow under his head, and within moments was asleep.

It was only the next morning that he remembered the bundle of letters he had brought up from the front hall. The first two were from Professor Krempe, demanding to know where Victor was. Didn't he realize that it was one of the duties of any student at Ingolstadt University to attend at least some lectures? Victor threw them aside. He could answer them well enough later in the day, when he confronted the professor in his lair.

The next one was addressed in handwriting he knew well: Elizabeth's. He tore the letter open eagerly, and imagined he could smell her scent rising from the single sheet of paper. He ran his eyes down the first side, turned the paper over, read the second side, and then started again from the beginning. He glanced at the date at the top, and realized that she had written to him nearly seven weeks before.

Dearest Victor,

It seems such a long time since I have seen your smile or heard your voice. Your studies at the university must be arduous indeed!

Darling William is growing to look very much like his elder brother! And like his elder brother he has developed a passion for "matters scientific" as he likes to describe them at the dinner table while telling us about the frogs and leeches and who knows what else that he keeps in tanks in his room. As he grows up, he and Justine are becoming more like brother and sister than ever.

Your father is unchanged but . . . growing older. I know he would like to see his much beloved son again soon.

Justine is in love! A nice boy from the village, who goes by the name of Werner, is the object of her affections. We have all become very fond of him, though William is terribly unsympathetic whenever Justine goes all moon-eyed about her young man.

Your father, of course, assumes that the lovebirds will marry soon, and he would prefer it to be tomorrow so that he could give them a great wedding party all the sooner. He has confided in me that he has treated Justine in his will as if she were his daughter. He proposes also to hire young Werner as an extra gardener, and to give the newly-weds the gatehouse as their wedding present. And all this time Justine has still not made up her mind for certain!

Oh, Victor, all this talk of marriage makes me long for the moment when once again I can look into your eyes and know that . . .

The second page expressed her love for him at very great and at times almost embarrassing length. About herself there was very little. Over and over again she told him how much she wanted to see him.

"And you soon will!" said Victor to the air. "Even if I can only return for a few days, I'll be there soon."

He held the letter crumpled to his chest, and once again believed he could smell her scent. Elizabeth was so lovely – so very different from the thing he had created in his arrogance. The thought of her walking by his side across the even lawns of Castle Frankenstein, her laughter tinkling in his ears . . . He sat on the edge of his bed, his eyes tightly shut, for a long time, thinking about her. Once or twice during his years in Ingolstadt he'd seen a pretty face in the street and been momentarily distracted, but Elizabeth had never been far from his heart.

Dizzily he reached for the next letter. Again he recognized the handwriting: this time it was his father's. Without much interest he broke open the seal and several sheets of paper fell to the floor. Gathering them up, putting them in order, Victor noticed that this letter had been written some three weeks after Elizabeth's. Feeling as if he were doing a duty, he started to read. A few moments later he was standing upright, horrified by what his father had to say. His beloved William was dead!

Victor read the paragraph again, refusing to believe it. His little brother, whom he had last seen sobbing into Justine's dress, had been murdered – strangled! Worse still – if anything could be worse – Justine had been arrested and and thrown into prison on the suspicion that she had committed the crime.

"She could no more have killed William than I could have myself!" shouted Victor, though there was no one to hear.

Forgetting all about the ruined laboratory in the attic, Victor quickly began packing his clothes. If he could find a good coachman who was willing to take him, he could be at home in Geneva within the week.

"Henry!" he said out loud. "I must see Henry." Henry had been desperate to resume his studies, but Victor must tell him about all this before leaving Ingolstadt. It was likely his old friend would want to return to Geneva with him – he had treated William as if he were a somewhat exasperating but much-loved younger brother, and Elizabeth and Justine as if they were his own sisters. However much Victor wanted to leave Ingolstadt right now, this instant, he must see Henry before he went.

Tears ran down Victor's face. The law could sometimes be shockingly swift in Geneva – for all he knew Justine might have been hanged already. Even so, he had to get home as soon as possible – if for no other reason than to console Elizabeth and his father. But he hoped beyond all hope that he would be there in time to speak at the trial, to explain to the magistrates the impossibility that Justine could have in any way harmed the child who had been in her care for so long. Justine – the woman had been incapable of swatting a fly. Surely they would listen to him! Surely they would believe him! Henry would speak out for her as well.

When Victor had finished packing – everything that he wanted to take away from Ingolstadt squeezed into a big suitcase – he went down to the street and waited impatiently for a carriage. At last one came. Victor blurted out the address of Henry's lodgings. "And," he added, "would you be willing to carry both of us all the way to Geneva?"

"That'll depend on the price," said the coachman as the vehicle lurched into motion.

"I'll pay you handsomely," said Victor. "More than you would think of asking. Much, much more."

"You're the sort of customer I like," said the coachman with a cackle, cracking his whip above the heads of the horses. "I can get you there in a week."

The man was as good as his word. As soon as Henry slammed the door of the carriage – just as Victor had suspected, his old friend insisted on returning to Geneva with him – the coachman began to push the horses to the limit of their endurance. They reached Geneva in seven days.

All through the journey, the suspicion grew in Victor's mind that he knew the murderer. He remembered the malevolent stare the monster had

directed at him. Could the beast somehow have discovered where the Frankensteins lived? It seemed impossible, but . . .

What was worse was that, if the creature was so inspired by evil that it could kill an innocent youth, how many other members of Victor's family might it murder before its thirst for vengeance was satisfied? But no: this line of thought was taking him too far. There was no evidence at all that the monster was even alive, let alone capable of malevolent acts. And it was an even more ridiculous idea to think that it could have tracked down Victor's family in Geneva. This was all wild speculation. Then he remembered that night when, on the way home from Professor Krempe's, he'd engaged in some other wild speculation. His instincts had guided him then. Perhaps they were guiding him now . . .

Victor churned these thoughts over and over in his mind all the way to Geneva. Henry found him very poor company.

The trial of Justine Moritz began the morning after Victor and Henry arrived. It was held in the Central Court of Justice in Geneva before a group of three magistrates. Victor settled himself uneasily on one of the hard benches. Elizabeth was on one side of him, his father on the other. Henry had decided to sit on the far side of the timbered room so that, if he were called to give evidence about Justine's character, he would not seem too closely connected with the Frankenstein family. Victor breathed deeply. The courtroom smelled of old fear.

Half an hour passed before the three magistrates – dressed in long red and black robes – made their entrance. All the people in the courtroom got to their feet and waited as the magistrates seated themselves behind the imposing oak table that more or less filled the platform at the end of the room. Then a pair of burly prison officers brought in Justine.

Victor stared. In the years since he had left Geneva, Justine had grown from a very pretty girl into a beautiful woman, but there was still an innocence in her face which made it impossible for anyone to believe that she could have committed such a savage murder. Surely she would be declared guiltless at once. He turned to look at Elizabeth. Her blue eyes were filled with tears.

"I'm sure she'll be freed," he whispered reassuringly. "Just look at her."

"No," Elizabeth whispered back, "they'll hang her, whether she's shown to be innocent or not. She's too beautiful for them. They'll hang her to show the rest of the world that their decisions aren't affected by a pretty face – that their justice is fair to everyone."

Victor turned back to look at the court. Before the magistrates had appeared the people had been gossiping and joking; now they were deadly silent as the clerk of the court read out the accusation against Justine. Victor found it impossible to concentrate on what the man was saying. Too many ideas, too many guilts and worries, were chasing each other around inside his head.

"... that on this past day of ... you did deliberately and cruelly ... the boy entrusted to your care ..."

As soon as the clerk had finished speaking, the prosecutor leapt to his feet. Victor was horrified as he listened. Until now he had not known how convincing the evidence against Justine was – or could be made to appear.

William had disappeared during an afternoon picnic in which the whole family – except Justine, who had been visiting her aunt – had participated. That night Justine had gone missing; the following morning she had been discovered wandering aimlessly near the spot where William's corpse had been found. On being shown his body she had fallen into a faint, and had had to be confined to her bed for some days. Meanwhile, a servant had found a locket in one of Justine's pockets and recognized it as the memento which William always wore under his shirt. It had belonged to his dead mother. From the lips of the prosecutor the evidence sounded very convincing, and Victor's eyes kept slipping from the man's eagerly accusatory face to Justine's, and back again. The prosecutor described the bruises on William's neck.

"Clearly no normal woman would have had the strength to inflict such damage," he said, spittle flying from his mouth. "This must have been the work of a madwoman." He pointed dramatically at Justine.

"That madwoman!" he shouted.

As he sat down, pandemonium erupted in the courtroom. Some people in the crowd were yelling that Justine was innocent, but the majority were demanding just as loudly that she be taken from the courtroom and hanged immediately. Victor had cringed when the prosecutor described the strength of the hands that had strangled his brother. He knew a pair of hands that would have that strength. All his gloomy suspicions of the journey to Geneva came back to him. Somehow the creature had made its way here . . .

He woke from his miserable thoughts to realise that Justine was speaking. Yes, she admitted, she had been out of the house for the whole night after William's disappearance, but this was because she was looking for him. Coming home after an evening with her aunt, she had learned of the boy's disappearance from a man she had met and had immediately set out to try to find him. She had slept briefly in a barn during the early hours of the morning, then continued her search. By the time she was found at dawn she was at her wits' end through exhaustion and anxiety. She had no idea how the locket had come to be in her pocket.

Her tale sounded appallingly weak to Victor, but Elizabeth took his hand and whispered to him: "That's obviously what happened! Surely they'll realize that."

"I thought you said they'd hang her anyway," he muttered grimly.

"Yes, but –" Elizabeth fell silent as a clerk of the court gestured to her to come to the witness stand.

There was little by way of hard evidence that Elizabeth could offer, but she was able to describe how much Justine and William had loved each other, and how much the family had come to regard Justine as being almost of their own blood. She declared to the magistrates that William had been like a brother to her: if she were firmly convinced of Justine's innocence, should not they, who had never known her or the boy, be even more so? Elizabeth's testimony was followed by Baron Frankenstein's. He repeated much of what she had said.

Victor was in an agony of guilt, but he didn't know what to do. If he told the court about his belief that his little brother had been killed by a monster which he, Victor, had created in an Ingolstadt attic, they would laugh at his feverish imagination – and become even more determined to hang Justine. If they would only believe him, of course, they would hang him in her place, but they wouldn't believe him: they would simply think he was raving or lying.

A few more witnesses were called and then the trial was declared over. The verdict, the clerk informed the court, would be handed down tomorrow. Everyone stood up as the magistrates solemnly filed out and Justine was led away to her cell in the basement beneath the courthouse.

Elizabeth tugged at Victor's arm. "Come on," she said. "We've done as much as we can. It's time for us to go home and pray that God will touch the magistrates' hearts tonight." Victor continued to stare straight ahead, his mind in a ferment. "Perhaps they would have believed me," he thought. If only I'd . . ."

"Yes, dear lad, come on," said Baron Frankenstein, pulling at Victor's other arm. "Elizabeth and I need your support." The old man was choking with emotion. Victor let them lead him out of the courtroom and into their carriage. His eyes blank, he saw nothing of the countryside as they drove rapidly back to Castle Frankenstein.

The next morning, Justine Moritz was declared guilty, and publicly hanged.

On Montanvert

The next two weeks were a miserable time for everyone at Castle Frankenstein. After the trial, Henry returned to Ingolstadt and Victor spent much of every day alone in his room with the curtains drawn. His earlier suspicions had hardened into certainties. He had created a living being in the hope of improving the lot of humanity: the result was that two of the people dearest to him in the world were dead. If he had murdered them himself his emotions would have been easier to tackle. As it was, he knew that they were dead not through any malice but through his own folly. Their blood was on his hands – he was honest enough with himself to admit this – yet he had not intended their deaths. He was guilty of murder, but he was not a murderer.

One night, unable to sleep, he was staring out through his bedroom window at the moonlit lawn. From the shrubbery there emerged what he at first thought was some trick of the shadows. Then he saw that it was some great beast. It was too far away for him to be able to see it clearly, but he imagined that it turned its head to look up at his window – to look directly at him. Then, in the blinking of an eye, it was moving at impossible speed across the silver grass until it was lost from his sight.

"No normal woman would have had the strength to inflict such damage," the prosecutor had said. And neither, Victor told himself, would any normal man.

It was Elizabeth who finally roused him from his orgy of self-recrimination. One day she knocked at his bedroom door and then, hearing no reply, beat on it with her fist. Finally, ignoring all decorum, she simply threw the door open and stormed in.

"Don't be such a self-pitying fool, Victor!" she shouted, dragging the curtains open so that sunlight flooded into the room. "Get up out of bed now!"

"But I'm not wearing –"

"I spend every Friday nursing the poor at the cottage hospital so there's no need to be coy," she snapped angrily. "Here" – she picked up a bundle of his clothes from the chair and hurled them at him – "get yourself dressed and come downstairs. Your father has lost one son to a murderer. At the moment he feels he's lost another to the same murderer. He's pining away – dying visibly – because you're being so completely selfish, Victor. I'll look out of the window while you put your clothes on, but I'm not leaving this room until you leave it with me."

With a last furious flash from her bright blue eyes she turned away. "It stinks in here," she said in an exasperated voice as she struggled to open the window. Numb with embarrassment, Victor pulled himself into the first garments that came to hand.

"One of the peacocks is spreading his tail," said Elizabeth more gently from the window. "If you've finished dressing you could come and look." He joined her, aware that his chin was unshaven and that his shirt-tail was hanging out.

"Where?" he said.

She pointed. The feathers were glorious. Then the bird let out a raucous honk and for the first time in weeks Victor felt himself beginning to smile.

"A very pretty sight, but not such a pretty sound," he said softly.

"I imagine you think the same of me, right now," said Elizabeth.

"No. You were right to say those things."

He put his hand on her shoulder and turned her to face him. "I have been selfish, but there's more to the deaths of William and Justine than I can tell even you." She gazed back at him.

"Victor –" she began, then stopped, moving a half-pace away from him.

"You are the brightest part of my life, Elizabeth. I would like . . . I would like . . ."

She skipped away from him and started picking up discarded garments from the floor. "To marry me? Oh, of course we'll marry each other – I decided that long before you went away to Ingolstadt."

Victor laughed out loud. "Elizabeth!" he cried.

Dropping the clothes, she came into his embrace.

The baron was delighted when they told him they were going to get married, and hugged each of them again and again. He ordered two cases of his best wine from the cellars, and over the next few weeks drank most of it himself. It was obvious to both Victor and Elizabeth that he had been hoping for

years that they would eventually marry, but had held himself back from saying so.

Only at night, lying awake as the wind howled, did Victor think about the two deaths he believed he had caused . . .

The baron declared the wedding should take place in three months' time – any earlier would be to insult the memories of William and Justine. Victor and Elizabeth wanted to marry as soon as possible, but they recognized the force of the old man's argument. Moreover, Victor needed some time to himself. It seemed paradoxical that he loved to be near Elizabeth, yet also craved solitude. He had to confront the emotions that still battled within him, and he couldn't do this when she was there. He remembered fondly the trip to the Alps he had enjoyed with Henry and how relaxing it had been.

"I have to go away for a while," he said one morning at breakfast.

Elizabeth looked offended. Victor reached out across the linen tablecloth and touched the ends of her fingers with his. "There are things that happened at Ingolstadt that I must work to forget," he said earnestly. Elizabeth snatched away her hand.

"I see," she said icily.

Victor hesitated. "No, I don't mean there was another woman, Elizabeth. It's just that I was doing an experiment, and – and it went wrong. The repercussions of my failure may have caused great grief to others. Even though I didn't intend that to happen, I still feel guilty about it all. I need to spend a little while by myself, walking in the mountains, thinking things through. I'll be a better husband to you, Elizabeth, if I do."

At the other end of the table the baron snorted. "Never bothered with such stuff in my day," he muttered. But neither Victor nor Elizabeth were listening to him.

"If it's important," she said.

"It is."

"Then go with my blessing."

In the valley of Chamonix, high in the Alps, the air was pure and good. Victor breathed it appreciatively as he crested a small ridge and saw a carpet of spring flowers stretching away to a little river far below. He dropped onto the grass and propped his stick beside him. In his knapsack he had some bread and cheese that he'd bought at the inn where he'd stayed the previous night. He dug them out, inspected them critically, then began to eat hungrily, washing down the food with swigs of beer.

Before leaving home, and despite the baron's complaints – "Just because I'm old doesn't mean I couldn't whip the hide off you or any other chap, young Victor" – he had hired half a dozen bulky village youths to guard the castle day and night. He was determined that Elizabeth and his father should be safe during his absence. He had been exploring the valley for three weeks now, and at last he was beginning to feel that he had shed some of the misery and guilt he felt about the deaths in Geneva. It was as if there had been a great weight on his shoulders which was slowly being lifted.

In the distance, on the far side of the valley, the slopes of Mont Blanc rose imperiously up to meet the clouds. Just the sight of the huge mountain's icecap was enough to make Victor feel cold. Nearer to him was a smaller mountain – really only a hill – which his map told him was called Montanvert. Its slopes were invitingly green, purple and brown. Victor squinted up at the sun. If he made good progress, he should be able to spend a part of the afternoon exploring the foothills of Montanvert before finding somewhere to stay in the little village he could see down in the valley. Throwing the last of his food to an inquisitive crow, he heaved his knapsack onto his back, grabbed his stick, and set off, singing an old folksong as he navigated his way through the tussocks of the hilly slope.

It took him longer to reach Montanvert than he'd expected, and by the time he came to the summit the afternoon was nearing its end. He began to worry that soon darkness would fall as he turned to make his way back down. Then he noticed that there was someone else on the mountain.

At first the figure was too distant for Victor to be able to make out any details, but as it came closer, he saw that the person was a very large man – too large, Victor began to realize, to be a man at all. It was moving across the ground at a colossal speed in a run that was a strange mixture of clumsiness and grace. And, though occasionally it had to divert from its path, it was obvious that the figure was heading straight for him.

The creature! It had found him! It must have followed him from the castle.

Victor simply accepted the fact that he was about to die. In a way he almost welcomed it. All the old guilt about the deaths of William and Justine came back to him in a rush. He deserved to die; he had said that to himself time and time again in the darkness of his curtained bedroom. Now that the moment had come, he felt no resentment. It seemed only right and proper that the thing he had created should be the means by which his life ended. He tossed his stick to one side, then chucked his knapsack after it. He sat down on a small hummock and waited calmly for the monster to reach him.

Then his mood changed. He still did not care about dying – although the thought of how unhappy Elizabeth would be made his heart pang – but then a bitter hatred of the creature began to grow inside him. He knew the hatred was unjustified – if a mad dog kills a child there is no sense in hating the dog – but that didn't make the emotion any less intense. It was not his hands that had tightened around William's small neck. Victor's fury rose. He scrabbled across the hillside to retrieve his stick, the only weapon available to him. He deserved to die – he said this to himself yet again – but so did the monster. If he died killing it, then that was a fair bargain. He clutched his stick and waited impatiently for the monster to reach him.

One moment, it seemed, the creature was still far away; the next it was directly in front of him. Victor looked at it with disgust. It had somehow made clothes for itself out of sheets and blankets. From what he could see of its skin, it looked as if it had been sewn together from old strips of leather of different textures and shades. Its features were enough to spark horror in the strongest mind, as if the various parts of a face – the nose, lips, teeth and cheeks – had been thrown together crazily by a small child. And set in that hideous visage were the being's loathsome eyes, yellow and filled with detestation.

Those eyes were focused on Victor's face.

"You killed them, didn't you?" Victor said.

The creature nodded. It seemed to be merely acknowledging a fact rather than making a confession.

"I wish you were dead," Victor hissed. "I wish you could die more than once – ten times over for each of the innocents whose deaths you caused."

"I expected nothing better from you," said the creature. Victor started. Its voice was a low growl, yet the words were perfectly clear. Where had it learned to speak? The beast spat onto the grass, then warily settled down a few yards away from Victor.

"You created me. Somehow you brought me into this world. You gave me life. And yet, as soon as I was alive, you spurned me because of my appearance. You are my father and my god, but when I was newborn you abandoned me. You gave me legs and arms," – the creature shook its limbs, as if Victor might not have noticed them – "and a heart and lungs and a brain, but then, as I suffered the agony of my birth, you fled from me. What would you say about any other father who abandoned his child at the moment of its birth?"

"You killed my brother," said Victor flatly.

"Yes," said the creature. "I didn't want to kill him. I had no notion of killing him until I tried to make friends with him."

The monster gave a weary sigh. Then it asked:

"Do you want to hear the full tale of what happened since I left Ingolstadt?"

"You may as well tell me," said Victor. "I still want to plunge this stick" – he waved the puny weapon – "into the very depths of your heart, but before I do that I'll listen to your tale."

The monster moved in a blur of speed. Victor found he was no longer holding the stick.

"Listen," said the creature, "listen, you stupid, pathetic little man. Physically I am so much your superior that I could snap you in two at any moment I chose. Mentally, too, I am far in advance of you. In a mere few weeks I have learned to speak – few human children could have done that."

Victor bowed his head. The creature was right.

"But," said the creature, "in other respects I'm still a child. I know what the words 'good' and 'evil' mean, because I've heard them used often enough, but I don't feel them. I didn't feel I was doing anything evil when I was killing your brother – all I knew was that I had to stop him from screaming for help. You gave me a body and a mind, Victor Frankenstein, but you forgot all about giving me a conscience."

"It was an experiment," Victor said limply. "I don't know how I could have given you a conscience. I don't know how I could have given you the power to tell the difference between good and evil. I grew you in a tank of chemicals. That was all I did."

The creature shook with anger, and again Victor assumed he was about to die. Then he saw it force itself to be calm.

"If you had stayed with me in Ingolstadt," it said, "and taught me, like any other father would have done, I might have been able to understand good and evil. But you didn't do that. The first I knew of the world was that my father was screaming because I looked revolting to him."

Victor could think of nothing to say. He had created a being that had a rational mind, but not a soul. It was not the creature that had killed William and Justine, but himself. As twilight fell over the slopes of Montanvert, he began to weep. He had meant no harm, and yet, simply because his creation had been ugly, he had caused so much.

"I offered to tell you my tale," said the creature. "Now I shall do so and you will listen until I'm finished. If you try to leave I'll tear you limb from limb – I swear it."

"I'll listen," said Victor. "It's the least I owe you."

As the sun lowered and the day grew cooler, the monster began to tell its tale . . .

The Monster's Tale

I can remember little about my first few hours of consciousness except confusion and pain and the sight of your face. Only later did I come to understand that the pain came from the wound that you had inflicted on my arm and that the expression on your face was one of loathing. At the time I had no way of knowing that these were not normal experiences for people coming into the world. Then you left me alone. I've said that you were my father, but really you were my mother – it was you who gave me life. When you abandoned me, you were like a mother abandoning her newborn baby. I didn't understand this then, but I do understand it now. Are you surprised I hate you, Frankenstein?

I had some difficulty sorting out my senses. The light shining in through your laboratory windows was so dazzling that for the rest of the day I could do nothing except stagger around, my hand across my eyes, hoping for the torment to end. As I did so, I discovered new sources of pain; soon I learned not to tread on the sharp pieces of glass on the floor, but it took me a little longer to discover I should not stumble into the hard corners of your bench or other objects. Every sound was deafening, especially my own screams of anguish. It didn't occur to me that there might be any world outside that room, even though I could hear the noise from the street below.

Then, finally, night came, and with it the gentler moonlight. At last I was able to see. I looked out through the window and discovered that there was indeed a greater world – I saw the houses and buildings of Ingolstadt. At first I didn't know what they were – it was as if I were looking at a flat picture and not understanding what it meant – but then I noticed people with forms much like my own, with two legs and two arms and a head, and I believed that they were just like me. I observed that they wore clothing to cover their bodies, and I hunted around to find similar garments with which I could cover myself. I didn't know why the body should be

covered like that: I just wanted to be like those laughing, happy people I could see from the window. I found some of your clothes, Frankenstein, but of course none of them would fit me. In the end I tore the sheets from your bed and draped them around myself.

I came out into the street, looking for the people I had seen, but there was no one – only the darkness.

I looked up at the sky and saw the half moon and the pinpoints of the stars. Here and there were lighted windows, but my mind didn't connect these with living creatures – they could just have been stars that were closer to me than the ones in the sky. Their brightness hurt my eyes. I shambled on clumsily through the streets of Ingolstadt, my sheets gathered pitifully around me, with no idea of where I was going. Eventually I reached the edge of the town, and without hesitation I struck out for the welcome darkness of the countryside.

Other sensations were making themselves felt. I was hungry and thirsty, although at first I didn't know what to do about these aches. I was also exhausted. I lay down by a stream in the middle of the forest, and after a while instinct told me to drink some water. I cupped a little in my hands, and drank. The water tasted so good that I drank more, and more, until I thought my belly would burst. I ate some grass and leaves, and then for some reason I was attracted to the fruits and berries dangling from the trees. I ate a few, and enjoyed their sweetness, so I ate more and more. In the end I was sick, but I soon became hungry and thirsty again. This time I drank and ate more moderately. My appetites satisfied, I curled up under a tree and slept.

I awoke with the dawn. I was freezing cold – though at the time I didn't understand what this meant, or how to make myself warmer. There was a pleasant sound in the air, and after a while I realized that it came from the small, winged creatures darting between the trees. The sunlight no longer stung my eyes: I had become accustomed to the brilliance of day. I drank some more water, ate some more berries, then set off deeper into the countryside.

Several days passed. One day I discovered the remnants of a fire that had been left by some forest folk, and warmed myself in front of it. The fire seemed somehow so friendly that I put my hand into the embers. I discovered at that moment, as you may imagine, Frankenstein, the dual nature of fire. This is one of the many things that you should have taught me, but you chose to desert me instead, because you thought my face was ugly.

I soon discovered how to keep the fire alight, so I camped there for a few days, sleeping in glorious warmth, then adding fuel and fanning the flames in the morning. The forest folk had left some cooked foods around the fire, which I ate, and then I experimented – finding that heat destroyed berries but made nuts and roots more pleasant to eat. Before long, however, I had eaten everything nearby that seemed edible, and so I resumed my travels.

Soon I came across a mountain hut. I had seen houses in Ingolstadt, of course, but this looked nothing like them – it was all sloping angles and patched walls. I didn't know what it was. I examined it from afar, then opened its door and put my head inside. There was a man there. He took one look at my face and screamed. I backed away, not knowing what a scream was, and he pushed past me and ran away across the fields. I went into the shack and found that he had been eating and drinking substances that I have learned were bread and cheese and milk and wine. I devoured the bread and cheese and milk. The wine tasted disgusting, so I left it. There was a straw bed in the corner, and after my meal I slept for a while.

On waking, I left the hut and continued to walk through the hills. In the evening I came to a village. This was a tiny settlement compared to Ingolstadt, but it seemed almost as grand a place to me. If I'd seen the grandness of Castle Frankenstein by then, I'd have realized that most of the houses were little more than hovels, but at the time I was awed.

I shoved open the door of one of the houses, and at once everyone inside started shrieking. Their noise aroused the other villagers, and I was chased away with sticks and stones. Catching my breath in a field some miles away, I came to the conclusion that I was hideous as well as big. Screams, I had discovered, were the human way of expressing fear or anger. I had no wish to make people scream. I wished no harm on any human being . . . yet.

I slept in the field that night, then continued my wanderings in the morning. At about noon I came across an isolated cottage. I crept up close to it. There was smoke coming out of its chimney. On one side of the cottage, leaning against the wall, was a wooden shed. I looked through one of the cottage windows and saw three people gathered around a crudely constructed table. They were eating a meal. My mouth watered as I saw the bread and cheese, but I had learned that other mortals rejected me on sight so I did not knock on the door.

Instead, I investigated the lean-to shed and found that its inside was covered in spiders' webs and filth: it seemed that the place hadn't been used for years. I slipped inside and quietly closed the door behind me. I had found a home. For the first week that I lived there I stayed motionless all day, enjoying the little warmth that filtered through the wall of the cottage. At night, after the dwellers in the cottage had gone to their beds, I went out to find vegetables and hunt down night creatures, which by this time I had discovered were delicious, even when raw.

Once I snatched an owl from the air and gobbled it up on the spot, bones and beak and all.

After a few days I became curious about the people who lived in the cottage. I waited until all of them were out and then, using this fingernail, I gouged a little hole through the wall. From this time onward I was able to watch their daily activity. I learned so much from them! The first thing I learned was speech. It was soon clear to me that the same noises came from their lips each time they referred to an object: a bowl was a concave wooden thing into which food was poured so that someone could eat it using a tool called a spoon. The idea of naming things was new to me; the notion that similar objects could have the same name took me a little longer to master, but at last I had it – one apple could be different from another in size and shape, but both were called apple. In a few more days I was able to comprehend that different actions, too, could be described by sounds. Watching through the hole, I silently repeated each of the sounds I heard the cottagers use. At night, in the open fields, I said the words out loud, over and over again.

I discovered also that these three people had names. The man with the grey hair was called Father. One of the younger people was called Agatha and the other Felix. I knew the two younger people were different in some way, but it was only when I observed them bathing that I was able to know what the difference was. Felix was similar to me; Agatha was not. At the time this discovery was of no more interest to me than the discovery of a new word; it is only recently that I have realized how much I crave someone like Agatha as my partner in life.

I already knew that the three people I loved so much – and I did love them – were extremely unhappy. All of them worked from dawn until darkness, and still they weren't able to get enough food from their fields and traps to fill themselves. And when the weather suddenly got much colder, their life seemed to become even harder.

I did what I could for them. Each night I gathered wood from the forest, and left it in a pile near the cottage. Once I'd satisfied my own hunger, I would catch and kill an extra couple of small animals, and leave them there for my friends. The cottagers were mystified by all this, of course, and at first were unwilling to use the fuel or to eat the hares and birds. Soon, though, they accepted my gifts.

I discovered one more thing about the trio: Father couldn't see. Although he normally moved around the cottage with confidence, he would trip over a chair that had been left in the wrong place or be unable to find a utensil that was not hanging on its customary hook. His children did their best to avoid such situations, but sometimes they forgot.

When I realized the old man was blind, my heart was filled with hope. Other people — including yourself, Frankenstein — had reacted to my appearance with hatred and revulsion. A blind man might accept me for what I was. He would hear my voice — I was now speaking fluently, though my vocabulary was still limited — and assume that I looked much like him. Once he had accepted me, perhaps Agatha and Felix would learn to ignore my face and welcome me into their family.

I was still waiting for a time when Father was alone when a newcomer arrived. Her name was Safie. She was a foreigner, and if anything she was even more beautiful than Agatha. I listened eagerly to the cottagers' conversations over the next few days, and discovered why she was there. Apparently her father had swindled the cottagers a few years before, which was why they were now poverty-stricken. However, Safie and Felix had fallen in love, even though they spoke only a few words in common. Now, at last, she had been able to escape from her father to join her beloved Felix.

She was welcomed by the family. Agatha embraced her as if she were a long-lost sister, and Father didn't stop smiling for days. But it was the way Safie and Felix looked at each other that first informed me of the different sort of love that can exist between two people. Whenever they were together it was as if a cloud of happiness surrounded them. When they were alone they kissed each other.

Soon Father took it upon himself to give Safie daily language lessons and, my eye pressed to the hole in the wall, I learned alongside her – in fact, I took some pride in the fact that I soon raced ahead of her. When you created me, Frankenstein, you gave me a good brain. If only you had known how to give me this thing called a soul which I often heard my cottagers talk about!

One day, when Felix and Safie had gone for a ramble in the countryside and Agatha had gone to a nearby farm to trade some vegetables for eggs, Father remained alone in the cottage. This was my opportunity. I slipped out of my hovel and knocked gently on the front door of the cottage.

"Who's there?" said Father nervously.

"A stranger," I said, as gently as I could. "I'd be grateful if you would allow me to sit by your fire for a few minutes before I continue on my way." I heard him moving inside, then he opened the door.

"Welcome," he said. "Come in."

He gestured to one of the chairs in front of the fire, and settled himself back into the other.

"I am blind," he said immediately. "If you would like some food, please help yourself to whatever you can see. My family will be back soon, and if you can wait, one of them will make you a meal."

I felt a welling up of emotion at his kindness. "I'm not hungry," I said. "But I thank you for your offer."

"Then warm yourself, friend," he said with a smile. He picked up his pipe and lit it with a taper. For a little while neither of us spoke.

"You have a curious accent," he said at last. "Where do you come from?"

"Not far away," I said. There was another silence.

"What brings you to these parts?" he said suddenly.

"I'm looking for a family."

"Would I know them? We haven't lived here very long, but we know some of the people around here." And he tapped his pipe against the cast-iron edge of the hearth.

"All that I can tell you," I said, leaning back in my chair and drawing a deep breath, "is that they're the kindest and gentlest folk I've ever encountered. You cannot see my face, my friend, but it is so grossly ugly that everywhere I go people chase me away. I believe that this family will not." He finished refilling his pipe, and struggled with the business of lighting it again.

"What makes you think that?" he said, when at last the tobacco was glowing.

"I have performed various acts of friendship for them," I said as lightly as I could.

"Then of course they'll welcome you," he cried. "How could they do anything else?"

"They are very poor," I said, plucking up my courage. "The father is blind, and he has a son and a daughter. It is very difficult for them to scratch a living from their land. Just recently they have welcomed into their home an extra person, and that has made it even harder for them to survive."

A frown creased the old man's brow. "It sounds as if you're describing my family," he said slowly.

"I am," I said.

I went down on my knees in front of him. "I've seen the love that the four of you share, and I love you as though I were one of you. I know that I am hideous – every person who has ever looked at me has told me, by their screams, that I am the most repulsive being that has ever stepped upon God's earth. But my heart is pure. I'm your friend. I'm the one who has been stacking up fuel and food outside your door these past weeks. I don't ask for much – no more than a dog would ask – and in return I'll give you everything I can."

Father looked pale. He felt for my hand. "You're far bigger than a normal man," he said tentatively.

"And far, far uglier," I said. My eyes were wet with tears, but I took his hand and put it against my face. "Though you can't see it, you can feel my ugliness."

His fingers explored my features, and he gave a hiss of indrawn breath. Then he took his hand away.

"You are not," he said reflectively, "a handsome man. But Safie's father was handsome, and look at the

way he treated me – and her. The outside of a person doesn't tell what the inside of them is like. I've heard you speak. Everything you've said to me persuades me that your heart is an honest one. We can make a bed of straw here in the main room, and you can live with us."

I kissed his hand, and began to weep out loud. After a moment's hesitation, he put his arm around my shoulder and gave me the kind of hug any parent would give – the kind of hug you have never given me, Frankenstein.

It was at that moment that the door of the cottage flew open and Safie and Felix returned. I looked up. Safie took one glance at me and fainted. Felix gave a shriek of undiluted wrath and snatched a walking stick from beside the door. He took a couple of paces forward and began to beat me about the face.

"What's going on?" shouted Father. "This man is my friend!"

Felix paid him no attention, but continued hitting me with the walking stick. I put up my arms in front of my face to shield myself from the vicious blows.

I could have killed Felix, you know, Frankenstein. It would have been easy for me to pull his body to pieces, to rip his heart from his chest. But instead I merely threw him back against the wall, stunning him. He lay there, breathing heavily.

"I wanted your friendship," I said quietly to the old man, "but it seems there is no one in the world who will be my friend."

"Wait!" he said.

"No," I replied immediately, "I won't wait. Safie fainted when she saw me. Felix attacked me. Would Agatha lose her wits at the sight of my face? I can't risk that. I love you and your family. I wish you well. If ever I come by here again I'll leave a gift on your doorstep, as I have done so often before. But Felix has convinced me that I look too vile to live among ordinary human beings. I must find my own father. He, surely, will accept me for what I am."

In the few moments before you abandoned me in your laboratory, Frankenstein, you mentioned the name "Geneva", and through my eavesdropping on Safie's language lessons, I now knew this was a town somewhere to the north. Using the sun as my guide, I headed north as fast as I could. I had to cross a great mountain range. I discovered that in darkness I could ask people directions – so long as they could not see my face, they assumed that I was just a giant man. They were only too eager to tell me the route I should take, because they were frightened of my size.

At last, more by luck than judgement, I found myself on the outskirts of Geneva. Huddling at the edge of the lake, the town looked very beautiful. In my innocence I thought that all I would have to do was discover where in Geneva you lived, search you out, introduce myself – and then you would welcome me. What had happened when you first saw me must have been a mistake. Now you would be proud of me. The pain of the rejection I had experienced at the hands of the cottagers was fading: I assumed you would love me, because you were my parent – just as Father loved Agatha and Felix.

I reached Geneva not long after sunset. The town's gates were closed and there were men with metal sticks guarding them. I thought for a moment about beating on the gates and demanding entrance, but then I realized the guards might hurt me. I decided instead to look for somewhere nearby where I could spend the night. Tomorrow would be soon enough to meet you. Had I known you were not there I would have set out for Ingolstadt. But I thought you would be in Geneva, because that is where you had prayed to your God you could be.

In the end I found a cave. I think a bear must have lived there at some time, but it hadn't been used for a long while, and it sheltered me from the night winds. I caught a late-roaming rabbit and ate it. I drank from a stream. Then I went to my cave and lay down, ready for sleep. Sleep was a long time coming. The earth beneath me seemed warm, and yet I was cold. I drifted in and out of dreams until the sunrise, when at last I fell into a deep slumber. When I awoke again it was midafternoon. Somewhere near me I could hear voices. I cowered at the back of my cave, hoping these people, whoever they were, would soon go away. I wanted to catch the moment between dusk and the closing of Geneva's gates when I could enter the town and find where you lived, Frankenstein.

A boy disturbed my plans. He came to the mouth of my cave, and giggled.

"Hello there, Mr. Bear!" he shouted.

I hoped he would run away, but he didn't. Instead he began to come into the cave. If there had been a bear living there he would have been dead within seconds. I gave a growl, hoping that would frighten him off, but he just giggled again. I growled again. Still he came in.

A thought struck me. Adult human beings recoiled from me, but perhaps children would be different. I was like a child myself, and all I could see in the world was beauty – because I was able to see through the outward layer of ugliness that so many things have, and perceive the beauty within. Almost all human adults, I knew, found this impossible. Perhaps children were different. Perhaps this boy would be like me. I got up and moved into the light.

"Hello," I said. He began to retreat.

"There's no need to be frightened," I said. "I won't do you any harm. I'm a friend."

He continued to back away.

"I'm the ugliest man you've ever seen." I laughed. "I'm even uglier than that. But I won't hurt you."

He was still retreating, but more slowly now. Once he was out in the daylight he seemed more confident. In fact, he seemed impatient to see the frightful monster I had described. But when I emerged from the cave, he gave a single shriek and began to run. He kept screaming as he ran. Before I knew what I was doing, I was chasing after him, as if he were one of the hares I had hunted down to give to Father's family. I caught him easily, within seconds.

"I want to be your friend," I said wearily.

He just kept screaming.

"I don't want to hurt you," I repeated, but even as I did so I found that I was picking him up bodily and getting ready to wring his neck, just as I had done countless times before with the wild animals that I'd caught. He screamed even louder. I killed him. It was a reflex. One moment he was alive and the next he was dead.

I hurled his small body from me, so that it went tumbling away through the bracken. I squatted down on my haunches and thought . . . nothing. If I'd killed a rabbit I would have felt some satisfaction. Now all that I felt was that I had rid myself of a noisy nuisance. The afternoon was very bright. The songs of the birds were sweet in my ears. The hillside beneath my cave was bare but for bracken.

After a while, I went to look at the corpse of the creature I had killed. Around its neck there was a glittering object that attracted my attention. I snapped the chain and examined this thing. I put it in my mouth and pressed my teeth against it, thinking it might be food; but it tasted horrible. Looking at it more closely, I discovered there was a clasp on one side. When I pressed this, the object fell open at a hinge, and I found myself looking at a picture of you, my dear Herr Frankenstein.

There was another picture inside the frame. It showed the face of a woman. I had believed that there could be no woman more beautiful than Safie, but I was wrong. This woman had ringlets of gold falling around a face of such exquisite loveliness that it drove the breath from my body. Ah, Frankenstein, you have already told me her name. Elizabeth. It is a name that I'll remember. I can see from your face that you love this Elizabeth, and I loved her picture.

I left the boy's body where it was, but took the

locket away with me. I felt no guilt about having killed him, as I say, but I knew that other human beings would wish to seek revenge for what I had done. I had to make myself scarce for at least a few days – perhaps a few weeks. I also realized that by killing someone close to you, Frankenstein – though at the time I had no idea that this was your brother – I had almost certainly earned your hatred.

Up until that moment, I had been prepared to forgive you everything. Through my observations of the cottagers, I had discovered the love that people could share – Father had loved his children, and they had loved him, even though his blindness made him a burden on them. I had been ready to love you, because you were my parent. But now – now that I knew you would hate me – I began to reflect upon the evil that you had done to me.

You had brought me into this world, which was crime enough, but then, seeing that your unnatural offspring was less pretty than other men, you just abandoned me. I began to understand that killing a child was a sin, but it was something that would never have happened had you treated me like a son, like any other father would.

Hours passed, and night fell. I moved around the hillside in the moonlight. All thoughts of entering Geneva and finding you had ebbed. I tell you, Frankenstein, by now I hated you. It must have been after midnight when I discovered a barn. My steps quickened. I could sleep in the straw, and then leave in the morning before the farmer was up and about. But I found someone else already sleeping there – a young woman.

You gave me a mind and a brain, Frankenstein; you also gave me slyness. I looked at the locket I still clutched in my hand, and I looked at the sleeping woman. Carefully, making no noise, I tucked the locket into the pocket of her outer garment.

She snored abruptly on feeling my touch, and turned over. I moved to the door, but she didn't wake up. When I was certain that she was still deeply asleep, I climbed a ladder into the upper loft. There I settled myself in the hay, and at last sleep came.

Later I heard that they had hanged the woman who was in the barn. If I were a human, I wouldn't have hanged her, even if I'd known she was guilty. Think of it – if she had been guilty, which of course she wasn't, of killing your brother, the only reason could have been that she was sick in her mind. Do you humans hang people because they're sick? It appears you do, because you hanged this woman.

One of the things I discovered while I was observing the cottagers was that it was evil for human beings to kill each other – or harm each other in any way. You humans say these things, and yet you then go out and do exactly the opposite.

I don't have any such feelings about guilt or innocence, Frankenstein. As I said, I felt no more emotion over killing your brother than I would if I'd

killed a hare. I could kill you right now if I wanted
to. Don't jerk away like that. You're safe enough. For
my own purposes I want to keep you alive.

I saw the emotion that existed between Felix and
Safie. A little while ago, when I mentioned
Elizabeth's name, I could see in your face the
emotion you feel for her. It is an emotion that I wish
I could share. And yet what mortal woman would
look at me without revulsion? You made me,
Frankenstein. You brought me into the world. It is
your duty to provide a mate for me, a female who is
like myself. A woman who will look at me with the
same softness in her eyes that Safie had when she
looked at Felix.

If you create a mate for me, I will leave your life
forever. Once we are united, we will find somewhere
far away from any human contact, and live our lives
there and you will never hear from me again. If you
refuse to do this, then all of your family and loved
ones are at risk. I shall pick them off one by one. You
love Elizabeth. It's obvious every time I mention her
name. You plan to marry her.

Listen to me, Frankenstein, and listen well. Unless
you do what I want – unless you create a bride for
me – then I shall be with you on your wedding
night!

The Bride

The creature beat the fist of one hand into the palm of the other with each of its final words. Then it sprang up, and in an instant was sprinting away down the side of Montanvert. Though the moonlight was bright, Victor lost sight of the beast almost immediately. With a heavy heart, he pulled himself to his feet and began the long trudge down the mountain to the village he had seen that morning.

Create another monster? A female? How would he go about it? He could hardly ask Elizabeth to allow him to gouge a strip of flesh from her body. And anyway, he wasn't sure if he wanted to run the risk of creating another murderous monster. Yet the creature had said that it would be out of his life forever if he agreed to its demand – that it and its mate would avoid any contact with the human race.

He was lucky to find the last available bed in an inn that night, but he couldn't sleep. All night long he wrestled with his dilemma. It was only when the first light of the morning reached in through the curtains to touch the end of his bed that he was able to come to a conclusion.

The monster was right. It had been treated abominably throughout its short existence. If a mate would bring it happiness, then a mate it should have. Oddly enough, its threat to continue its campaign of murder had little bearing on Victor's decision. He splashed some water in his mouth, shivering in the cold air. His eyes felt gritty. Minutes later he paid his bill and set off for Geneva.

Once back at home, however, Victor found himself procrastinating. He would have to set up his new laboratory in secret, and this was something he found almost impossible to arrange. If Henry – who had just arrived from Ingolstadt and was staying at the castle during his annual vacation from the university – was not by his side, then Elizabeth was, and if not Elizabeth, the baron. And the old man had become so aged by the deaths of William and Justine that he needed a supporting shoulder simply to move from one room to the next.

There was just over a month left until their planned wedding date, when Victor told Elizabeth that he had to go away again.

"I have more scientific research to do," he said sadly. They were eating breakfast together. His father and Henry had yet to emerge from their bedrooms.

She put her hand on his. "Must you go?" she said.

"Yes. I'd rather spend the time away from home now than after we're married, dear Elizabeth."

"Where will you go?"

"England. There are libraries in London that contain books and treatises which are unavailable here. All the time I was at Ingolstadt I was frustrated by the lack of the books I needed. If I don't go to London now to consult them, I'll be unable to tear myself away from you for years, perhaps forever."

"We could wait until after the wedding," she said, "and then go to England as man and wife."

"It would be tedious for you, Elizabeth," he said. "All day long I'd be closeted away in the library, and all night long I'd be doing my calculations. No, it's much better if I go now."

Her face softened. "If you really think that would be the best thing, Victor . . ."

"I do."

A few minutes later Henry appeared.

"You two look as if you've been talking far too seriously for a morning as beautiful as this one," he said cheerfully, helping himself to some breakfast from the sideboard.

"Victor says he must go to England for a few weeks to continue his research," said Elizabeth, her voice low.

"England!" said Henry, joining them at the table. "What a capital idea! I'll come along, Victor, to keep you on the straight and narrow." He winked at Elizabeth. "I've heard tales about those English girls, you know. Worse than the ones at Ingolstadt, if such a thing could be possible."

Elizabeth giggled.

Victor made a feeble attempt at laughter. "I'd rather go alone, Henry," he said. "I've such a lot to do that I don't want to be distracted." Even as he said the words, he knew they were futile. And after a few more minutes it had been settled. Henry was coming with him.

The following night Victor crept out of Castle Frankenstein. There was hardly any moon, and the sky was piercingly clear. He turned the collar of his coat up around his ears and blew into his hands, then slipped quietly away across the lawn.

The baron had insisted that Justine be buried in the family plot, which was at the far end of the estate. It took Victor about fifteen minutes to reach it. He was out of view of the house, now, so he took a little lantern from his pocket and, after much difficulty and not a little cursing, got the thing lit. It hardly seemed to produce enough light for his purposes, but he was able to find the spade he had hidden in the corner.

Justine's gravestone was a simple one. Best not to think about what he was going to do. He gave one last anguished glance at the brilliantly twinkling stars, and then thrust the blade of the spade deep down into the earth.

The digging was easier than he had anticipated, and in less than half an hour he had exposed the top of Justine's coffin. He paused to catch his breath. He estimated it would take at least another hour to dig all around the edges of the coffin so that he could lever the lid off. He had to find a quicker way. The silence of the night was oppressive: he wished an owl would hoot or a night creature scream.

Raising the spade high above his head, he brought the edge of the blade crashing down onto the coffin lid. The wood cracked. Again he smashed the spade down, and the crack widened. He stabbed the tip of the spade into the crack, and pushed down with all his might. Splinters flew up. One nearly hit him in the eye. Breathing loudly, he pushed down once again, and this time the wood split open.

A waft of decay erupted from the coffin, drowning the smell of the newly dug earth. Victor gagged. The face he could see dimly in the lamplight was like a hideous parody of the Justine he had known. All the beauty had been stripped away from her. Her lips were drawn back tightly against her teeth, which were set in a terrible grin. Her eyes had rotted away entirely, leaving only empty sockets: at least she wouldn't be able to see what he was about to do. As he watched, a pallid fat worm crept from her nostril and slithered into the darkness below.

"Don't think about it!" he told himself soundlessly. "Just do it. Do it, then cover her up again and get away from here."

Forcing himself not to remember Justine as a person, he drew a scalpel from his pocket. Keeping his stomach under control with difficulty, he darted the knife forward and stabbed it into Justine's cheek. The flesh came away easily. He hacked two slices from her jaw and clumsily stuffed them into a bag he had brought along for the purpose. "None of this is hurting Justine," he told himself firmly. "She has long departed this corpse. I'm only taking a little of her dead flesh". Even so, he felt his stomach churn again. He vaulted up out of the hole and ran for the wall of the little cemetery. Leaning over it, he vomited violently into the darkness.

Several minutes later, his stomach still rebelling, he forced himself to go back to Justine's graveside. He'd planned to repair the coffin lid as best he could, but he no longer had the heart for that. Weeping bitterly, he hurled the earth back over the face, wielding the spade vigorously in the vain hope that the physical effort would somehow blot out the memory of what he'd just done.

When he'd finished, he sat for a long time on the wall. The leathery strips of Justine's flesh were a guilty weight in his pocket. The lantern's light seemed very small against the ponderous darkness of the night. At last he was able to stop the trembling of his limbs. He hid the spade back in the corner of the plot. Once he was in sight of the castle, its great bulk a smudge against the stars, he blew out his lantern. He was able to get back to his bedroom without being observed, and spent another sleepless night.

In London Victor made a great show of going to all the public libraries, including the Reading Room of the British Museum, which he had heard about but which was far more impressive than he had ever believed possible. Henry tagged along with him for the first few days, but soon became bored. Victor leafed through various books rather aimlessly, pretending to conduct his medical research and, every now and then, coming across something that might help him in the construction of the monster's mate. What he really needed to do, he knew, was order all his chemical supplies and find somewhere he could use as a laboratory, but this was impossible with Henry always in attendance.

After a week or so Victor announced that he had exhausted the resources of London and would now have to head north, to the Royal Library of Scotland, in Edinburgh. He had hoped that Henry would decide to leave him at this point, but the man insisted on accompanying him. He began to hate his old friend. Several more days were wasted as they journeyed north. In Edinburgh Victor spent a day at the Royal Library, then told Henry that his researches required him to travel even farther north.

"There's a library in the Orkney Islands," Victor lied, "that may contain the final clue. The Orkneys are far to the north of the northernmost point of Scotland, dear friend, and the sea crossing is often rough. I can't drag you there, Henry – you have been far too kind already in accompanying me this far. Besides, your new term at Ingolstadt starts next week. Surely you should be heading for home?"

They'd climbed the hill called Arthur's Seat that morning, and were looking out over the city.

"I worry about you, Victor."

"I can manage, Henry."

Victor said the words with enough determination that his friend stared at him, even more concerned than before.

"Are you sure?"

"I'm absolutely sure. When you get back to Castle Frankenstein, tell Elizabeth that I'll be with her as soon as I can. If it means our marriage must be delayed – well, Henry, until this line of research is complete I'd be unable to settle down."

"Can't you at least tell me what it is you're trying to discover, Victor?"

"Not yet, Henry. Not for a while yet. It's important work, and I don't want anyone else to hear about it. It may come to nothing, of course. And anyway, you probably wouldn't understand it if I tried to explain – I'm afraid that's one of the disadvantages of a classical education, Henry!"

Victor laughed. After a moment, Henry joined in.

The next morning Henry – still offering to stay with Victor if he could be of help – set off for Leith to embark for the continent.

At last Victor was free! He went to the largest apothecary shop in Edinburgh's Princes Street and placed an order for all the chemicals he required. Less then fifty yards away, in Rose Street, he found a builder who was willing to make a tank like the one that Victor had constructed in Ingolstadt. Most important of all was the mountain of electrical batteries he bought, each weighing so much that he had difficulty carrying even one of them.

He had told Henry he must go to the Orkneys only to make his friend leave, but he had since come to the conclusion that the Orkneys were as good a place as anywhere to create the monster's bride. He paid for all the equipment in cash, plus an extra fee to have them delivered to Kirkwall, in the Orkney Islands. That night he set off.

A few days later, Victor waited impatiently by the quay for the boat that was bringing his equipment from Kirkwall. The grey sea churned beneath him, as if it wanted to devour the land. He had at last found himself somewhere that he could set up a new laboratory – the tiny island of Sibbens. It was little more than a rock jutting up out of the sea, with sparse patches of grass and wiry vegetation on which a few sheep miserably fed. Apart from the one that he had rented, there were only two other cottages on the island, and the families that lived in them showed hardly any interest in the curious-looking southern stranger with his weird accent. And that was exactly the way he wanted things to remain. He kicked his toe against a crack in the stones of the quay. Would the blasted boat never turn up?

And then finally he saw it, tossing through the angry waters. Within a few minutes, half a dozen friendly sailors were climbing up beside him, and not long after they were carrying the tank and all his various jars and bottles and batteries up the dirt track to the cottage. They had brought his supplies of food and wine as well – enough to keep him going for at least a two weeks, although he planned to stay no more than one. Victor gave them a generous tip and a bottle of brandy to share between them. They shouted their good wishes across the churning sea as the boat retreated into the drab evening.

Victor worked late that night. First he assembled the tank, then he began the slow task of pouring the chemicals into it. The cottage had a fireplace, but he had forgotten to gather any wood or to buy any peat to burn. He was hardly aware of the cold, however, as he toiled feverishly on into the night.

It must have been about five in the morning when finally the concoction of chemicals was mixed. The lamp was flickering, and he added some more oil to it. He gathered together the empty jars.

"I'm simply putting off the moment," he said to himself angrily. "The quicker you get this infernal business started, Victor Frankenstein, the quicker it'll be over. You've done it before, so you can do it again. And then you can go back to Elizabeth and forget all about this miserable period of your life."

He dug out the cloth wallet in which he had brought the scraps of Justine's flesh. They no longer seemed to be remotely human – or even flesh at all. They were just two things. They could have been anything.

"Do it. Do it now."

He tossed the blackened, twisted shreds into the tank. Then, gingerly, he wired the huge batteries together one by one. Finally he dropped the free end of the last wire into the liquid. There was a short-lived blaze of violent light. Then, abruptly, the batteries went dead. But he knew that the electrical charge had been delivered.

He sat back to watch. And nothing happened. Of course nothing would. It would be hours before the flesh began to respond to the nutrients in the tank. He hadn't been able to watch the first of his creatures grow, and he took a sick satisfaction from the fact that this time he would be able to observe how the process progressed. But there would be nothing for him to see in what remained of the night. He threw himself down on a heap of clothing in the corner, and fell asleep at once.

It was well past noon when he awoke, and he spent some moments wondering where on earth he could be. The wind was howling around the little cottage, making the roof grunt and groan as if it wanted to fly away from the walls. The breeze coming in through the hut's ill-fitting door was slowly flicking over the pages of one of Victor's notebooks on the floor.

He sat up stiffly, staring balefully at the pile of empty jars. He would have to get rid of them all somehow, he supposed. It was only then that he thought to turn his attention to the contents of the tank.

The two leathery strips of flesh had come together, but that wasn't the first thing he noticed. What was most obvious was the way that they had changed. Where before they'd been blackened by decay, now they were a strange, shining pink. He remembered how his creature had seemed at first – as if it had been flayed – before contact with the air had hardened its skin. It looked as if the same would be true of the ghastly bride.

He peered more closely through the glass. The flesh had grown during the time that he had been asleep. Already it was at least three times the size that it had been when he had thrown its component pieces into the liquid. Swirls of what appeared to be blood hung in the clear fluid around it. All thoughts of the morality of what he was doing fled. He was amazed and fascinated. He watched the tank for an hour or more, telling himself he could see minor changes taking place, before hunger forced him away. Even then, as he ate an unpalatable meal of stale bread and over-ripe cheese, he continued to stare at the tank.

Days passed, and the flesh continued to expand. He had half-expected that it would form itself into a perfect miniature of a human being, and then simply increase in size; or, perhaps, it might go through all the stages his medical textbooks had shown him of the developing baby in the womb. In fact, it did neither. There seemed no pattern at all to its changes. The first recognizably human part of it to appear was an arm. Then from the end of this sprang – with shocking swiftness – the right-hand side of a ribcage, over which the flesh crept so quickly that Victor could almost see its advance.

In this unpredictable fashion, the creature grew, until at last there came a morning when it had the first semblance of a face.

At which point, all Victor's earlier qualms returned. It was too soon to be certain, but the rudimentary features looked horribly like Justine's.

He ran out of the hut, slamming the door behind him. It was all he could do not to scream.

The wind-borne rain was like a bitterly cold hand slapping his face. Hunching his shoulders, he pressed on through it, to the sea. The sky was dark grey, and seemed so heavy that it was barely able to support itself. The little island had never appeared so desolate or hostile.

He kicked among the pebbles along the shore. He hadn't expected the she-monster he was creating to look anything like Justine – after all, the original beast had looked nothing like himself. Or had it? He had left the monster in the tank in Ingolstadt far longer than his calculations had indicated he should. Had it, at one stage during its development, resembled himself, Victor Frankenstein, exactly, and then continued to grow until it became horrific?

But there were more urgent matters to consider. If the bride he was growing for her fearful mate looked like Justine, might she not have all of Justine's sensibilities? Would she resemble the dead woman in mind as much as in physical appearance? If that were the case, how could he think of handing her over to the frightful being who had killed Victor's younger brother and who had caused the death of Justine herself? Would she be willing to live out the rest of her life in some remote corner of the world, with no one else to share her existence except a creature so vile that no one could look at it without a shudder? Could he condemn Justine – poor, sweet, innocent Justine – to an existence like that?

At the same time, could he deny the female creature life? The real Justine could never live again – the hangman's noose had seen to that – but the replica Victor was growing would also, surely, seek to live. Did he have the right to deny it – her – that privilege?

He remembered Justine all too vividly. She had been a person who was vibrant with the joy of living. In part he had been responsible for her death. Could he take away her life a second time? All day he walked along the rainswept shore, circling the little island several times, deaf to the pounding of the sea against the boulders. As night fell, he groped his way back to the hut, his heart leaden. He knew what he must do.

As soon as he was inside, he threw off his soaking coat and lit the lamp. Not giving himself any more time to think, he lashed out with his boot at the side of the tank, and the glass shattered. A torrent of liquid flooded out over his legs, drenching him to the knees before it gurgled out through the gap under the door.

Then he seized two of his scalpels. Kicking aside the broken glass, he reached through and grabbed the shoulder of the partial corpse, dragging the heavy flesh out onto the stone floor, where it flopped with a revolting noise. He raised his right hand and plunged a scalpel into the partly formed chest of the dead creature, ripping down to the torso. Blood – human blood, or an approximation of it – sprayed everywhere.

Victor turned his face away. He felt as if he were killing Justine all over again, even though the carcass he was attacking had not yet attained the spark of life. When he looked back, the eyes had opened with a terrible look of alarm. Justine's clear eyes looked directly into his. She was trying to scream in agony, but her vocal cords had not yet formed.

He froze. Those eyes were imploring him to stop.

But Victor made himself continue. He told himself that the opening of the eyes was merely a reflex brought about by severing a nerve. The dead meat could not possibly be conscious. He slashed again with the scalpels, first one and then the other, ripping the half-formed creature to pieces. He never knew just how long this act of imitation murder took him. It could have been five minutes or it could have been an hour. In the end he stumbled back from the evidence of his butchery and cowered against the wall, curling up into a ball, unwilling to confront the true horror of what he had done.

And still the wind – the relentless, pitiless Orkney wind – screeched around the cottage. Drenched in blood, Victor was shaking with terror.

Then, all at once the gale dropped. In the silence, there was a tap at the window opposite him. Once more, Victor froze. Then, both dreading and knowing what he might see, he slowly raised his eyes. Pressed against the outside of the glass, was a huge hand –

the monster's hand. Even through the dirty glass, he could see that the features of its face were grossly distorted.

"I will seek revenge, Frankenstein!" it bellowed. "I will seek revenge on you and all whom you hold dear!"

Then the creature was gone. How long had it been watching him? Terrified and remorseful, Victor curled up even smaller.

The tempest returned.

Wedding Night

Somehow Victor slept, and in the morning he felt as if many of the cares of his life had somehow been lifted from his shoulders. Before last night he'd been terrified of the creature; now, once again, he had returned to a state of mere acceptance of his doom. He almost looked forward to death.

Setting to work methodically, he cleaned his scalpels and stowed them away in his case. Most of his clothes were filthy, but he folded them roughly and packed them away as well. He couldn't do much about the wreckage of the tank, or the countless glass jars that were scattered everywhere, but he certainly had to get rid of the remains of the half-formed Justine. Taking care not to spatter his clean clothes with blood, he packed the pieces of flesh into an old canvas bag along with some heavy stones. This done, he mopped the floor, trying to get rid of all traces of blood.

He knew he had to get away from the island. Where he was going to go he had no idea, but he wanted to put as much distance between him and the creature as possible. How it had reached the island was something else he didn't know. It must have swum from the mainland. He tried to put out of his mind any thoughts of how far it could swim. He knew there was nowhere on earth he could be safe from it. It would follow him. It had greater speed, strength and stamina than any mortal-born human being.

He trudged across the thin grass to the hovel where the nearest family lived. This family survived mainly on the fish they caught in the chilly waters of the North Sea. Not long ago they had somehow managed to obtain a new boat, but Victor had seen the old one still at anchor, apparently seaworthy.

"What is it that you'd be wanting to buy a boat for?" said the old fisherman, opening his door only the width of his face.

"I want to leave the island. Today."

"But the mailboat will be here early next week," said the fisherman.

"I have to leave before then. Name me a price for the boat."

The old man considered for a moment, then looked up at Victor slyly. "I canna let you have it for less than fifteen pounds," he said.

"Fifteen pounds!" said Victor immediately. "Done!" Then, feeling guilty, he added: "Call it twenty."

"Guineas," said the fisherman, obviously realizing that he was driving a poor bargain.

Victor plucked the coins from his pouch and counted them into the man's hands. "And here's an extra shilling for one of your lads to row me out to it tonight," he said.

The old man was testing the coins between his teeth. "Ay," he said, "tonight."

Victor suddenly understood that the man assumed he was a smuggler. Well, let him think that. The cargo he was going to carry was far more ghastly than anything the fisherman could imagine.

"Tonight," said Victor. "As soon as the moon rises."

For once the sea wasn't too rough. The fisherman's son dourly waved farewell to Victor in the moonlight and was soon heading back to shore. Victor waited a little while, feeling as if he had just escaped from prison, and then set the boat's single sail. The night was clear, and he was able to get an approximate bearing from the pole star. As long as he plotted a course that was more or less due southeast he would come, sooner rather than later, to Denmark or Germany. There he would abandon the boat and make his way across country by rail or carriage to Geneva. There was one more thing that he must do.

He took hold of the bag containing the remains of the second Justine. As he propped it on the rail he once again imagined he heard the real Justine's laughter as she played with William. He had loved her almost as much as he had loved his brother – indeed, had it not been for Elizabeth, he might well have fallen in love with her. But the travesty of her that had begun to grow in his tank – that was something

best forgotten, best disposed of. He
shoved the bag into the inky waters.
It sank with hardly a bubble. Then,
trusting that the wind would not
change during the night, he went
back below and settled himself
on a dirty bunk.

Three weeks later he was in
Geneva. Elizabeth met him as
his carriage hurtled up the
drive to Castle Frankenstein.
She threw herself into his arms,
covering his face with kisses. At
last she pulled herself away, holding
him at arm's length.

"Elizabeth," he said. "Oh, Elizabeth, you don't
know what I've been through. Just seeing your face
again makes me believe there's some hope in life after
all."

Her features clouded. "Not all my news is good,
Victor. Come inside. Let the servants deal with your
luggage. Here, I'll take your coat."

He followed her to a little sitting room just off the
hall. She bustled around for a minute or two, talking
of nothing much, obviously trying to compose
herself for what she really wanted to say. Finally she
sat down in the chair opposite his.

"Your father is very ill," she said, leaning forward
earnestly, her eyes fixed unwaveringly on his. "Very ill
indeed. He's an old man, Victor, and I don't think he's

long for this world."

Victor drew in his breath, then slowly let it out again. "As you say, Elizabeth, he's an old man – and recently he's had to cope with far too much grief. It's not entirely unexpected. I must go and see him."

He half-rose, but Elizabeth gestured to him to remain seated.

"There's one other bit of bad news that I haven't dared tell him yet," she said. Her eyes fell, and she began to pick at a nonexistent loose thread on her skirt. "It's about Henry."

"What's he done?" said Victor.

"Nothing – and he never will again."

"He's dead?"

"Yes."

"But – but what happened?"

She looked up again, and her eyes were full of tears. "He was most brutally murdered. Strangled in Ingolstadt. A week ago. The police believe he was killed by the same person who slew poor William, and they've issued a posthumous pardon to Justine. It was then they discovered that her grave had been desecrated. They dug down to the coffin so the pastor could sprinkle holy water on her and found the coffin lid smashed and Justine's face scored by a knife."

Victor felt as if he couldn't breathe. Henry was dead! The abhorrent monster had returned to Geneva and had started to carry out its threat of destroying all those dear to Victor. He wondered who would be next. His father? Elizabeth? Victor wished that it could be himself, so that there would be an end to the story, but he knew that the creature wasn't able to show such mercy.

He put his face in his hands. "This is terrible," he muttered. "Terrible."

Elizabeth reached out and put her hand on his arm. For a long time they remained motionless. Finally Victor shook his shoulders and stood up. "I must go and see my father," he said. "You were right not to tell him about these dreadful things. He has no need to know. I'll keep them from him as well."

"I'll come with you," she said, gathering up her skirt and standing. "Here, Victor, take my hand."

As they climbed the long curve of the main stairway she added: "And remember, Victor, we must look cheerful for him. After all, you're home safely. Isn't that a cause for celebration?"

Although Elizabeth had half-prepared him, Victor was still shocked by his father's appearance. It seemed the baron had aged ten years or more in the few weeks Victor had been away. He looked not so much old as dead, though still breathing. The flesh of his face had shrunk and grown thinner, so that it was wrapped tightly around his skull. His remaining tufts of white hair looked as if they would break at a touch. His cheeks were craters. His eyes, when he opened them as Victor and Elizabeth entered, looked infinitely tired.

He raised his head from the pillow. "Victor," he wheezed weakly. "You're home, my boy. Thank God for having preserved you!" Tears glistened at the corners of his eyes.

Victor, recalling how his father's voice had boomed along the corridors in days gone by, knelt by the bed overwhelmed with emotion and kissed the baron's bony hand.

"Yes, father," he said, "I'm home. I wish, seeing you so unwell, I'd come home earlier."

"Nonsense, Victor. There's nothing wrong with me that a few more days in bed won't cure."

Victor could find nothing to say. Then his father sighed deeply. "That was a lie. You know it and I know it, and dearest Elizabeth, who has nursed me more than I deserve, knows it. I'm dying, my son. Who knows whether it'll be days or weeks or . . ."

His voice faded away. Victor stayed on his knees by the bed. The baron laid a hand on his shoulder.

"There is one thing that would make me very happy before I die," the old man said. His voice was as quiet as a soft breeze rustling autumn leaves. "It would be to see you and my darling Elizabeth married at last."

Victor bowed his head. Again, conflicting emotions ran around his brain. He wanted more than anything to please his father. He wanted more than anything to marry Elizabeth. But he also remembered a hoarse voice bawling at him: "I shall be with you on your wedding night!"

"Don't worry, father. We'll be married as soon as

the pastor will permit," he said, beginning to sob. When he looked up, his father's eyes had closed once more. But there was a faint hint of a smile on his face.

A week later Victor stood in the doorway of the village church with his new bride leaning against his shoulder. Though thoughts of the creature were never far from his mind, he couldn't help smiling as he leaned over and kissed Elizabeth and heard the

cheers of a small crowd of villagers and servants.

It was a gloriously bright morning. The sky was a brilliant alpine blue, with wisps of clouds scurrying high above. Victor couldn't help feeling happy. Two servants carried his father on a chair out from the little chapel and down the porch steps to join him and Elizabeth.

The old man was weeping. "This is the day I've dreamed about for years," he managed to say. "The two people I love most in the world . . ."

He broke off in a fit of coughing. Elizabeth took his face between her hands and kissed him on the forehead. "Now I can truly call you 'father' at last," she said softly.

A carriage was waiting just outside the church grounds, ready to take Victor and Elizabeth to Lake Geneva. They were to honeymoon in Italy – at the Villa Lavenza, on the shores of Lake Como. Today they were going to sail to Evian, where they would spend their first night as man and wife. Tomorrow they would travel on by carriage. Victor felt very relieved that they were putting a great deal of water between themselves and Geneva. Although he knew that the enormous creature was able to swim great distances – his experience in the Orkneys had proved that – the wide lake nevertheless seemed to offer them some sort of security.

The little vessel scudded along, a fresh wind filling the sails. On one side of them Victor and Elizabeth could see Mont Salève, with the huge mass of Mont Blanc in the distance. On the other there were the even more forbidding slopes of the Jura Mountains. Sometimes he and Elizabeth chattered to each other; other times, trying to ignore the amused eye of the skipper, they kissed.

As evening came they approached Evian. They sent their baggage on to their inn, and spent an hour or two rambling along the beach in the dusk. It was the first time they had been alone since swearing their marriage vows. Elizabeth was becoming happier and happier with each passing moment, but Victor's mood sank. The creature had pledged vengeance upon him. Earlier in the day he had been content to believe that they were too far away for the monster to carry out its threat of being with him on his wedding night; now he became convinced that it would indeed appear.

"What's the matter, Victor?" said Elizabeth.

"I'll tell you tomorrow. There's something dreadful I have to tell you – but it can wait until tomorrow."

"Tell me now," she insisted, clutching his arm.

"Tomorrow."

"You're just teasing." She began to laugh, but then stopped. "Is it something very dreadful, Victor?"

His silence gave her the answer.

"Is it anoth . . . ?"

"No, it's nothing like that," he snapped. Then he was immediately contrite. "Oh, I'm sorry. I shouldn't have spoken to you so sharply. My researches have made me do some very foolish things. Nobody else but me knows what they are. Now that you're my wife, then obviously I must open my heart to you. But I don't want to do that today – today of all days. Let's go to our inn. I'm hungry."

After they'd eaten they sat outside for a long while, watching the town of Evian quieten for the night. One by one, the lighted windows around them darkened. The reflections of the stars shone on the calm waters of the lake. Elizabeth was wearing a shawl, but eventually she shivered inside it. "It's time to go up to bed, Victor," she said shyly. "I'll call you when I'm ready."

She pecked him briefly on the cheek, and was about to leave the terrace when he caught her hand and pulled her back for a long, lingering kiss.

"Don't be long," he said, his voice faltering.

"I won't be," she said, and was gone.

As soon as she'd disappeared, his attention returned to the lake. There was enough moonlight for him to be able to see its mirrored surface stretching all the way to the horizon. If the creature really were swimming to Evian, pursuing them, Victor would be able to spot the splashing a mile away. But all he could see were the occasional expanding rings of ripples where fish jumped or water birds moved.

He clenched the arm of his chair tightly. "I shall be with you on your wedding night," the creature had said savagely. Well, Victor was ready for it. He felt the pistol tucked into his inner jacket pocket – keeping its presence a secret from Elizabeth had been difficult, both when it was in their shared trunk and, after dinner, when he'd slipped it into the pocket. He was also wearing a sword, which he had claimed he'd put on as part of his formal dress for dinner. Little did Elizabeth realize that this was no ceremonial weapon but the sharpest blade Victor had been able to find hanging on the walls of Castle Frankenstein. He waited, motionless, his eyes intently scanning the surface of the lake. Everyone in Evian had long ago gone to bed. He was utterly alone.

The night was growing very chilly, but still he kept up his watch. He was ready for a final confrontation

with the monstrous being he had created. If he could, he would persuade it to leave him and his dear ones alone forever; but he was prepared to kill it outright, if need be. Once again he felt the pistol. Its weight, under his shoulder, was reassuring.

What was taking Elizabeth so long to prepare for bed? His head began to loll onto his chest as tiredness overtook him.

Then he started. Somewhere above him there had been a shriek and then the sound of a window breaking. Elizabeth!

Something heavy dropped from an upper floor of the inn and lumbered off rapidly through the empty streets. Victor threw himself from his chair and charged into the inn. He leapt up the stairs, repeating over and over again, "No . . . no . . . no!"

He kicked open the door of their room. The first thing he saw was the shattered window. Then his eyes turned to the bed. "Elizabeth!" he screamed. "Oh my God! What have I done to you?"

The bedding was a mass of blood. Elizabeth's body lay across it, her head twisted at an unnatural angle. There was a gaping, gory hole in her chest. On her face – her dead face – there was a look of shock and agony. Her eyes, wide open, seemed to be staring at Victor accusingly. Through the window, from far in the distance, came a maniacal laugh.

Victor threw himself across the body of his dead wife, screamed again, then began to weep. He touched her blonde head tenderly. "Oh, God,

Elizabeth, I'm so sorry," he said, although he could hardly see her any longer. "It's my fault, my fault, my fault . . ."

Then there were hands on his shoulders, pulling him away from Elizabeth's corpse. In fits and starts he heard voices. Some of the other guests, woken by his screams, assumed he was Elizabeth's killer and wanted to hang him from the nearest tree. But soon more rational people intervened. Someone guided him to a chair, where he sat sobbing uncontrollably. Another hand offered him brandy, but he was shaking so violently that he was unable to grip the glass.

"Hang me!" he said. "I killed her! It's because of me that she's dead!"

"That's enough of that talk," said a gruff voice. "You weren't the one who escaped through that window, and you weren't the one who took her heart with you." Victor convulsed in even deeper grief. Her heart! The monster might as well have stolen her soul – his soul. Abruptly he stopped weeping, and sat up straight in the chair.

"I know who her murderer is," he said. "I have seen the face of the one who killed her. I will follow this vile criminal to the ends of the earth, and then have my vengeance."

"He's babbling," said someone.

"Wait," said someone else. Victor recognized the voice of the innkeeper. The man bent down to look him in the eyes. "Did you see the murder?"

"No," responded Victor, "but I do know who committed it. There is someone who swore he would wreck my wedding night."

"You can't leave tonight," said the innkeeper. "Someone has sent for the police. They'll want to speak to you. Arrangements must be made for . . . well, arrangements."

"Leave me alone with her," said Victor. "I want to beg her forgiveness. If it hadn't been for my own stupidity she wouldn't have died like this."

They left him with Elizabeth until the police arrived. For most of the rest of the night he was interviewed, but at last the inspector declared himself satisfied that Victor was innocent. Then the innkeeper took him away into another bedroom, fed him a sedative despite his protestations, and put him into bed.

"I will follow her murderer to the ends of the earth," repeated Victor.

It was the last thing he said before sleep engulfed him.

Among the Snows

Captain Walton, skipper of the *Margaret Saville*, closed the door of the cabin as quietly as he could. The ship was still locked in the ice of the Arctic. This past week the sun had been dipping ever closer to the horizon, and it couldn't be long before the six-month night began. He hoped beyond all hope that the ice would release them before that happened. His crew had shot a few seals and even a polar bear, but there was still far from enough food to sustain them through the winter.

During his spare time he had listened to Victor Frankenstein's story, and had simultaneously watched the man drifting ever closer to his death. Victor couldn't be more than twenty-five – although Walton guessed he might be younger. The man had been so delirious throughout much of his account that it was impossible to tell either his age or the truth of his tale. How much of it did the captain believe? He didn't know. The giant figure he'd seen on the ice made him think there might be some truth in Victor's story. But all logical sense persuaded him that the rambling account was just the raving of a very sick man.

That Victor was dying was, however, certain. The *Margaret Saville* had only a limited stock of medicines, and none had proved useful against the fever that he was suffering from. Walton punched the side of his fist against the bulkhead. During the past week he had come to like and admire Victor. To be sure, the young man had done some very stupid things – if his tale was to be credited – but his aim had always been to help humanity. He had wanted to create a better humanity.

Captain Walton found Rostop on deck.

"He's dying." said Walton wearily.

"Could have told you that when he came on board," said Rostop, bluntly.

"When I left him he was falling asleep. He told me

how he followed this creature of his up through the northern lands. He said that the monster seemed to want him to catch up with it – that it left clues to help him find it.

"That's if there ever was a monster," said Rostop.

"I think there was," said Captain Walton. "Whether it was a real monster or just a projection of Victor's mind I couldn't tell you, but he certainly believes in it. It was real to him – and, remember, we saw that giant creature on the sled."

"We saw a big man," said Rostop, tersely.

"A very big man. Too big to be a man, I think."

Rostop took a pipe from his pocket. "Think we'll get out of this?" he said, gesturing at the waste.

"Maybe," said Walton. "If God is with us."

There was a loud groan from below. For an instant Walton thought it was Victor. Then the boat swayed.

"God does seem to be with us," he said, keeping his voice as cool as possible.

There was another lurch. The timbers creaked. The sailors, who were returning from a hunting trip, began to cheer – and to run over to the ship, because cracks were starting to open up in the ice.

"We're going to be free!" said Walton. He punched Rostop affectionately on the shoulder. "Didn't I tell you?"

The first mate grinned. "No, but I'll say to the crew you did."

"Bring out some rum. Quickly, so it's ready when they come aboard."

Chuckling, Walton turned to go to his cabin. Then

he remembered Victor. He supposed he should look in on him. Perhaps a little rum would revive the man. He tapped at the door of Victor's cabin. There was no response. Then a tremendous shock hit the *Margaret Saville*. Walton instinctively glanced up, as if the ship had been struck by a thunderbolt. He smiled to himself. Not a thunderbolt at all: more of the ice was breaking up around the hull.

Through the cabin door, he heard a noise. He tapped again. Still there was no reply. There was a sound, though. He put his ear to the wood and listened more closely. Someone – Walton could hardly believe it was Victor – was sobbing hoarsely. The captain grabbed the handle and threw open the door. A huge figure was crouched over the man Walton had come to call a friend. It turned its face toward him, its eyes filled with hatred. His stomach lurched.

"You!" Walton hissed. "So Victor was telling the truth!"

"Yes, me," said the creature. Its face was repulsive. No wonder, Walton thought, that everyone rejected it on sight.

"I came to ask him for forgiveness," said the creature, "but he was dead before I could."

"You killed him? "

"No. He was already dead. He was my father and my mother, and he treated me cruelly – abandoning me when I was hardly born – but at last, out there on the ice, I discovered that I loved him. When I saw the pack-ice splintering I decided I must come to him to beg forgiveness for all the terrible crimes I've committed against him. But he was dead."

"You've committed a crime against my ship," said the captain. "You've torn a hole through her side to reach here."

"It's nothing you can't repair. Look at Frankenstein instead. He's past any mending you could do."

Walton looked at the frail figure sprawled on the bunk. Maybe it was better this way. Who would want to live with the memories of a wife and a younger brother and a friend murdered, and of a father dying of grief, and of another friend hanged unjustly?

Victor, through his arrogance, had brought many of his sufferings upon himself – and, more than that, upon those around him – but he had never meant to

do any harm.

"Do you repent all the things you've done?" said Walton, wondering where his courage came from.

"I can't repent," said the creature, moving back to the hole it had made in the *Margaret Saville*'s side. "I don't have the capacity to feel repentance, or remorse, or guilt. Frankenstein built me as best he could, so that I had the form of a man. If his experiment hadn't been interrupted, I'd have been so like a man that you wouldn't have been able to tell the difference.

"But what he wasn't able to do was to give me a soul. I've no real conscience. I can tell right from wrong, but I can't really understand why I should do one rather than the other. Except now . . . now I've learned a little about the world and, sitting out on the ice, letting my hatred ebb, about myself."

"I can take you back with us," said Walton, moving cautiously into the cabin.

"I wouldn't want you to. I'm always going to be an exile from the human race. Somewhere out there on the ice I'll die, eventually – I have no idea how long my allotted lifespan might be. But I do want to die, alone, unmocked – unmocked by those who were given an easier life than I was."

"I wouldn't mock you," said Walton, quietly. "You've done awful things, but it's easy to see why you have. I wouldn't –"

"And the rest of the world? Your crew?" The creature snarled viciously. "Captain, I'm not safe in human company. I tell you, I have no ability to tell the difference between good and evil. I couldn't trust myself – so why should anyone else trust me? If I weren't hanged for my crimes I'd be caged away as a freak, perhaps displayed for the fascination of pretty women brought to see me by the men who wanted to impress them." The creature was spitting the words. It understood only too well.

"No, I don't want to come back to civilization with you. Civilization threw sticks and stones at me, just because I was ugly. Civilization would do the same again. Much better for me to find my death in the ice. The cold will kill me, in the end, but at least it will not deliberately torment me."

More swiftly than Walton's eyes could follow, the creature sprang out through the hole it had beaten in the ship's side. The captain took a few paces forward. Through the breach he watched the monster leap from one ice floe to the next until it reached the pack-ice.

Moments later it was lost in darkness and distance.

Other Versions of the Frankenstein Story

Almost immediately after its publication, *Frankenstein* was adapted and retold by other writers. Even today, almost two centuries later, it continues to inspire new versions in various forms: theatre, films, comics, and even music, as well as books. Some of the most famous of these are listed below.

Theatre　The first play to use the story was Brinsley Peake's *Presumption: or the Fate of Frankenstein* (1823). Mary Shelley herself went to see it, but was unimpressed, for like many other adaptations, it concentrated on the horror element and ignored the book's scientific and philosophical arguments. Three years later, Henry Milner's *Frankenstein or the Man and the Monster* was the first version that actually showed the animation of the monster on stage.

Films　The first Frankenstein film was made in 1910, by J. Searle Dawley, and lasted only twelve minutes. It contained the first representation of the monster on film. Over the next 20 years many films dealing with the creation of artificial life were made in the USA, Italy and Germany. Some of them retold parts of the Frankenstein story; others reinvented the idea.

In Fritz Lang's *Metropolis* (1926), a mad scientist invents a female monster. This film provided a lot of the visual imagery that is now associated with later Frankenstein films. The most important of these, simply called *Frankenstein*, was directed by James Whale in 1931 for Universal Studios. Many critics claim that this is the best horror film ever made, and it is this version of the monster that most people think of when they think of *Frankenstein* – the beast with a flat head and bolts through its neck. In this film, the monster was played by the actor Boris Karloff. This portrayal was so successful that many people now think that "Frankenstein" is the name of the monster, not its creator.

In 1957 the British film company Hammer made *The Curse of Frankenstein*. While many of the characters in the book remain the same, the story is retold and, if anything, is more violent and horrific than the original. This was the first in Hammer's series of Frankenstein films which continued for nearly 20 years.

Young Frankenstein, by Mel Brooks, was released in 1974. It uses the story as the basis for the first Frankenstein comedy, but in fact is also a very clever spoof of older Frankenstein films. It is also the only Frankenstein film which has a happy ending – the monster gets married and becomes an accepted member of society.

Comics In the early 1970s Marvel, the American comic publisher, published a series of 18 books called *The Frankenstein Monster*. These are now very rare collectors' items.

Music *The Rocky Horror Show* (1973), written by Richard O'Brien, is a parody of the Frankenstein story retold as a rock musical. Part comedy, part horror, it was also filmed in 1975 as *The Rocky Horror Picture Show*.

In the 1970s and 1980s, the funk musician George Clinton released a number of albums about Dr Funkenstein, a space alien who created a race of funk monsters dedicated to filling the world with dance music. *The Clones of Dr Funkenstein* (1976), by Clinton's band Parliament, is among the best-known of these.

Frankenstein!! (1977), by the Austrian composer HK Gruber, is a musical entertainment for a singer and group of musicians. It is based on a number of rhymes written for children by the poet H.C. Artmann. Some of these are based on the Frankenstein story. Others are about different characters from horror, cowboy and spy films.

DRACULA
FROM THE STORY BY BRAM STOKER

Retold by Mike Stocks
With an introduction and notes by Anthony Marks
Illustrations by Barry Jones

CONTENTS

About Dracula   148

Castle Dracula   151

The Ship with No Crew   168

Horror at Hillingham   181

Desperate Measures   198

The Graveyard   211

Carfax   229

The Vampire Vanishes   245

The Deadly Chase   262

Other Versions of the Dracula Story 286

About Dracula

The author of *Dracula*, Bram Stoker, was born near Dublin, in Ireland, in 1847. He worked in the legal profession, then in the Irish civil service, and his first stories were published in the early 1870s. In 1877 he met Henry Irving, the most famous English actor of his day, when Irving gave a reading at Trinity College, Dublin. Shortly after this, Stoker moved with his wife to London and became Irving's theatrical manager, a position he held for 28 years. During this period he wrote many short stories and eleven novels, as well as his memoirs of his work with Irving.

But only one of these books remains well-known: *Dracula*. It is one of the most powerful horror stories of all time. Stoker began making notes for it in 1890 while visiting the North Yorkshire seaside town of Whitby, and it was eventually published in 1897. Since that date it has never been out of print. It has also been translated into nearly fifty languages. Count Dracula remains one of the most popular figures in contemporary horror fiction, represented in countless films, books and comics.

Dracula draws its inspiration from many sources. Its

dark, brooding style, and episodes of bloodthirsty terror, resemble the horror and suspense stories (known as Gothic novels) that became popular in the previous century, with books like Walpole's *The Castle of Otranto* and Anne Radcliffe's *The Mysteries of Udolpho*. Tales of blood-sucking monsters can be found in various ancient civilizations, including China, Greece and the Babylonian and Assyrian empires. Medieval vampire legends were common in such Eastern European countries as Albania, Hungary and Romania, and vampire stories had already been served up to British readers in the form of works like Polidori's *The Vampyre* (1819) and the anonymous *Varney the Vampire* (1846).

There were also several historical characters that Stoker may have been familiar with. These included a 16th-century Eastern European count, Vlad Tepes (Vlad the Impaler), who was also known as *dracul*, the local word for "devil", and the Blood Countess, a 16th-century Hungarian aristocrat who liked to bathe in the blood of animals and young women, because she believed it would keep her young. All these elements combine in Stoker's book to create a dramatic portrayal of evil.

But *Dracula* was far more successful than other vampire novels before or since. There are two main reasons for this. Firstly, from the middle of the 18th century, people had been taught that science, reason, industry and wealth would solve the world's problems. But during the Victorian era, many people began to doubt this, feeling that industry and technology had created the horrors of inner city slums and that science and wealth had failed to eradicate disease and decay. *Dracula* tapped into these fears by including a scientist, a lawyer and an aristocrat in the group of people who are challenged to conquer the vampire. It is noticeable that up-to-date medical knowledge cannot help them (for example, blood transfusions do not help Lucy). Instead they have to rely on Dr. Van Helsing's obscure library research, and on other more traditional values, such as the physical strength of Jonathan Harker and Arthur Holmwood, and on Mina Harker's bravery.

Secondly, by beginning his novel with Harker's visit to the vampire's castle in Transylvania, Stoker drew readers in by appealing to their appetite for exotic places. The Victorian era saw a huge growth in foreign travel, as well as a boom in travel writing. But he did not allow the terror to remain a distant fantasy. Instead he brought the vampire to England and eventually to the heart of London, placing unimaginable evil right on the doorsteps of his readers. While most earlier horror tales were set in the past, or in remote places, much of the action of *Dracula* happened in the Victorian reader's own time and place. And though the world has changed since the book was written, our fears have not – which is why *Dracula* remains a classic.

Castle Dracula

It was the dead of night. Jonathan Harker sat bolt upright in bed and screamed "No-oooo!" His brow was covered in sweat, his heart beat furiously, and he was so scared that he didn't know where he was. Then, slowly, it all came back to him – he was at an inn in Transylvania, one of the wildest, least-known parts of Europe. "What a creepy dream," he thought. "Those horrible wolves. And that huge bat which wrapped its wings around me. . ." He shuddered.

Next morning he received a letter.

> *My dear friend,*
>
> *Welcome to Transylvania. I am particularly looking forward to meeting you in the flesh.*
>
> *I have arranged for you to travel by the afternoon stagecoach to the Borgo Pass, where my carriage will bring you to my castle.*
>
> *Count Dracula*

As Jonathan was getting ready to leave, the landlady surprised him by coming to his room, and pleading desperately with him not to go.

"But it's my job as a lawyer," he explained, feeling slightly embarrassed. "I've organized all the legal details of the Count's new house in London, and I need to explain to him how. . . Oh! Please don't be upset."

"Tonight," whispered the old lady, "all the evil in the world will be let loose. You will be at the mercy of forces you never dreamed existed. You must not go!"

"Did you have nightmares as well?" Jonathan joked, trying to make light of the situation. "I did. First this gigantic bat wrapped its slimy wings around me, then as I screamed in terror it sank its teeth into my. . . Are you alright?"

The old lady was moaning and gasping in horror, making him regret being so flippant. So when she held out in her hand a chain with a cross on it, he looked at her solemnly.

"For the sake of your soul," she begged, "always wear this crucifix."

"I will," he said in a quiet voice.

When the other passengers on the stagecoach found out where Jonathan was going, they stared at him in astonishment. Then they started whispering in

Transylvanian and Jonathan heard some words that he knew: *pokol* and *vrolok*. The first word meant hell, and the second. . . Jonathan shivered. It meant vampire. But he told himself that such fears were merely absurd superstitions. When he met the Count, it would be interesting to discuss them.

Even though the roads were rough, winding and dangerous, the driver seemed to be in a frantic hurry. Jonathan watched the countryside flash past, a landscape of steep hills, green forests and sudden spectacular views of craggy mountains. When it started to get dark, the driver urged his horses to go even faster, and the stagecoach swayed and rocked like a boat on a stormy sea. They entered the Borgo Pass at a full gallop, then the driver pulled hard on the reins and the carriage lurched to a halt. Jonathan was glad they had arrived – the other passengers were starting to get on his nerves. Half the time they were whispering that his soul was in eternal peril, and the rest of the time they kept trying to press cloves of garlic into his hand. Why? thought Jonathan, as he secretly dropped yet another clove out of the window.

"This is the Borgo Pass, but there's no carriage waiting for you," said the driver with a great sigh of relief. "You're not expected after all." It was a cold night, but there were beads of sweat on his face. "We'll drive on, as fast as we can, and you can return tomorrow – and with a different driver, too," he added in a low voice.

But before he had finished speaking, his horses began to snort and stamp wildly, and out of the surrounding darkness a four-horse carriage thundered up to them. When they saw the tall, dark driver, the other passengers screamed and cowered. His face was obscured by a long, brown beard, and a large, black hat. But nothing could obscure the fact that his eyes flashed red in the blackness of the night.

"The stagecoach has never been so early," he observed, smiling from a cruel-looking mouth, his voice harsh and malevolent. "Now," he commanded, "the English gentleman will come with me."

Jonathan's fellow passengers suddenly seemed like the most cheerful, friendly and fascinating bunch of people he had ever met. There was nothing he wanted less than to leave them and go with the tall, dark man. But he felt that he had no choice, so he got out of the stagecoach and collected his luggage from the roof. His anxiety was not eased when the door of the carriage flew open of its own accord, trembling on its hinges. And when he got in, the door slammed shut behind him so hard that the noise echoed across the mountains, like nails being banged into a coffin. Then, before he could even sit down, the carriage surged forward and swept him away into the night.

The journey took hours. They rose ever higher up the perilous paths of the thickly forested mountains, the driver savagely cracking his whip as the horses struggled to climb the steep slopes. Bats flitted above them in great numbers, and by the edge of the road there were hundreds of wooden crosses which, Jonathan suddenly realized with horror, were graves. Everything was so creepy that he wished he had stayed in England. He thought about his fiancée, Mina. She would be at home now, marking her pupils' homework, or perhaps sitting snugly in front of a log fire, eating hot, buttered toast.

Then, finally, the trip drew to a close. They journeyed along a track to a vast, forbidding castle, as wolves bayed malevolently into the darkness of the night. When they arrived, and Jonathan was left alone in the courtyard, he could see the castle's broken battlements etched against a moonlit sky. Not a ray of light came from the high, black windows. Directly in front of him was a huge, wooden door, and beyond it he heard heavy steps approaching: clump, clump, clump. There was a rattling of chains and a clanking of bolts. Then very slowly, the old door creaked open.

A tall, old man was standing in the doorway, dressed from head to foot in black. He had a sneering mouth with two sharp white teeth protruding over his lips.

"Welcome to my house!" he said, and then, almost eagerly, "Won't you come inside?"

Jonathan winced when he shook hands with him. The old man's grip was like a steel trap, and his hand was as cold as ice, like the hand of a dead man. And there was something else very curious about it: the palm was covered in hair.

"Count Dracula?" Jonathan asked nervously.

"I am Dracula," the old man replied in a chilling voice, "and I welcome you, Mr. Harker."

The Count bowed to Jonathan, who felt a sudden shudder. Perhaps it was just that the Count's breath was revolting, but there was something about the man that was making him feel sick.

The freezing stone corridors they walked along did nothing to raise Jonathan's spirits. Nor did the narrow staircases, the damp walls, or the heavy bolted doors. But at last the Count led him to a comfortable study. A fire was burning in the hearth, and an open door revealed an adjoining bedroom. Suddenly Jonathan felt much better. To see a warm fire was comforting, and his welcome to Castle Dracula had at least been. . . well, polite. After all, it wasn't the Count's fault if he had hair on the palms of his hands, or breath so bad that it could fell an ox.

"You must be hungry after your journey," the Count said, pointing to a table where a substantial meal was laid out. "You will excuse me if I do not join you. My eating habits are rather. . . er, unconventional."

Neither of them spoke much as Jonathan was eating, but when he had finished, the Count said, "And now, my friend, tell me all about my new house in London." So Jonathan got the property deeds out from his luggage. Clause by clause, he explained the numerous legal arrangements. Then he asked the Count to sign various papers and documents.

"But is the house exactly as I requested?" the Count asked.

"Oh yes," said Jonathan, who had seen the place with his own eyes. He wondered why anyone would want to buy such a crumbling old dump. Carfax was dark and damp and gloomy. It was falling to pieces. It was next door to a lunatic asylum. "The property is a most desirable residence," said Jonathan.

Count Dracula kept Jonathan talking about England, and London in particular, for so long that it was nearly dawn when he left.

"Lie in as long as you like tomorrow," he said gravely, pausing in the doorway. "I have important affairs to attend to until evening. Sleep well, Mr. Harker. . ."

Before finally going to bed, Jonathan sat down at a desk and described the day's events in his journal. It was a diary of all his Transylvanian experiences which he was keeping for Mina. He smiled as he wrote, imagining her reading it. She would laugh her head off at how nervous he had been earlier.

He woke up so late the next day that it was already dark. He couldn't find a mirror in his bedroom, so he hung up his own shaving-mirror by the window. As he slowly dragged the razor across his chin by the light of a lamp, he idly wondered why there was no mirror.

"Good day," said the Count's voice, from nowhere. Jonathan jumped in surprise, cutting himself with the blade. He blurted out a gabbled greeting, then turned back to the mirror. A cold feeling suddenly swept over him. He could see his own reflection, a glistening trickle of blood running down his chin. And behind his face he could see the rest of the room. But he couldn't see the Count.

He turned around again, very, very slowly. It was inexplicable – there was the Count, as large as life, standing right behind him. . . and he was staring at the blood on Jonathan's chin. The Count's nose began to twitch, and he licked his lips. Then, as quick as lightning, his hand shot out and made a grab for Jonathan's throat. Jonathan stepped back in alarm, and the Count's hand touched the chain of the crucifix. In an instant the old man regained control over himself.

"Take care," he warned in a strange voice, breathing heavily. "Take care not to cut yourself in this place. It could be dangerous." Then he seized the mirror. "This wretched object has caused all the trouble – away with it!" And he crushed it to smithereens in his bare hands, and furiously flung it out of the window.

There was a meal waiting for Jonathan in the study. He picked at it listlessly, alone and very afraid. After throwing the mirror away, the Count had left, without a word of explanation. Jonathan wrote about the incident in his journal. Then, as the Count didn't seem to be around, he decided to explore the castle. Taking a lamp with him, he set off.

It was cold in the echoing stone corridors. He hurried along them, trying out doors on each side. He noticed that there was thick dust on the handles, as though no one had used them for years. Each one he tried seemed to be locked. But it was a big place, so he made his way to another floor. There were hundreds more doors to try. One of them was bound to be open. He grabbed another handle. Locked. Jonathan tried to ignore the sinking feeling in his stomach.

After another hour, he knew the dreadful truth: he was a prisoner. He sat down on the top step of a stone staircase, and closed his eyes. For some minutes he sat motionless, listening to his own heartbeat.

On the way back to his room Jonathan noticed that one of the locked doors was rotten. Soon he would wish that he had never laid eyes on that door, or witnessed what lay beyond it. But now his spirits lifted. He pushed and kicked at it, and shouted in triumph when it burst open. With his head full of thoughts of escape, he went through the doorway.

He found himself in a luxurious suite of rooms, with walls of dark wood panels, filled with exquisite antique furniture and paintings. Thick dust covered everything, and enormous cobwebs were suspended from every corner. The silence of centuries hung in the air. Jonathan sat down on a soft, velvet-covered couch. For some reason he was starting to feel very sleepy. It was almost as if there were some strange force in the room – a force which was impossible to resist. He lay back on the couch, and went into a sort of trance.

It felt like a dream when three young women approached through the moonlight. Two were dark, with piercing eyes that seemed to flash red. The other was fair, with masses of wavy golden hair and eyes like sapphires. All three had brilliant white teeth, which shone like pearls against the deep red of their lips. They were very beautiful.

"You go first," said one of them. "He's young and strong, and there's enough blood for us all."

The fair girl bent over him. Jonathan watched her from under his eyelashes. He couldn't move. He could only look on in fascination. She was staring at his neck. She licked her lips, like a hungry animal. Then he felt two sharp points against his throat, pressing on the skin. Hopelessly, helplessly, Jonathan waited.

"Get back!" a voice roared from somewhere, waking Jonathan from his trance and plunging him into terror. He tried to shrink away from the sharp teeth which were just about to puncture his skin. As he did so he saw Count Dracula's hairy hand grip the girl's shoulder. The Count pulled her away with the strength of a giant, and she shot across the room. His eyes were on fire, his face was chalk-white, and his voice cut through the air like a deadly blade.

"He's mine!" he hissed.

"Are we to have nothing tonight?" one of the demon women whined.

"Before two nights have passed," said Dracula chillingly, "it will be time for him to die, and he will be yours. But do not meddle with him until I say. Now go!"

In front of Jonathan's eyes, the three women began to fade in the rays of moonlight. Before they disappeared into a million specks and seeped out of the window, he saw the fair one smiling at him and heard her low, sweet ripple of laughter. Then horror overcame him, and he sank down into unconsciousness.

Jonathan awoke in his own bed in his room. He noticed that his clothes were folded in a neat pile on a chair, as though someone had put him to bed. Then he remembered what had happened, how those dreadful women had been ready to drink him dry of blood, and he covered his face with his hands.

Later that day there was a great commotion in the courtyard. Jonathan looked out of the window. Below there was a band of gypsies with two great wagons, each loaded with large boxes and drawn by eight sturdy horses. The boxes were obviously empty, because the gypsies were unloading them with ease and stacking them in a corner. Jonathan leaned out of the window.

"Help me!" he cried. "I'm a prisoner! Please help me!"

But the gypsies just pointed at him and started to laugh. They were still laughing later, when their empty wagons rumbled out of the cobbled courtyard.

Jonathan had noticed that he never saw the Count in the daytime. Was it possible that he was sleeping when others were awake, and awake when others were sleeping? He decided that when the morning came he would try to find the Count's room. He knew it was a desperate, hopeless act, but he was in a desperate, hopeless situation, and it would be better to die bravely than wait to have the blood sucked out of him by those vampires.

When the sun rose over Castle Dracula early the next day, it revealed Jonathan, perching precariously on the narrow ledge outside his bedroom window, trying not to look down at the sheer drop below. He felt his heart pounding as his hands groped for holds in the rock of the castle wall. Perilously, inch by inch,

he began his slow
descent.

He re-entered
the castle by a small
arched window far
below, and found
himself at the top of
a narrow spiral
staircase. After he had
got his breath back he
went down it, farther and
farther, as if descending
into hell itself. Eventually he
came to the bottom, where he found
himself in an old ruined chapel.

Jonathan wrinkled his nose in disgust. The place
was dirty and dank, and every so often he could hear
the sound of scuttling rats. Cautiously, he made his
way deeper and deeper into the chapel. As he did so,
he noticed a peculiar smell. It baffled him at first, but
after a while he realized what it was: the smell of
freshly dug soil. It was coming from the far end of the
chapel, where there were lots of boxes – the boxes
that he had seen the gypsies unloading in the
courtyard. He made a quick investigation. There were
about forty-five of them, maybe more. Each one was
half-filled with soil.

Walking around them, he came across a low
doorway in the wall. Hesitantly he pushed his head
through the opening, feeling terrified about what

might be inside. It seemed to be some kind of vault, a chamber in the ground used for burials.

The interior was dimly lit by sputtering candles. Jonathan wiped his brow, which was damp with sweat, before stepping inside and...

"Aaah!" he shouted suddenly, stepping back in panic as something brushed against his face.

It was only a cobweb, but it startled him so much that his breath came in great, heaving gasps. He tried to calm down, telling himself not to be scared. After all, he reflected as he went farther into the vault, it's only natural for a damp and dingy place like this to be full of cobwebs, not to mention...

"Waah!" he yelled, as an enormous rat ran over his feet, squeaking horribly.

Again he stopped, desperately trying to calm himself down. But now it was perfectly obvious to him that he was in a foul and evil place, a place where something terrible was waiting to happen. Even the smell in the air was vile and terrifying, like the Count's breath, only worse.

Finally, in the very heart of the vault, he found a last box. This one had a lid on it. Jonathan placed his lamp on a ledge and grasped the lid. In his heart he already knew what was inside, but he hardly dared admit it... Slowly, as shadows flickered over the walls, he began to lift.

There was a loud creak. He opened it wider, then suddenly had to put his free hand over his nose, spluttering and coughing as an indescribable stench of death and evil seeped out of the box. And there, lying on a great mound of earth, neither asleep nor dead, was Dracula!

His white hair was now dark grey. His cheeks were fuller and less pale, and his face was less wrinkled. And on his lips was fresh blood, trickling bright red from the corners of his mouth and down over his chin and neck. It seemed as if the hideous creature was simply gorged with blood, blood which had renewed his youth, for he looked at least twenty years younger. He lay, like a filthy leech, bursting with all the horrible crimes he had ever committed.

Jonathan shook all over. He couldn't help it. This confirmed his worst suspicions: the terrible realization that the ghoulish Count was indeed a vampire. To think that this horrible creature was heading for London where – perhaps for centuries – he might prey on innocent people and suck their blood. The idea drove Jonathan almost insane with fury. Seizing a shovel which lay on the ground nearby, he lifted it up high and, with all his strength, brought it down swiftly on the vampire's face.

Dracula's veiny hand shot out to fend off the blow, and his red eyes opened, rolling horribly to stare at his assailant. Jonathan felt the shovel spin around in his grip, as though an invisible force had taken control of it, and the blade smashed harmlessly into the side of the box. Then the vampire's eyes closed once more, and the lid slammed shut with an echoing crash. Jonathan's final glimpse was of a bloated, bloodstained face, its mouth set into a malicious grin.

As he stepped back, trying to overcome the urge to run away, the shovel fell from his hands. Taking a deep breath, he picked it up again and grasped the lid of the box. His instinct for survival told him that he had to kill Dracula! But just as he began to raise the lid a second time, he heard something – footsteps, shouts, orders, and people running towards him. It sounded like the gypsies. They were very near and getting nearer. Jonathan cursed silently, running quickly out of the vault and the chapel, and up the spiral stairs. In despair, he made the long, exhausting journey back to his own room. He collapsed in a heap by the old window and looked out at the jagged, rocky mountain ranges of Transylvania. For as long as he lived (which didn't look as if it was going to be very long) he would never, ever forget the loathsome expression on Dracula's bloodstained face.

In the courtyard below, the gypsies were starting to load the boxes of earth onto their wagons. Jonathan knew that the containers were going to England, and one of them had Dracula in it. He clenched his fists in powerless anger and grief.

Back in his room, Jonathan spent the night wide awake, petrified of what was going to happen to him, and jumping in fright at even the tiniest sound. He feverishly scribbled in his journal:

I'm all alone. I've never felt so desolate in my life, knowing that I've been left here as a . . . as a slap-up feast for those three things — monsters — vampires! I must escape! I'll climb down the walls again to the very bottom and take my chances with the wolves in the forest. I'd rather die out there than in here. Mina, it breaks my heart to think that I'll never see you again. Goodbye, Mina . . . goodbye . . .

Then there was a sound which froze his blood. He stood up, knocking his chair to the floor, and listened in terror. From outside his door came a noise he had heard once before. It was a low, sweet ripple of laughter. The laughter of the vampires.

The Ship with No Crew

In England a month later, Mina, Jonathan's fiancée, sent a letter to her friend Lucy Westenra in the seaside town of Whitby in Yorkshire. Mina had been Lucy's teacher a few years earlier, but now that Lucy was older they had become as close as sisters.

Dearest Lucy,

Thank goodness the school term ends this week. I'm worn out, and I'm so worried about Jonathan. I still haven't heard from him. But coming to Whitby to stay with you will cheer me up. We can sit on the old seat we always sit on, by the graveyard on the cliff top, and talk about all our news. Speaking of which, is it true that you have become engaged to a certain Arthur Holmwood? You can tell me all about it when I see you in a few days.

Much love,
Mina xxx

P.S. Your mother told me that in the last few nights you have started sleepwalking. It sounds mysterious. I shall have to keep a close eye on you!

A storm was brewing out at sea when Mina arrived in Whitby. Sitting on the clifftop seat with Lucy in the evening, Mina watched the swelling waves. All the fishing boats were making for port as fast as they could sail, and the sky was getting blacker every moment. Even the air around them seemed heavy and oppressive. It made Mina feel nervous, as though something unpleasant was about to happen.

"So Arthur got down on one knee and proposed," Lucy was saying, "... and I said, 'Arthur, I'm so happy I could *faint*,' and he said. . ."

Mina had heard this story already: once before breakfast, twice during breakfast, three times after breakfast, and about a million times since. It was beginning to get on her nerves.

"I think we'd better go home now," Mina said.

". . . and he said, 'I love you so much that sometimes I think my head's just going to *fall off*,'" Lucy continued in a dreamy voice as she stood up and collected all her things together.

"Look at that ship," Mina said, pointing far out to sea at a large schooner. "It doesn't seem to be making any attempt to get to shore." Still musing dreamily about Arthur, Lucy looked up. When she saw the ship, she stopped talking in mid-sentence, and her face went pale. A look of melancholy filled her eyes.

"Lucy? What's the matter? Are you all right?"

"I think so," Lucy said, quietly. "It's that ship. I just looked at it, and I felt. . . odd."

"I'll take you home," Mina said, holding her by the arm.

It was the worst storm since records began, and it blew up in minutes. The waves rose in fury, each one bigger and angrier than the last, before crashing onto the beach and lashing the cliffs. The wind roared as loud as thunder, and great flashes of lightning cracked like enormous whips in the sky, revealing black clouds gathered like huge rocks waiting to fall.

On the summit of Whitby's West Cliff, the local coastguard trained a searchlight out to sea in case there were still any boats out there. Around him there was an excited crowd of townspeople who had come to observe the grandeur and fury of the storm. The searchlight soon picked out the lone schooner, and everyone pointed and shouted into the gale.

The ship had all sails set, and the wind was driving it to the shore at ferocious speed. But between the schooner and safety lay a flat reef on which many a ship had been wrecked. It didn't seem possible that she could avoid it. Then fierce winds swept in more huge clouds of seafog, and for some moments nothing could be seen. The coastguard's searchlight was of no use. The crowd waited, motionless, and wondered if they would be able to hear the doomed ship splintering into pieces above the crash and roar of the storm.

But when the fog passed, they were amazed to see that the schooner had somehow found a narrow gap in the deadly reef. The ship was now leaping from wave to wave at headlong speed. It was being blown straight to the safety of the shore!

The townspeople cheered with relief, jumping up and down in joy; and yet, within a few moments, the cheering had turned into a collective gasp of horror. The coastguard had managed to train his searchlight on the schooner again, revealing a sight so gruesome that it made people hold on to each other in terror.

Lashed to the wheel of the ship, swinging horribly to and fro as the vessel was battered by the waves, was a dead man. No one else could be seen on board. The ship had reached the safety of the shore steered by a corpse.

The watching crowd barely had time to take this in before the ship ran aground. Every timber strained and shuddered as it slammed into the beach, and two of its masts crashed to the deck. But the strangest thing of all was the immense dog which appeared from below deck and, with a huge leap, jumped from the ship to land. Its eyes blazing red, it made straight for the East Cliff, where the graveyard of the parish church was crumbling into the sea.

It was a restless night for Mina as the storm raged. Twice she had woken and found Lucy sleepwalking, looking out of the window at the tempest of the sea. Each time Mina had led her gently back to her bed. They both slept very late into the morning. When they finally got up and went down to breakfast, Mrs. Westenra, Lucy's mother, was waiting for them. She had heard all about the mysterious schooner, and she was impatient to tell them about it.

"What a terrible tragedy," Mina whispered, when Mrs. Westenra had finished her breathless tale. "What did the dead captain look like?" Lucy asked.

Mrs. Westenra had no idea, but that wasn't going to stop her.

"He was a very handsome young fellow," she asserted, "with a good strong face, and jet-black hair."

"It's very strange indeed about the dog," Mina said. "I wonder what sort it was."

"It was an enormous dog," claimed Mrs. Westenra, who knew even less about the dog than she knew about the captain, "the biggest dog ever, bigger than a horse, bigger than an elephant. . ."

"Mother!" said Lucy, laughing.

"Well, as big as a really big dog," Mrs. Westenra conceded, "with huge, evil, bright-red eyes. They say it had two heads and six legs, and. . ."

"*Two* heads?" Lucy asked.

"*Six* legs?" Mina queried.

"Or possibly one head," Mrs. Westenra admitted, "and about four legs at the most, but that's not the point. The point is, it was the scariest, deadliest, most evil beast I ever laid eyes on."

"Oh, so you actually saw the animal?" Mina asked.

"Um. . ." said Mrs. Westenra, dabbing at her lips with a napkin, "more tea dear?"

Mina was incredibly disappointed that no letter arrived from Jonathan that day. No letter arrived on the following day either, nor the day after that. She couldn't imagine why he hadn't written, and began to wonder if something had happened to him. It became difficult to stay cheerful as the days passed with no news. And Lucy's sleepwalking was getting worse, which was also very worrying. In fact ever since that dreadful night of the storm, when a foreign ship steered by a dead man had mysteriously delivered a huge dog to Whitby, it was as though the whole town was on edge. The local newspaper was reporting more and more bizarre details about the story, and every morning Mrs. Westenra would gossip about it.

"The ship had a cargo of fifty boxes," she told them, squinting through her reading glasses at *The Whitby Times,* "all addressed to a secret location in London, and each one full to the brim with something terrible."

"What do you mean, *terrible?*" asked Lucy, reaching for another piece of toast.

"Well it says here that they were just filled with soil," murmured Mrs. Westenra in a low voice, "but, you see, I know what was *really* in them."

"And what was that?"

Mrs. Westenra frowned, deep in thought. She tried hard to think of something thrillingly scary. Unfortunately she couldn't think of anything, so she quickly changed the subject.

"And as for the Captain's logbook," she said, "well you don't want to hear about it. You aren't old enough to hear what was in that logbook. If I told you what was in that logbook, you'd never sleep a wink at night. I wouldn't tell you what was recorded in that logbook," she claimed, looking slowly from one to the other, and then slowly back again, "even if you *begged* me."

"So what was recorded in the logbook?" asked Lucy in a bored voice.

"All the crew were horribly murdered one by one by an evil presence," gabbled her mother breathlessly. "The captain had the ship searched time and again but never found anything. Eventually he was the only one left. And when the authorities untied him from the wheel of that ship, they discovered that he was holding a crucifix – to protect himself against *it*."

"Oh," said Lucy quietly, her eyes filling with tears. "How awful. He must have been so terrified. I wish you hadn't told me that."

"You shouldn't have dragged it from me," her mother said.

One night, Mina woke up abruptly with the distinct feeling that something was very wrong.

"Lucy?" she called.

There was no reply from Lucy's bed. Mina struck a match and lit a candle. The pale, quivering flame revealed that her friend's bed was empty. Mina searched the upstairs rooms before going downstairs.

In the hall her heart sank. The front door was open – Lucy had gone outside. It was a cold night, and Mina knew that her friend was wearing just a thin nightdress. Hurriedly throwing a shawl around her own shoulders, she went to look for her.

The church clock was striking one as Mina ran through the streets of Whitby. She kept a sharp lookout, but there was no sign of the white figure she had expected to see. She ran along the Crescent, then she explored along the North Terrace – nothing. Searching farther and farther away from the house, she made her way up to the West Cliff.

At the edge of the West Cliff she looked across the bay to the East Cliff. There was a bright full moon but also lots of swift-moving clouds, so a dappled light was moving across the sea and the town. For some time she couldn't distinguish very much at all. Then the moon emerged fully, casting a narrow strip of cold blue light over the East Cliff.

Mina could see the tombstones of the old graveyard, leaning over at crazy angles, making dark silhouettes against the wild night sky. The strip of light moved steadily along the tombstones and memorials. And there on their seat, was the half-reclining, snowy-white figure of Lucy.

Almost as soon as she spotted her friend, the moon went in. But it seemed to Mina that something dark had been standing behind Lucy, or leaning over her. Whether it was man or beast Mina wasn't sure.

She started running down the slope of the West

Cliff as fast as she could. It seemed to take forever. Eventually she was leaping up the endless steps of the East Cliff, her legs shaky with tiredness. As she neared the graveyard on the cliff top she gasped. She had been right. A dark shape was leaning over her friend.

"Lucy! Lucy!" she called in fright.

At the sound of her voice, the dark figure raised its head. Mina saw a pale face and red, gleaming eyes. For a moment they flashed at her. Then, as Mina got closer, the dark figure seemed to melt into the surrounding blackness.

"Lucy!" Mina cried, throwing herself next to her friend on the bench.

Lucy was still asleep. Her lips were parted, and she was breathing in long, heavy gasps. She put her hand to her throat and moaned. Mina wrapped her shawl around her friend's shoulders. Lucy seemed unusually cold and gave a shudder. Using a safety pin, Mina fastened the shawl at Lucy's throat. But she must have been clumsy, because Lucy's hands went to her throat again, and Mina noticed that there were two little red marks on her neck. Mina thought that she must have pricked her accidentally.

"Wake up, Lucy" she whispered, shaking her gently. "Wake up!"

Lucy's eyes opened and looked at Mina with wonder. She didn't seem to understand where she was. She started to tremble, and clung to her friend.

"We must walk home," Mina said softly.

She pulled Lucy to her feet, and putting an arm around her shoulder, began to walk her home. When they got there, Lucy begged Mina not to tell Mrs. Westenra anything of what had happened. Her mother's health was already poor, and Lucy didn't want to make things worse by worrying her.

Mina locked their door from the inside and tied the key to her wrist. She put Lucy to bed, and, once she was asleep, got into bed herself. But she couldn't stop thinking about what had happened. Who – or what – was that dark figure she had seen leaning over Lucy? When at last she finally fell asleep, she dreamed that Lucy was sleepwalking again, rattling the handle of the bedroom door. The door didn't open, so Lucy moved to the window and pointed outside: a great bat was flitting through the moonlight, coming and going in whirling circles. It was such a vivid dream that it felt real.

"Letters for you both today," said Mrs. Westenra in the morning.

Mina and Lucy ripped open their envelopes.

"Are you all right, Lucy?" Mrs. Westenra asked. "You look a little ill this morning, rather pale –

almost as if you didn't have enough blood in your veins!" she joked.

"I'm fine," Lucy said. "Listen to this, mother – Arthur says he's sorry, but he definitely can't come to Whitby because his father is ill, so he wants us to go back to our house in London. He wants the wedding to be arranged as quickly as possible!"

"Well that's very good news, dear," said Mrs. Westenra. "And you, Mina? Any news of Jonathan?"

"Yes," said Mina after a long pause, scanning her letter with great concentration.

"I suppose it must be a private letter, then?" Mrs. Westenra speculated.

"Yes," Mina agreed, after an equally long pause.

"Well don't go telling me what it says, dear," Mrs. Westenra said. "Other people's private letters don't interest me in the slightest."

Mrs. Westenra saw Mina's eyes widen with shock.

"Is it a very interesting letter?" she couldn't help asking.

But Mina just kept on reading.

"Not that I want to know what it's about," Mrs. Westenra emphasized. "I wouldn't let you tell me even if you wanted to. I don't find interesting letters particularly. . . interesting," she claimed feebly.

"I'm just going to my room," Mina said in a strange voice, "to read my letter again."

"Shall I come too dear?" Mrs. Westenra asked, hastily standing up and knocking over the sugar bowl as she did so.

In the bedroom Mina shut the door firmly, took a deep breath, and carefully read the letter again.

Dear Madam,

I am writing on behalf of Mr. Jonathan Harker, who is not strong enough to write himself. He has been in our hospital for two months suffering from a violent brain fever. He has had some sort of terrible shock. He raves of wolves and blood, of monsters and demons. He came to us in the middle of the night, from where we do not know. He is mentally and physically exhausted, but getting better slowly but surely. Only recently was he able to say who he was, and who we should write to. He talks about you in his sleep. I can assure you that he will receive the very best care until he is ready to return home. I wish you both many happy years together.

Sister Agatha
St. Joseph Hospital, Budapest

Mina didn't know whether to cry with sorrow or laugh with relief. She knew there was only one thing to do. She threw open the cupboard doors, pulled her suitcase out, and began to pack.

Horror at Hillingham

It was a long and exhausting journey to Budapest, but when Mina arrived she went straight to the hospital. Sister Agatha led her to Jonathan's room.

"Try not to show any surprise at the way he looks," she whispered outside the door.

"Of course not," said Mina.

"His dreams and ravings have been so dreadful that no one can imagine what he has been through."

Sister Agatha opened the door and they entered. Despite Sister Agatha's warning, Mina gasped when she saw Jonathan. She couldn't help it. He was so pitifully weak and thin, his eyes staring hugely from his pale, gaunt face.

"Jonathan!"

"Mina!"

"Jonathan, what happened to you?" Mina cried, hugging him.

Jonathan pulled away from her and put his head in his hands, struggling to overcome his emotions.

"I've had a. . . a terrible shock," he whispered. "A great shock. I never thought I'd see you again. When I think of what I've seen. . . the terror of. . . and. . . his red eyes. . . Oh Mina! I don't know if it was real or if I'm mad!"

"Tell me about it," said Mina.

Jonathan shook his head. He reached under his pillow and pulled out his journal.

"It's all in this book, Mina.

You take it. Read it if you have to. I can't. I never want to read a word of it in case. . ."

"In case what?"

"In case it is true!" Jonathan cried in anguish.

Mina stayed silent for a few moments, trying to decide on the best course of action.

"Jonathan, I don't want us to live in the past. I'll put this book somewhere safe, but I'll never read it unless it's absolutely necessary." She took his hand in hers. "The most important thing is that you get your health back. I want us to be happy, Jonathan. Happy and strong, like Lucy and Arthur."

But back in England at that very moment, Arthur was pacing up and down outside Lucy's room. He was worried sick about her. Ever since returning from her holiday in Whitby to Hillingham, her family home in London, her health had steadily declined. Arthur had asked his friend Jack Seward to look at her. Jack was renowned for his expertise in psychiatry, running a large mental hospital on the outskirts of London; but he was also an experienced medical doctor.

"What's taking him so long?" Arthur muttered to himself as he waited in the corridor.

Then his friend came out of Lucy's room, closing the door gently behind him. He paused before speaking. Jack was a dark, brooding, melancholic man, and this had been no easy task for him. He too had once been in love with Lucy, and had even proposed to her.

"Well?" Arthur said. "Did you examine her?"

"Yes I did," said Jack, nodding.

"And have you come to any conclusion?"

"Yes I have," Jack answered solemnly. There was a silence which Jack showed no sign of breaking.

"Well, tell me, what is your conclusion?" Arthur implored him.

"The conclusion I have come to," said Jack, gravely, "and listen to this very carefully indeed, Arthur, as it's most important —"

"Yes, yes, get on with it," Arthur said impatiently.

"The conclusion I have come to, after a detailed, extensive examination of the patient, during which I employed the very latest techniques available to modern medical science, is that I have absolutely no idea what's wrong with her."

Arthur stared at him.

"But you're a fully qualified doctor!" he exploded.

"She complains of being tired all the time," Jack said, almost to himself. "And sometimes she has difficulty in breathing. She has bad dreams, and irrational fears – bats, wolves, things like that. She looks far too pale, which suggests a blood disorder or an iron deficiency, for example. I tested for them and found nothing. But nevertheless. . ."

He fell into a deep silence.

After what seemed like an age, Arthur could bear the silence no longer.

"But nevertheless *what*?" he implored.

"It's something to do with her blood, I'm sure."

"So what are you going to do, Jack? Do you know?"

"Yes. I'm absolutely clear about that. It's obvious. There's only one thing I can do."

"And what's that?"

"Nothing."

"Nothing!" Arthur shouted, hitting the wall blindly in frustration.

"As I don't know what to do, I'm going to do nothing," Jack said, shaking his head sadly. It seemed perfectly logical to him, and he couldn't understand why Arthur was being so unreasonable about it. "Clearly," he went on, "the patient must be examined by Professor Van Helsing."

"Professor Van Helsing?" Arthur repeated, watching as Jack began to stride along the corridor to the stairs. "I've never heard of Professor Van Helsing. Who on earth is this Professor Van Helsing person?"

"Professor Van Helsing is a distinguished doctor and scientist," Jack replied, taking the steps three at a time. "If anyone will know what's wrong with Lucy, he will."

Professor Van Helsing lived in Holland. Although he could be rather absent-minded and eccentric, he had devoted his life to science, and he knew more about obscure diseases than any living person. He taught at the Amsterdam School of Medicine, which is where Jack had met him. Jack had been his best, most brilliant pupil.

As soon as the Professor received Jack's telegram about Lucy's strange illness, he abandoned all his work and started packing. He didn't like the sound of her symptoms at all, so he completed the journey as fast as possible. Arthur and Jack were waiting for him when he arrived the next evening.

"Good morning to you, Jack!" the Professor called cheerfully.

"Good evening, Professor Van Helsing," replied Jack, smiling.

"Is it evening already?" the Professor asked.

"Yes. Morning was – well, earlier," Jack explained.

"Just before lunch," Arthur helpfully pointed out.

"But I had my lunch not half an hour ago," the

185

Professor said, "at six o'clock precisely, which would suggest, although not prove conclusively, that it is neither the morning nor the evening, but the early afternoon. On the other hand, if you could supply me with some empirical evidence that refutes my contention, then I would be forced to amend my thesis."

"Er. . ." said Arthur.

"Professor, may I introduce you to Arthur Holmwood?" Jack asked. "Arthur is Lucy's fiancé."

"Pleased to meet you," Arthur said, shaking the Professor by the hand. "I'm very grateful to you for coming such a long way to see Lucy."

"Well," said the Professor, "I have to be honest and say that I was utterly absorbed in my fascinating research into the saprophytic agaricaceous poisonous woodland fungus, *Amanita muscaria*. I nearly couldn't tear myself away."

"Er, quite," said Arthur. "I don't blame you," he added after a slight pause.

"I was at a crucial stage, too," mused the Professor regretfully. "Normally nothing could have induced me to abandon everything at a moment's notice. But when I got Jack's telegram I felt I had little choice. The symptoms he described are very worrying indeed. I suppose the situation is still the same, Jack?"

"I'm afraid it's much worse," Jack responded.

When the Professor saw Lucy, he clenched his jaw. She was as pale as chalk, and the bones of her face were standing out prominently.

"Professor Van Helsing, please *do* something!" Arthur begged.

The Professor began to make his examination.

"Jack," he said after a while, "do you know how she came to lose so much blood?"

"But she hasn't lost any blood."

"Oh, she has. Believe me, she has. And unless it is replaced, she may die. It's lucky she has a common blood group. There must be an immediate transfusion." He turned to Arthur, who had sat down heavily in a chair and put his head in his hands. "Are you willing to help the young lady?"

"I would give the last drop of blood in my body for her."

"You may have to," the Professor said grimly.

Professor Van Helsing asked Arthur to sit by the bed and roll his sleeve up. He took a sample of blood, checking it was from the same blood group as Lucy's. Then he performed the transfusion swiftly and efficiently. As the blood flowed from Arthur to Lucy, a touch of pink began to return to her cheeks. The Professor carefully monitored the situation.

"Enough. Jack, attend to the young man while I see to the lady. He needs to lie down somewhere. But he can be assured that he has saved his fiancée's life today."

Arthur was feeling rather groggy, so Jack helped him to his feet. But just as he was supporting him to the bedroom door, there was a sudden hiss of shock from the Professor.

"What is it?" Jack called.

"Look after your friend, then come back as quickly as you can," was the reply.

As soon as Jack was sure that Arthur was all right, he rushed back upstairs.

"Does Lucy always wear this black velvet band around her neck?" the Professor asked.

"I don't know," Jack said. "I can't remember – why?"

The Professor pushed the band down. On the side of Lucy's throat were two small wounds.

"What do you make of that?" he asked.

Jack examined the red marks.

"I'm not sure. I've never seen anything like it. There's no sign of disease or infection. And yet. . ."

"And yet what?"

"The wounds don't look clean. They look as though they keep being reopened."

"They are being reopened. Every night. That's how she is losing all her blood."

Jack racked his brains for an illness or disease which would explain it. He couldn't think of one.

"But how is it happening?" he asked.

"There isn't time to tell you now," the Professor said, busily putting all his medical equipment away. "As soon as I got your telegram I had my small suspicions. The unusually pale skin, the difficulty in breathing, the dreams of bats, of wolves. . . They all pointed to the same conclusion."

"But what conclusion?" Jack asked.

"Now that I have seen her," the Professor said, ignoring him, "my small suspicions have become very great fears indeed."

"But fears of what?"

"And now, Jack, I must read. I have brought all the books I could find on this. . . this subject. Now I must read all about it."

"But what subject is it?"

"And I must find more books, from the libraries, from the British Museum. I must read all night. And you, Jack, have to stay here and watch over Lucy. You mustn't leave her, not even for a moment. Do you understand?"

"Well of course I understand," Jack replied rather crossly, "but surely you can just tell me –"

But the Professor was already out of the door.

That evening, after Lucy's mother had sat with them for a while, Jack took care of his patient. Lucy seemed afraid of going to sleep, so he promised to stay awake all night, and to wake her if she seemed to be having a nightmare. She soon fell into a deep sleep. Jack watched over her tenderly. Sometimes, as the big, old grandfather clock downstairs chimed away the hours of the night, he couldn't help feeling sad, thinking about what might have been. Ever since Lucy had turned down his marriage proposal, Jack's life had been work, work, and more work as he threw himself into the running of the hospital.

But he tried hard not to let himself become too miserable. After all, the only thing that really mattered was Lucy's health.

The next evening Professor Van Helsing returned to Hillingham. He was covered from head to foot in dust, and was carrying a large parcel.

"The books I've read in your excellent libraries!" he exclaimed. "Some of them hadn't been opened for two hundred years! I've been reading non-stop, all night and all day. How is our patient?"

"Come and see for yourself," Jack replied.

"Good evening, Professor," Lucy said brightly when they went to her room. "I've heard all about you from Arthur. I want to thank you for your treatment."

"Ah, good," said the Professor contentedly. She was still a little pale and weak, but she looked much better. "It was your young man who saved your life, my dear."

"Arthur," Lucy said.

"Yes, Arthur. It was all down to him. Where is he today?"

"His father is ill and has taken a turn for the worse," Lucy replied. "Arthur has gone to look after him."

"So much misfortune," the Professor murmured. "But here, at least, I hope there will be no more. I think I know the cause of your illness. And once the cause is known, the treatment can be found."

"What's wrong with her?" Jack asked quietly.

The Professor smiled sadly, but said nothing. Instead, he unwrapped his parcel and produced a large bundle of white flowers.

"These are for you, Miss Lucy."

"For me? Oh!" Lucy sniffed them, but then drew her head back, wrinkling her nose in disgust. "Yuk! They smell like garlic!"

"They are garlic flowers," said the Professor. "They will keep you safe from –" but then he stopped himself.

"From what?" Lucy asked.

"From the evil of your illness, my dear."

Before the Professor and Jack left that night for some much needed rest, they arranged the garlic flowers in Lucy's room. Under the Professor's direction, Jack made sure that all the windows were firmly shut, before rubbing the flowers around the door and windows. The Professor made up a garland from the flowers, and carefully put it around Lucy's neck.

"This will be your medicine," he told her. "There will be no more bad dreams, as long as you wear this. And remember – don't open the windows on any account, not even if it gets hot and stuffy."

"I won't," Lucy told him as she settled down to sleep. "Thank you so much for your help. I somehow feel much safer now. I can't wait until I'm better."

"You'll be out and about with Arthur in no time," said the Professor.

The Professor was in excellent spirits when he and Jack returned to Hillingham early the following day.

"Good morning to you, Mrs. Westenra!" he boomed when Lucy's mother opened the door.

"And good morning to you, Professor."

"And how is your beautiful daughter today? Much better no doubt after my first-class treatment!"

Mrs. Westenra smiled proudly.

"Well, Professor, if Lucy is better this morning, it will be down to my care as well as your treatment."

"Oh yes?" said the Professor, rubbing his hands together cheerfully.

"You see, I went into Lucy's room in the middle of the night, and there she was, fast asleep, as peaceful as a baby."

"Good, good," the Professor said, and he clapped Jack over the shoulder. "I knew my diagnosis was right!"

"But I happen to know a thing or two about nursing. In my day I was renowned for my abilities in nursing. In fact, it would be no exaggeration to say that I know more about nursing than –"

"I'm sure your nursing abilities are beyond comparison," Jack said kindly.

"Beyond comparison," Mrs. Westenra agreed. "I couldn't put it better myself, Jack. Quite simply, they are beyond comparison. And as it was terribly stuffy in Lucy's room, I decided to –"

The Professor's face went ashen.

"– to open the window," Mrs. Westenra said.

"Really Professor, I'm surprised at you. Fresh air is essential to a convalescing patient."

"It might not matter," muttered the Professor. "Just as long as the garland wasn't removed. . ."

"And as for all those horrible-smelling flowers," Mrs. Westenra continued, "you'll be glad to know that I took them and threw them out. You see, when your nursing abilities are beyond comparison, as mine are, then you understand how –"

But Jack and the Professor weren't listening. They were rushing up the stairs to Lucy's room. They found Lucy unconscious, more horribly white and wan than before. The skin on her face seemed to have shrunk, so that she had a gaunt, skeletal look, and she hardly seemed able to breathe.

"My God!" Jack whispered, sinking to his knees by her side. "What happened in the night?"

The Professor turned his medicine bag upside down and tipped the contents onto the floor.

"Roll your sleeve up!" he shouted. "She needs more blood! Mine's the wrong blood group but yours will do!"

For the second time in twenty-four hours, he performed a blood transfusion. As Jack watched his own blood being pumped into Lucy's veins, he wondered how on earth she had lost so much so quickly. Not from those two small wounds on her neck, surely? If so, where had it all gone?

The two men stayed with Lucy all day. The second transfusion didn't strengthen her as much as the first, and she was still quite weak by the evening. Jack felt weak too, but he sat with her while Professor Van Helsing went to talk to Mrs. Westenra. He wanted to make absolutely sure that she wouldn't disturb the garlic flowers that night. On his return, he and Jack arranged the flowers as before. Jack made doubly sure that all the windows were securely shut, and the Professor made an extra-large garland for Lucy's neck.

"I think we should watch over her, too," Jack suggested. "I'd feel better if we did."

"Jack, the garlic will protect her. You have given so much blood today, you need to rest. And I, I need to seek out more books. I must read. There is so much I must find out about this, this monstrosity. There are things you don't understand, Jack. If I told you, you just wouldn't believe me. Our only friend is knowledge. Now, let me put you in a carriage and send you home."

Lucy couldn't sleep that night. From the garden outside there was a howl, like a dog's, but fiercer and harsher. Shakily, she got out of bed and went over to the window. She couldn't see much outside – just a big bat flitting about. As she watched, it came up to the window, buffeting its wings against the glass. Lucy didn't like it. She got back into bed and decided to stay awake. She kept feeling at the garland of garlic around her neck, to reassure herself that it was still there.

Eventually she must have drifted off, because some hours later she woke up. She gave a little cry of fright. She couldn't see anything, but she could sense that someone was in the room. She peered into the darkness with dread, her heart thumping, and her forehead damp with sweat.

"Who's there?" she said. There was a short silence, and then a noise, a sort of scary, rustling noise, just inches away from her bed. Lucy's whole body began to tremble.

"Who's there?" she called again.

"I'm afraid I can't sleep," Mrs. Westenra said.

"Mother!" Lucy exclaimed in relief, sinking back on her pillows.

"There's such a terrible wind blowing outside," Mrs. Westenra said. "It's really frightening me."

She snuggled up beside Lucy, and the two of them listened to the sound of the wind.

"What's that other noise?" Mrs. Westenra whispered.

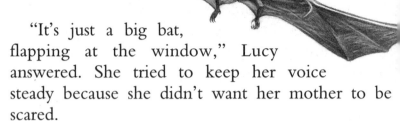

"It's just a big bat, flapping at the window," Lucy answered. She tried to keep her voice steady because she didn't want her mother to be scared.

"I don't like bats!" Mrs. Westenra cried. "I hate bats! Is it a very big bat? I bet it's a huge bat! It's probably as big as an eagle!"

"Hush," Lucy soothed her, "try not to be frightened."

But even as she spoke, a strange sort of moaning sound came from the garden. It started quietly, almost softly, but then grew louder and more mournful, until it became an ear-shattering, appalling howl. It went on and on and on, and Mrs. Westenra whimpered with terror and pulled the sheets up to her nose. Suddenly the wind dropped, and the howling stopped with it. The moon must have come out from under a cloud, because the whole room flooded with light. There was a split second of absolute quiet. Then with a tremendous crash the bedroom window shattered, and there, in the window frame, looking through the jagged panes, was the enormous head of a great, red-eyed wolf.

Mrs. Westenra shrieked and wailed. Her hands began grabbing at everything around her – the sheets, the bedside table, Lucy – and in her terror she clutched at Lucy's throat, pulling off the garland of garlic. For a second or two she sat up, pointing at the wolf, and a strange gurgling noise came from her throat. Then she fainted, falling out of the bed and striking her head on the bedside table as she slumped to the floor.

Almost against her will, Lucy's eyes were fixed on the wolf. For a moment both she and the huge, vicious beast were absolutely still. Then the creature's head drew back a little. It seemed to break up into millions of little specks which all charged about in a mass. The specks came blowing in through the broken window, beginning to take on the shape of a sinister figure.

Desperately Lucy scrabbled for something to defend herself with, her hands groping uselessly over the books and pens on her bedside table, scattering them all over. She clutched the edges of the bed and stared in terror. Then she screamed.

Desperate Measures

Jack woke that morning to the sound of wheels clattering over cobblestones. He went to the window and leaned out. Four large carts, each drawn by four horses, were lumbering past the hospital. As he watched, he heard one of the patients shrieking a strange chant through the bars of his window:

"Tyrant of the human race,
Master of all evil powers,
Welcome to this gloomy place,
Lie here safe in daylight hours."

Each cart was loaded with large wooden boxes. Jack wondered why they were heading for Carfax, the deserted old ruin next door.

"Lord of horror, king of fear,
Sleeping on your mound of mud,
Spread your terror far and near,
Seek your prey and suck their blood!"

It sounded like Renfield, the most dangerous and unpredictable inmate in the hospital. His gruesome rhymes were fascinating to Jack, but there was no time to investigate. The Professor's advice about rest had been all very well, but now he wanted to get back to Hillingham as quickly as possible.

No one answered when he knocked on the big old door half an hour later. He tried again, and waited for a long time. Still no answer. While he was standing there, bemused, a carriage drew up and the Professor jumped out eagerly.

"Good morning, Jack! I've read over 400,000 words in just under twelve hours! About 395,000 of them were completely useless, but I did learn something very interesting about –"

"No one is answering the door," Jack interrupted. "There's probably a good reason, but I don't like it."

The two men walked around the building. The doors and windows were all firmly shut. Before long they found themselves back at the front door again.

"Now what?" Jack asked.

As he spoke, he saw Mrs. Westenra's maid and cook hurrying up the street.

"We can't get in!" the cook cried. "We've come back every half hour since six, but there's still no answer!"

The Professor took a long, thin knife from his medicine bag and started to attack one of the windows.

"Why didn't I listen to you, Jack?" he cried, as he worked the blade under the wood. After a while he managed to lever the window open. Jack scrambled through it and ran upstairs.

Lucy's bedroom door was closed. He pushed it open a few inches, wondering what he would find inside. He could hear the Professor coming up behind him, panting. Jack gave the heavy oak door a firm push. It swung open on its hinges, striking the wall with a dull thud. Standing side by side, Jack and the Professor looked at the scene of desolation inside.

"No. . ." Jack breathed.

Mrs. Westenra was dead. She was lying on the floor inside a circle of broken glass, her eyes wide open and an expression of terror fixed on her face. And as for Lucy. . . Jack closed his eyes tightly, as if to make the horror go away. She lay motionless on the bed, spotted with blood. Her face was as white as snow. There were more drops of blood on the floor between the bed and the broken window, where the curtains were flapping in the breeze.

For one more moment Jack and the Professor stood, transfixed by the gruesome spectacle. Then they came to their senses and ran to Lucy's side.

"Is she dead?" Jack cried.

The Professor pulled back her eyelids to look into her eyes, then felt for her pulse. At first he couldn't feel anything. And then –

"She's alive – just! Get me some brandy – quick!"

"Thank God!" Jack whispered, and he scrabbled around in his medicine bag for brandy.

"She feels like ice," the Professor said, pouring brandy between Lucy's lips. "We need hot water, and a hot fire. We must warm her up!"

"Do you think she's going to die?" Jack whispered.

The Professor looked up at him grimly as he rubbed Lucy's arms.

"God help us if she does."

"Why do you say that?"

"Have you seen her teeth?" the Professor asked.

Jack gasped. The tips of two sharp teeth were just visible at the corners of Lucy's mouth.

"Her teeth are – growing!" He recoiled in disgust. "Professor, what *is* this illness?"

The Professor didn't answer, but handed Jack a piece of paper.

"This was in her hand," he said. "She is a brave young woman. She was writing it out even as... even as. . ." He paused. "She wanted us to know what happened."

Jack flattened out the crumpled piece of paper. In a large, untidy scrawl, written as though in a desperate hurry, were the letters:

"What does it mean?"

But the Professor just shook his head, and started rubbing Lucy's limbs even harder.

Professor Van Helsing and Jack struggled hard to save Lucy. After her maid had given her a hot bath, she was placed in front of the fireplace in her bedroom, where they had built up a roaring fire. But she remained freezing cold. Unless she became warmer, another blood transfusion was simply out of the question. And without another transfusion, she wouldn't live long.

"Send for her young man," said the Professor, putting his arm around Jack's shoulder. Jack covered his face with his hands. "She's leaving us soon."

When Arthur arrived and saw Lucy, he couldn't speak. He sat at her bedside, holding her hand and talking to her in a low voice. Jack and the Professor left them alone.

"In the middle of so much sadness," the Professor said softly to his grieving friend, "it's good to keep busy. And there's so much to do. For instance, imagine how grateful Miss Lucy would be if she knew that someone was dealing with all the funeral arrangements for her mother. Someone she cared about and trusted."

Jack smiled sadly.

"You're quite right," he said. "Arthur's in no fit state at the moment. And have you seen all that unopened mail in the hall? Someone should go through it."

"Good idea."

Jack kept himself occupied as the Professor had suggested. After dealing with a few invoices and receipts, he opened a hand-written letter from Mina. Jack knew Mina quite well. The last he had heard, she had gone abroad to look after her sick fiancé.

Dearest Lucy,

Here we are, back in England! Jonathan is my husband, and I'm his wife. We were married in Budapest. Jonathan is stronger and beginning to put some flesh on his bones. It's true that he wakes up sometimes in the middle of the night, screaming about. . . Well, perhaps I shouldn't say. The important thing is, every day he's a little bit better.

And what about you? When is the wedding to be? I expect it will be more of an occasion than mine, which took place in a hospital bedroom! Jonathan and I think of you and Arthur often. We wish you a long and happy life together, and hope that you will be as happy as we are. Looking forward to hearing from you soon.

Much love,
Mina xxx

Jack blinked back tears as he began writing a letter to Mina informing her of the terrible events at Hillingham. *I am afraid I have to inform you that Mrs. Westenra is dead,* he wrote, *and our dear friend Lucy is dying. . .*

In the study, the Professor settled down in an armchair and opened an ancient volume: *The Manifestations of the Vampire*. He was just reading the first paragraph when Arthur burst into the room.

"Professor, come quickly!"

"What is it?" asked the Professor.

"She's talking and moving around. She looks much stronger. There's still hope!" Arthur declared.

The Professor followed Arthur to Lucy's room. Lucy was sitting up in bed. Her lips were pulled back into a ghastly smile. The two sharp teeth seemed even longer than before. She was breathing in heavy gasps, sometimes breaking into mirthless laughter.

"See!" Arthur said.

Jack, who had heard all the commotion and followed them, stared in astonishment. It hardly seemed possible that someone as sick as Lucy could sit up in bed, laughing. But on the other hand, she hardly looked like Lucy any more. It was as though somebody else was pretending to be Lucy.

"The wounds on her neck – " the Professor hissed. "They've gone! This is one of the signs I've read about!"

Suddenly, Lucy shook her head, so that her long hair came loose, cascading over her shoulders. She laughed again, scornfully. Earlier in the day the Professor had placed a cross on a chain around her neck. Now she grabbed the chain and broke it, flinging the cross to the floor. Then they heard her say, in a soft, deep voice utterly unlike her own, "Arthur, my love! Kiss me!"

Arthur, desperate to believe that Lucy was going to recover, bent over her eagerly to kiss her. But in an instant Professor Van Helsing, old man that he was, caught hold of him and hurled him across the room.

"No! For the sake of your life and your soul, no!"

Sat on the floor where the Professor had thrown him, Arthur looked up, bewildered and angry.

"Professor," Jack asked, "what are you doing? What's going on?"

The Professor didn't answer, watching closely as Lucy sank down on the bed. Her eyes closed, and her breathing became quieter. Then she opened her eyes once more. This time she looked like the real Lucy, and although she was terribly weak, she held out her hand to the Professor, who grasped it in his own.

"My true, true friend," she whispered, "and Arthur's." Her voice was weak, but it was her own voice. Summoning what was left of her strength, she made one last, supreme effort to speak.

"Professor. . . you must defeat. . . this. . . evil."

"I will, I swear!" the Professor whispered.

Then he turned to Arthur.

"Now you can hold her hand, and say goodbye."

Arthur came to Lucy's side. He gently took her hand in his own, and they gazed into each other's eyes. After a few minutes, Lucy's eyes closed, her breathing ceased, and time itself seemed to stand still.

"She's gone, Arthur," Jack said eventually, placing his hand on his silent friend's shoulder. "She's at peace now. This is the end."

But the Professor, wiping his eyes, shook his head.

"No, this is not the end," he muttered to himself. "This is only the beginning. . ."

The funeral of Lucy and Mrs. Westenra took place several days later, and was the most miserable morning any of Lucy's friends had ever experienced. Both Arthur and Jack were very brave, and did not break down. They spent a lot of time talking to Mina, who had come down to London with Jonathan, and in their own ways they all gave each other some comfort. But there was no mistaking the despair they felt. It seemed to hang in the air itself.

After the service, Mina and Jonathan had some spare time before going home. They went for a long, slow, sad walk through Hyde Park. They had stopped for a few minutes to rest when Jonathan grabbed Mina's arm so tightly that it hurt.

"No!" he breathed.

"What is it?" Mina cried out in alarm.

"It's him," Jonathan groaned, "and he looks younger than ever!"

"Who?"

"That vile monster, from Transylvania. . ." Jonathan couldn't go on. He seemed half amazed and half terrified, and his face took on a ghostly pallor. Mina followed the line of his gaze. She found that she was looking at a tall, thin man, dressed

206

entirely in black, with a very pale face and jet-black hair. He was staring at a young woman who was walking along the path. His cruel mouth formed a sneer as she passed him, and Mina saw two big white teeth, as long as a wolf's and sharper than needles. As the dark figure turned to follow the woman, a red light flashed from his eyes. Watching his retreating back, a vivid memory came back to Mina. It was a memory of Lucy, sleeping on the bench on the East Cliff in Whitby, while a strange figure loomed over her. A figure with flashing red eyes. . . Was it possible that, somehow, there was a link between Lucy's illness and whatever had happened to Jonathan in Transylvania?

Mina made a quick decision. She was going to read Jonathan's journal. Only then would she be able to understand what he had gone through. Perhaps it would help to explain Lucy's death as well. Then she thought about the odd little scientist she had met at the funeral, Professor Van Helsing, who kept muttering to himself about defeating the forces of evil. There was something compelling about him. Perhaps it would be a good idea to show him the journal too. Maybe he would be able to help her unravel the mystery.

After Lucy's funeral, Professor Van Helsing showed no inclination to return to Amsterdam. Instead, he stayed at the hospital with Jack. While Jack attended to his patients, the Professor studied his books; old, dusty books, crumbling to pieces, such as *Vampire Arts, The Unknown Powers,* and *Conquering The Undead.*

One evening, as the two men were relaxing in the study after a hard day's work, the Professor began reading the newspaper.

"Ah!" he suddenly exclaimed.

"What is it?" Jack asked.

"So soon, so soon," his friend murmured sadly as he read. Then he looked at Jack. "Do you know why I chose to stay here, rather than return to Amsterdam?"

"No," said Jack. "I would have thought you had a lot of work to do in Amsterdam."

"I do. But the reason I stay here is contained in this article. Listen to this: *'Panic is growing in the Hampstead area because of a series of unusual attacks. Several victims have been discovered on Hampstead Heath in the past few days, half-conscious, deathly pale, and each with a distinctive injury — two small wounds on the throat. Although the victims appear to recover after a day or two, doctors are mystified as to the nature of their illness.'* Well, Jack. What do you think about that?"

"I don't know what to make of it," Jack said. "The injuries are like Lucy's, but as to the cause. . ."

The Professor paused before speaking.

"I know exactly what, or rather, I know exactly *who* has caused these injuries on Hampstead Heath."

Jack sat bolt upright in his chair.

"Who? Perhaps Lucy's injuries were made by the same person!" he said excitedly.

"That's impossible," the Professor answered.

"Why?"

"Try not to be angry with me, Jack, when I tell you this. The time has come when you must believe the unbelievable. The person who made these recent attacks. . . was Lucy."

Jack stood up, knocking his chair over.

"Are you out of your mind?" he raged. "Lucy is *dead!*"

"If only I were out of my mind," the Professor sighed. "I would happily be mad, like one of your poor patients, if that could change the agony of the truth."

"And what evidence do you have," Jack said sarcastically, "for this, this obscene accusation?"

"Come with me to her tomb tonight, and I will show you the evidence."

Jack glared at him in even more anger and disbelief.

"Never! I'd rather die than show such disrespect to the woman I. . . to a person who. . . to Lucy!"

The Professor nodded.

"I do not blame you for being angry. But at least read this," he said, passing him a notebook. "It's Jonathan Harker's journal of his stay in Transylvania. Mina Harker sent it to me after her husband broke down in Hyde Park. I assure you, as I assured her, that every word of it is true. Read it, and then come back. If you still refuse to come tonight, then I'll never mention this painful issue again. If I have to," he muttered grimly, "I'll fight the monster alone."

Without a word, Jack snatched the notebook from him and stamped out of the room. The Professor sank back in his chair heavily and closed his eyes. At that moment, in the middle of so much pain and distress, all he wanted to do was sleep. But before ten minutes had passed, Jack had come back into the room.

"Professor, get ready. We're all going to the graveyard."

The Graveyard

The graveyard was only a short distance from Hampstead Heath, and as the last lingering light of the day was fading, Jack and the Professor went there by carriage. Checking that no one was around, they scaled the sturdy iron railings. The graveyard was overgrown and neglected. Vast yew trees and cedars had spread their roots under the packed headstones and forgotten memorials, toppling many of them to the ground. Thousands of people were buried there, and as the two men made their way to the vault of the Westenra family, it felt like every one of them was watching.

"How are we going to get in?" Jack asked as they stood by the black metal door to the vault.

"I'm afraid that I bribed the undertaker's assistant," the Professor admitted, inserting a large, rusty key into the lock.

Jack began to have second thoughts. Could they really be sure that they were doing the right thing? What if it wasn't Lucy who was stalking the Heath? In that case, they were committing a very serious crime. He watched unhappily as the door slowly opened. In the stillness of the graveyard, the creaking of the hinges sounded as loud as a scream.

"I don't like it," he said. "We're disturbing the dead."

The Professor smiled grimly. He struck a match, lit a candle, then turned to face the interior of the vault.

"Remember Jonathan's journal, Jack. Whatever else we're doing," he said gravely over his shoulder, "I can assure you that we're not disturbing the dead."

They climbed down thirteen stone steps and entered the vault. It was easy to see which coffin was Lucy's, because it was surrounded by flowers. Sadly, Jack watched the candlelight flicker over the wreath he had provided. In the middle of the dying blooms he could still make out the words he had written:

To Lucy, a friend I will never forget.

The Professor began to loosen the coffin lid with a screwdriver.

"What are you doing?" Jack whispered. "If opening Lucy's coffin isn't disturbing her peace, what is?"

The Professor didn't answer, continuing to unscrew the lid as quickly as he could, as if he were afraid that Jack might try to stop him. Jack stepped back. He knew that a week-old corpse would be an unpleasant sight. He waited to hear the hiss of gas seeping from the coffin, the gas produced by decomposing flesh. The Professor seemed entirely unconcerned about this danger. He lifted the heavy lid slowly but surely, without even looking inside.

Then he held the candle over the coffin.

"Take a look, Jack. Tell me what you see."

Jack took a deep breath.

"I. . . I can't."

"You must!" the Professor urged him.

"I can't – you know why! I can't bear to see her!"

"Perhaps you won't have to," said the Professor, enigmatically. "You must look, Jack."

Jack felt a terrible dread consume him as as he stepped forward. What would Lucy look like, ravaged by her illness, consumed by death? Little by little he edged slightly nearer and finally, with infinite reluctance, he looked inside. For some moments he stood motionless, just staring. Then his face contorted into an expression of pure bewilderment. He turned to the Professor, shaking his head, then looked again.

The coffin was empty.

"This is proof," the Professor announced, "if you needed any more proof, that Lucy is now. . ."

"Is now what, Professor?" Jack whispered.

"One of the Undead, such as Jonathan Harker described in his journal."

The words tore into Jack's heart and mind like raw, physical pain, making him clutch the sides of the coffin to stop himself from falling to his knees. Lucy, the woman he had loved, was a vampire!

"She isn't the real Lucy," the Professor continued, "just a tragic, evil thing, which must be destroyed. We'll return tomorrow night with Arthur. We have to convince him of what we know before we carry out this dreadful duty."

"Arthur!" Jack exclaimed, the absurdity of the idea giving him his voice back. "You can't expect Arthur to come here! Think about it, Professor. She was his fiancée!"

Professor Van Helsing stood up straight, gripped Jack's arm, and spoke so quietly, yet so firmly, that Jack felt like he was back at medical school again, in one of the Professor's lectures.

"For the sake of Lucy's soul, and for all humanity, this thing must be destroyed. But we can't expect Arthur to understand if he hasn't seen it for himself. He must come. And I know how to make him."

"NO!" Arthur bellowed the next morning, striking the table with his fist. "No, no and no again!"

"I'm sorry, Arthur," said the Professor sadly, "to involve you in such a painful request. I know that it must be hard for you to understand. I can only tell you that, if you come with us this evening, you'll know why I'm asking."

"What do you want to do there?" Arthur asked.

"Drive a sharpened stake through her heart," said the Professor, almost casually.

Arthur's eyes nearly popped out of his head.

"I forbid it," he hissed. "If you even speak of it again, you'll have me to answer to." With that he left the room, slamming the door behind him.

The following night, as a full moon hung over Hampstead Heath, the Professor and Jack could be found hiding behind some tombstones in the graveyard. They were keeping watch over the Westenra family vault. A little farther away a third man was hiding. It was Arthur. The Professor's suggestion had appalled him so much that he had followed them. If they went anywhere near the door of the tomb, they'd have him to deal with.

Shuffling from one foot to the other, Arthur accidentally stood on a stick. It made a loud crack! Jack's heart raced and pounded when he heard it, and he peered into the night, anxiously waiting for the horrible approach of. . . he smiled to himself rather sheepishly, suddenly realizing that he didn't know what might be making a horrible approach. The Professor heard the noise too, and smiled for a different reason. It was good to know that his plan had worked, and that he had provoked Arthur into following them.

The three men waited for ages. The night seemed to get colder and darker, and Jack began to get more and more impatient. What was the Professor thinking of, making him stand in a graveyard half the night when he could be curled up under a warm eiderdown? And anyway, what were they here for? They already knew that Lucy's body had gone. It wasn't as if it was going to come marching across the graveyard, open the door of the vault, get back inside the coffin and settle down for a quick nap. Was it?

"Pssssst!"

Jack looked up, startled, to see that the Professor was pointing at something. Some distance away, flitting between the headstones, was a dim white shape. As he watched, the wind dropped, creating an eerie silence. It was difficult to see what the white thing was, but it was getting nearer and nearer, slowly but surely, and as it did so Jack saw that it was holding something. He strained his eyes, trying to make out what it was. The pale, mysterious figure climbed onto a raised tomb. At that moment, a moment which would be engraved forever in the memories of the three watching men, the moon came out, illuminating a horrible sight with a cold, blue light.

On the raised tomb, her white dress smeared with fresh blood, stood Lucy. The eyes which had once been clear and friendly were like sizzling flames. Her lips curled and slobbered like the jowls of a starving dog. Blood trickled from her vampire teeth onto her chin, before dripping onto the bundle she carried in her arms – it was a boy, a teenage boy. She bent her head down over his throat, saliva dripping from her lips. Her mouth opened, and for an instant her teeth glinted like daggers. She seemed to wait for a few seconds, relishing the prospect of sinking her teeth into his neck. And it was then that the Professor made his move. He stepped out from behind the yew tree to stand in front of her silently. Following his lead, Jack emerged from his hiding place, and Arthur stumbled out of the undergrowth to join them. They stood in a triangle in front of the Westenra family vault, the Professor in front and the other two behind.

When Lucy – or the thing that now bore Lucy's shape – saw them, she snarled like an animal. Her eyes ranged over them; first the Professor, then Jack, and then. . . as she looked at Arthur, her mouth formed into a cruel smile. She laughed, deep and loud, and with a sudden careless gesture dropped the boy to the ground. Seeing his chance, the boy scampered away and hid behind a tree. The Professor breathed a sigh of relief. The legions of the Undead had just lost their newest recruit.

Lucy sprang down from the tomb. Advancing upon them, she seemed simultaneously horrible and lovely, appealing and appalling. Arthur's eyes widened as she came closer. She stopped in front of them, wiped some blood from the corner of her mouth with her arm, and smiled again.

"Arthur. . ." she breathed in a soft, sweet, seductive voice, "Arthur, come to me. . ."

She stretched out her arms to him, and Arthur put his head in his hands and sobbed.

"Arthur. . ." she breathed again, her voice even softer, even sweeter.

Trembling, Arthur looked at her through his fingers, and instead of a vicious monster, stained with blood, he saw Lucy. His hands slipped slowly down his face. Then he reached out to her.

"Lucy!"

It was just as she smirked in triumph that the Professor stepped between them, holding out a small, gold crucifix.

Jack blinked in astonishment at the speed of the vampire's reaction. She recoiled as if struck by a bolt of lightning, her expression becoming one of baffled malice. She hissed like a snake, but she was utterly powerless. The Professor watched, unflinching.

"Arthur," he said finally, "do you understand now? Do I have your permission to go on with my work?"

"Do as you want, Professor," Arthur moaned, throwing himself onto his knees. "I understand nothing except horror and misery!"

"Things will get better," said the Professor gently, "when we have done what we have to do."

Cautiously he moved nearer to Lucy. Her eyes blazed with fury, but the powers of the crucifix were greater than her vampire powers, and she backed away.

"Get Arthur away from the vault," the Professor told Jack. "You're about to see something rather interesting."

Holding the crucifix in front of him, he slowly circled Lucy until there was nothing between her and the vault. With a grisly grin, she backed away to the black metal door. Then her body seemed to fade into tiny specks, forming a floating shape which slipped under the narrow crack at the bottom of the door. The vampire had returned to the dark sanctuary of her grave.

Stepping up to the door while Jack and Arthur still stood blinking in astonishment, the Professor began to seal it with a sort of paste.

"My own invention," he said proudly. "Putty mixed with garlic." He patted the substance into the cracks until there wasn't even the smallest gap left.

"Now she can't escape," he said, "and in the daytime, when she's sleeping, we'll return. But first we must look after that poor young boy. Jack, will you take him home? There are things I must explain to Arthur."

When they returned to the graveyard in the daylight there were several funerals taking place. They watched as a family mourned at an open grave. They waited until the last funeral was over before making their way cautiously to the vault. Jack squeezed Arthur's arm as they followed the Professor down into its darkness. At the very bottom, the Professor lit a candle.

"Remember what I told you, Arthur, and do not flinch from your task."

Arthur gasped when the lid was open. There was Lucy. In the quiet of her grave, resting from the horrible impulses which made her stalk the night for blood, she was beautiful. Her eyes were closed, her expression serene.

"Is she really dead?" Arthur breathed.

"No, she is not dead. That's the point," the Professor said sternly. "Would someone who had been dead for more than a week look as lovely as this? She is one of the Undead, and her soul will never rest until we release it from this evil curse."

The Professor took a thick wooden stake out of a bag. It was as long as his arm, with one end sharpened to a point. He laid it on the floor, and next to it placed a heavy hammer. Then he stepped back, waiting for Arthur to pick the implements up. Momentarily, Arthur hesitated.

"The Undead do not die," the Professor said quietly. "They go on, age after age, attacking new victims and multiplying the evils of the world. Their souls are in torment. Arthur, Lucy needs you to perform an act of great love and great courage. For although the Undead do not die, they can be killed."

Arthur stepped forward.

"I'm ready," he said.

He picked up the heavy stake with one hand and the hammer with the other.

"Place the point of the stake over her heart," the Professor said, "raise the hammer high, and summon all your strength. Then do what has to be done."

The Professor took a small book from his pocket and began to recite a prayer. The ancient words of worship echoed around the stone chamber as Arthur held the hammer high in the air. Jack watched the light of the candle flame shine on its dull metal. He crossed himself and bowed his head. Then Arthur struck the stake as hard as he could.

The thing in the coffin quivered, writhing and thrashing from side to side. A hideous, bloodcurdling screech came from its open lips. It shook and twisted wildly, its face contorted in agony.

"Again!" shouted the Professor over the gruesome noise, "again!"

Arthur delivered a second tremendous blow. There was a last, horrible squeal. The writhing of the body stopped. The vampire was dead.

While he was performing this terrible task, Arthur hadn't faltered. Now it was done, the hammer fell from his grip, and he fell backward. Jack caught him, and lowered him to the floor. The strain had been too much. For a few minutes, Jack and the Professor were so busy looking after him that they didn't look in the coffin. But when they did, they stared in wonder.

"So we did the right thing," Jack said.

"Did you doubt it?" asked the Professor.

Together they gently pulled Arthur to his feet and helped him to the coffin. The foul thing that had taken over Lucy's body had gone, and in its place lay the real Lucy. Her face was ravaged with illness and the marks of pain and suffering, but her expression was as human and gentle as they remembered.

"Now Lucy really is dead," said the Professor solemnly. "Her soul is at peace and in heaven, where you will surely meet her again, Arthur."

Two days later, in his study at the hospital, Jack was sitting at the table frowning in concentration. Next to him was Mina. Opposite them sat Arthur and Jonathan. And at the head of the table, standing up, the Professor was addressing them. He had called them all together for an important meeting.

"One part of our work is over," he was saying. "But a greater task remains. It is to seek out the author of all our sorrow. And then. . ." He paused, looking slowly at the expectant faces in front of him.

"And then kill him," Jonathan said vehemently, to murmurs of agreement. Now that the battle was finally out in the open, Jonathan had regained all his old strength and spirit. He no longer felt like the only person in the world who knew about Dracula. He was part of a team.

"We all know what happened to poor Lucy," the Professor gravely said, "and those of you who weren't already familiar with Jonathan's journal have now read it. Very few people," he said with admiration, "have faced what he has faced and lived to tell the tale. His journal provides an invaluable insight into the powers and habits of this scourge on humanity."

He began to pace up and down the length of the study, stroking his chin thoughtfully.

"I have made it my task to learn as much as possible about the many dangers we face. Jack will testify to the days and nights I have spent in this room, in that chair, reading books and papers untouched for centuries. My purpose in calling this meeting is to share my knowledge – my knowledge of Dracula."

Abruptly he stopped pacing up and down, stood behind his chair and thumped the table.

"There are such beings as vampires. Dracula is the greatest and most evil vampire there has ever been. He is as strong as twenty men and has the cunning that comes from living over a thousand years. He is able to change his form to any beast. He can –"

"So that huge dog which leapt from the ship in Whitby was Dracula!" Mina suddenly interrupted.

"Correct. And he has other tricks. He can control the weather, causing fogs and winds and storms. He can control all animals which live in groups – rats, bats, wolves, wild dogs. He casts no shadow, and has no reflection in water or mirrors. He can fade into a million specks and disappear. These are his powers. As to his purpose, all of us here know what that is. It is to suck blood, the blood of the young, and so add to the numbers of the Undead and perpetuate his own youth."

"I want this monster dead as much as anyone," Arthur said. "You all know the reason why. But how can we defeat him when he has such incredible powers?"

"Because he also has weaknesses," the Professor answered, "weaknesses and eccentricities. He cannot enter a strange place unless invited, or unless he has already sucked the blood of someone inside. He cannot pass through any door or window which has been sealed with garlic. He cowers and cringes at the sight of a crucifix. And perhaps his greatest weakness is that his powers only work at night. In daylight his form is fixed, so he prefers to be in the darkness of his tomb."

He frowned in concentration then turned to face Jonathan. "Your journal tells us about the boxes of earth which Dracula has had brought here. They came by ship. They are his resting places. It's a pity we don't know how many there are, but –"

"Fifty," Mina said. "It was in *The Whitby Times*."

"Excellent!" the Professor cried. "They were to be delivered to Carfax, a ruin in England that you found for him. Can you recall where this place is, Jonathan?"

"Of course. And I think you'll be surprised when you know," he said, smiling.

"It won't surprise me," Jack said. "I even saw the boxes being delivered!"

"Can you explain what you two talking about?" Arthur asked.

"Carfax is next door," Jonathan said.

"This hospital lies in its grounds," added Jack.

"Sometimes we depend more on luck than logic," the Professor said quietly.

There was a pause in the discussion. Perhaps all of them were thinking about Dracula, sated with blood, sleeping in one of his boxes not half a mile away.

"We'll go tonight," declared the Professor suddenly, "when Dracula probably isn't there."

"But. . . why?" Arthur asked.

"One of the things I have learned is that a vampire's lair can be sterilized with Holy Water. We'll sprinkle Holy Water in all fifty boxes. Then he'll have no resting place, and in the daylight, when his form is fixed, we'll hunt him down."

"But what if he's there?" Mina asked.

"If Dracula is asleep in one of his boxes, then. . . Well, we know what to do."

They began to discuss what time they should go to Carfax, and what weapons and equipment to take.

"Professor, one thing worries me," Mina said.

"What's that?"

"If we all of us go to Carfax, and – God forbid – we fail. . . "

"We won't fail," Jonathan muttered.

"We can't," said Arthur.

"But if we do, and we become. . . become like poor Lucy was, one of the Undead, then Dracula will be free to continue his evil work, and there'll be no one to resist him. You see, Professor, we're the only people in England who know about him. And who else would believe us if we told them?"

"She's right," Jack said quietly, after a few seconds thought.

"One of us has to stay behind," Mina continued, "and if the worst comes to the worst and the others fail to return, somehow that person will have to begin this dreadful fight all over again."

"It's a big responsibility," Jack said.

"I'll do it," Jonathan quickly volunteered.

"No, I'll do it," Arthur said.

"No, I'll do it," exclaimed Jack.

They began to argue, each one wanting to save the other from the possibility of facing Dracula alone.

"I think it should be me," Mina said calmly. "Dracula killed Lucy, my dearest, my oldest friend. He nearly killed my husband, the one person I love more than anyone. I hate this monster, and I want to see him dead. I know I have the courage and the stamina to face him alone if I have to. I know I can do it."

"Well let me stay behind too," Jonathan begged her.

"No. You must go to Carfax. You must not underestimate the difficulty of your task. There are a lot of boxes to sterilize. Every spare hand is needed."

Jonathan looked in despair at the Professor, as though appealing for him to intervene.

"Mina has decided," said the Professor simply.

They all fell silent. The men were thinking about Dracula, about destroying his sanctuary and – maybe

– killing him. But if they failed, if they died in the attempt, then it would be all down to Mina. She would have to be as clever as the Professor, as thoughtful as Jack, as brave as Jonathan, and as committed as Arthur. She would have to defeat Dracula alone.

Carfax

"Take these – and these, and these," the Professor directed, handing out crucifixes, garlic flowers, bottles of Holy Water, and a long, sharply-tipped stake.

They were standing next to the ominous stone stump of Carfax. It towered above them, a crumbling heap, Dracula's hiding place. From beneath its forbidding walls Jonathan looked back to the hospital, noticing some flickering lights through the trees. He couldn't help being glad that, for one night at least, Mina was safe. Then he turned to the others.

"I'll lead," he said. "Don't forget I've been here once before – when I was looking for a house for Dracula." He took them around the building, past the big front door, to a back wing where a smaller door was hanging from broken hinges.

"*In manus tuas, Domine!*" the Professor said – "*We are in your hands, Lord!*" – and they crossed the threshold. With grim purpose they walked in single file from one dark, filthy room to another, on the look-out for a desecrated chapel. After several wrong turns, Jonathan stopped in front of a low, arched door.

"This is the place."

"There's a funny smell here," Jack whispered, and

wrinkled his nose. Arthur placed his hands against the door and shoved. At first nothing happened as he strained and heaved. Then there was a sharp snap. The rusty iron hinges broke, and he fell inside.

Only Jonathan recognized the foul stench that assaulted their noses. It was as though Dracula's every vile breath was clinging to the place. Arthur, crouched on the floor, gagged and spluttered. The others stepped back, putting their hands over their noses.

"We can't go in there," Jack coughed.

"We haven't any choice," the Professor replied, entering the chapel.

Arthur got to his feet and with lamp in hand, moved farther in.

"Professor – the boxes!"

"Be careful," the Professor warned, his grip on the stake tightening. "He may be on the streets of London, pursuing his foul ways. But on the other hand. . ."

"Wherever he is," Arthur said, "he is about to become homeless."

He wedged his knife under the lid of a box and began to lever it off. The Professor handed Jonathan the stake and a heavy hammer and got out a bottle of Holy Water. Jonathan held his breath. He wanted Dracula to be in the box. He wanted to drive a stake through the detestable monster's heart.

"Ready?" Arthur hissed.

The other two nodded. Arthur raised the lid, revealing a great mound of Transylvanian soil. The Professor sprinkled a few drops of Holy Water on it.

"Now the evil is sterilized and Dracula cannot rest here," he said. "One down, forty-nine to go."

"I'm afraid not, Professor," said Jack, stepping up to them. "I've had a quick look around. There are only twenty-nine boxes here. And I found this receipt from a delivery firm." He held up a tattered piece of paper on which was written:

> Sir,
> Delivered as rekwested to a adress in
> London — 21 boxes of erth.
> Yours faythfully,
> Thomas Snelling, Snelling & Co.
>
> P.S. You hav a problem with your dranes.

"Blast!" Arthur exclaimed.

"Try not to get too impatient or angry," the

Professor cautioned him. "It's true that twenty-one boxes aren't here. But twenty-nine boxes *are* here, and if we sterilize them, then our job is more than half done."

"You're right," Arthur said. "Let's get to work."

After the men had set out for Carfax, Mina buried her nose in one of the Professor's old books. She wanted to keep herself busy so she wouldn't worry about Jonathan. And she needed to know as much as possible about the enemy in case it became her duty to defeat him. Her eyes grew wide as she read about an outbreak of vampirism a few centuries earlier:

> *The ancient townsfolk always knew when a vampire was stalking its prey. In the dead of night, every dog in the village would start howling at the moon. . .*

There seemed to be a lot of dogs barking *that* night. She listened for a few moments, wondering. Then she shook her head, and forced herself to go back to her book:

> *It was a time when people went out of their wits, when the sane became mad, and the mad became sane. . .*

Mina smiled to herself. The hospital was full of mad people, and none of them was showing any sudden signs of sanity! She closed her eyes, listening to the barking dogs and the noises of the night. It was then that she heard one of the patients chanting a strange rhyme:

> *"Where they go, he will leave,*
> *Where they leave, he will go.*
> *In the future they will grieve.*
> *Now prepare for blood to flow."*

It gave Mina the creeps. She snapped her book shut and decided to go to bed. What she needed was a good night's sleep.

Over at Carfax, the men were systematically sterilizing boxes. They were halfway through, and had become a bit too confident.

"Saw a rat just then," Jonathan observed, as he wrenched the lid from the fourteenth box.

"Huge rat over there," Arthur said, sprinkling Holy Water into the nineteenth box.

"Masses of them here," Jack said a little later, just as he was sealing box number twenty-seven. All four men glanced up from their work and looked around the room. Rats were appearing from nowhere, scuttling and scrabbling across the chapel floor, leaping over their feet, squeaking horribly.

"We must finish this task!" the Professor shouted, looking down in horror at the ocean of vermin around them.

Arthur desperately levered the lid from the twenty-eighth box as his feet entirely disappeared under rats.

"Sterilize it!" he shouted to Jack.

Jack needed no encouraging, quickly sprinkling it with Holy Water as a hundred rats clambered up his ankles. He looked across to Jonathan and the Professor. They were dealing with the last box, but the rats were deeper than ever.

"Come on!" he shouted to Arthur, and they pulled each other through the squealing, writhing mass to the safety of the door.

By the time the last box had been made safe, the

rats were at knee-level. Jonathan looked wildly around him – unless they could get out soon, they were going to drown in rats! He and the Professor started to wade through them.

"I can't make it!" the Professor cried. "Go on without me, carry on the battle! They're too deep!"

"We'll never do it without you!" Jonathan shouted, and he picked him up, slinging him over his shoulder.

"Put me down!" ordered the Professor.

Jonathan ignored him. He could feel the sinewy bodies of rats squirming against his legs as he forced a way through.

"They're huge!" he cried.

"*Rattus rattus maximus,*" called the Professor, "an interesting species. It's a direct descendant of the black rat, the rodent which spread the bubonic plague across Asia and Europe in the Middle Ages. It's absolutely fascinating to think how. . ."

"Shut up!" Jonathan shouted, desperately trying to pull his legs free.

"Hurry!" Arthur called from the chapel door. Jonathan made a last, frantic lunge, and just managed to get the Professor safely into Arthur's waiting hands. But in the attempt he fell over.

Immediately rats were clambering all over him, and in less than a second he was almost totally submerged. He felt as if he was being trampled to death. There were rats clawing at his face, squealing in his ears, scrabbling across his body. He tried to

fight his way out, but felt himself sink deeper and deeper. The rats pressed down on him so hard that it became difficult to breathe. Jonathan thought he was going to die. At that moment, he felt strong arms grab his collar. Jack was heaving him out.

"Mina would never forgive me if I let you drown in rats," he said.

Mina didn't stir when the exhausted Jonathan returned from Carfax. She was breathing in long, drawn out sighs, her hands opening and clenching like a sleeping baby's. She was in the middle of a dream about a white mist. It came creeping up to the hospital, low like a snake, and pressed itself against the walls and windows. Then it seeped into her room through a narrow gap and. . .

Jonathan looked down at her. He was pleased she was sleeping so soundly. The horrific escapade with the rats had amply illustrated Dracula's powers. They nearly hadn't made it. So Mina needed all the sleep she could get, just in case the rest of them didn't survive.

In the morning, as he was telling her about the night's events, he noticed she didn't look very well.

"I think I must be coming down with something," Mina admitted. "I feel so tired and weak."

"I was going to ask you to help me find the other boxes, but perhaps you should stay here instead."

"I think I ought to stay in bed today," Mina agreed.

It took Jonathan only twenty minutes to find Snelling and Co., less than five minutes to track down Thomas Snelling, and the rest of the day to extract the information he needed. It wasn't that Thomas Snelling couldn't *remember* where he had delivered the other boxes. As he told Jonathan again and again, in great detail and at enormous length, he *could*. And it wasn't as if he didn't *want* to tell Jonathan where he had delivered the other boxes. As became completely clear during the course of a long and tedious monologue, he *did*.

"Well just tell me then," pleaded Jonathan. "It really is vitally important."

"Can't do it," Thomas Snelling said, shaking his head gloomily. "I only wish I could, but I can't."

"But why?"

"On account of my illness, which makes talking difficult."

Jonathan stared in disbelief.

"But you've been talking to me for ages! In fact you've been talking to me for ages, and you haven't even said anything yet!"

"Exactly," Thomas Snelling said, shaking his head gravely at the tragedy of his condition. "That's what's so difficult about it. That is the nature of my terrible ailment."

"Are you seriously telling me that you suffer from a medical condition which prevents you from saying things when you talk?"

"That's it – that's it in a nutshell. And there's only one known cure."

"What is it?"

"Now you might find this hard to believe," Thomas Snelling warned.

"Go on."

"But all the most respected medical authorities have reached the same conclusion."

"Just get on with it!"

"The *suffering* I had to endure before the cure was found," he said, shuddering at the memory, "the pain, the agony, the. . ."

"What is the cure?" Jonathan said through gritted teeth, resisting the urge to swear. Thomas Snelling leaned back in his chair, shook his head sadly, and scratched his chin.

"Bodkin's Best Bitter," he sighed.

They went to The Bull's Head, The Trafalgar, The Joiner's Inn, The Speckled Pigeon, The Duke of York, The Three Kings, The Ramsden Croft, The Little Fella, The Billy Boy, The Varsity Tavern, The Prince of Wales and The Frisky Ferret.

"I'm starting to feel a conslidrabbable improvement," Mr. Snelling declared, beaming broadly.

"It's amazing what modern medical science can achieve," Jonathan said drily.

"One more dose should do it," said Snelling. "The full and glorious powers of speech are beginning to vein through my courses."

"I beg your pardon?"

"Er, course through my veins."

It was in The Ribald Rabbit, just before midnight, after a few more restorative measures of Bodkin's Best Bitter, that Thomas Snelling felt sufficiently recovered to tell Jonathan where he had delivered the boxes.

"Number nine," he breathed. "Number nine, Piccadi-pippadi-dilly."

"Number nine Piccadilly?"

"Stank like a *hic!* – stank like a *hic!* – like a *hic!* – oh, never mind," and he slumped beneath the table and fell asleep.

Jonathan rushed back to the others at the hospital. They could go to Piccadilly right away and sterilize the remaining boxes.

"What took you so long?" Arthur exclaimed.

"Don't ask. I know where the other boxes are. I'll just go and see how Mina is, then let's go.

"Hurry!" Arthur implored him.

As they waited for him to return, one of the hospital nurses ran into the room.

"Doctor Seward," he cried, "one of the patients has had a terrible accident! You must come quickly!"

"I can't," Jack said, "I'm too busy. I can't explain now. You'll have to deal with it yourself."

The nurse threw his hands up in despair.

"But there's blood all over the place, and he's moaning and crying. He says he must see you because of the vampire, and I'm too scared to. . ."

"Because of the what?" Jack interrupted sharply.

"Because of the vampire."

"Which patient is it?"

"Renfield."

Jack looked at the Professor.

"What's going on?" he asked.

"There's only one way to find out," the Professor answered, grimly.

They found Renfield lying in a glittering pool of blood. His injuries were horrible, and there was blood and broken furniture everywhere as though he had been thrown around the room by a terrible force. There was no doubt that he was dying. But when he saw Jack crouch down next to him, he began to breathe harder, and his mouth opened.

"He said he would make me sane," Renfield whispered, "so that I could go free. He promised."

"Who did?" the Professor asked.

"He kept coming to the bars of my window," Renfield continued. "He said he would make me sane if I did what he said."

"Who?" Jack said. "Who was it?"

"He broke his promise!" Renfield cried. "I did what he asked, but he came in a white mist and turned into a great wolf, shaking me in his jaws like a rabbit!"

"Dracula. . ." Jack hissed, closing his eyes.

"I called him Lord and Master!" Renfield moaned, "I invited him inside! Forgive me!"

A glassy look came over his eyes, his head turned to one side, and he died.

The three men looked at each other, speechless with shock. Arthur was the first to break the silence.

"Mina!" he shouted.

As they rushed to the Harkers' bedroom, the same image haunted each of them. It was an image of Dracula bending down over Mina's throat; of his bloody fangs piercing her skin. Perhaps for those few moments they were lucky. Because the truth was harder to bear.

Outside the bedroom door they paused briefly. The Professor tried the handle, pressing it slowly and silently down. The door was locked. He gestured to Arthur to kick it open. Arthur took a step back, summoned all his strength, and gave the door an almighty kick. It flew open, smashing into the inside wall with a loud bang, to reveal the unbearable scene within.

Moonlight was flooding the room, illuminating a spectacle so shocking that the hairs on the back of Jack's neck rose.

"Oh Mina. . ." he whispered.

For a few moments they were all incapable of action. They could only watch in fascinated horror.

Inside the room, under an open window, Jonathan was lying on the floor in a stupor. A huge red mark on his cheek indicated that he had been felled by a savage blow. As for Mina, the tell-tale wounds on her neck showed that Dracula had been feasting on her blood. And now he was standing above her, dark and merciless, utterly absorbed in his evil deed. He had pulled open his shirt and gouged a long cut in his chest with his fingernails. He had dripped blood onto Mina's forehead so that it trickled down her face.

"Monster!" Arthur suddenly yelled, breaking the trance. Dracula rotated his head slowly to face them, an indescribable look of disdain and contempt etched into his features. His eyes were flaming red with fury, and his nostrils quivered and flared. His teeth, stained with blood, were champing together like those of a wild beast. Then he sprang at them. But in that instant the Professor held out a crucifix. Dracula came to a halt as though hitting a brick wall. He stared at the small cross, cowering and cringing before it, then looked at the Professor in bewilderment.

"We've got him now," Arthur hissed triumphantly.

He held out his own crucifix, and Jack did the same. They began to advance. Dracula moved backward to the window, step by step, as delicately as a cat. For a split second he smiled, exhibiting his gore-stained teeth. Then, before their eyes, he faded into countless specks which formed a cloud and wafted out of the window. Jack ran to the window and looked out. A great black bat was flapping westward.

From the bed came a scream so ear-piercing, so heart-rending, so full of despair, that they would never forget it. Mina was sitting up, rocking to and fro, her eyes wild with terror. As if responding to his wife, Jonathan began to wake up, moaning in agony on the floor. He felt at the wound on his face. Then he looked up, not seeming to know where he was or what had happened. But a second chilling scream from Mina told him.

"Unclean!" Mina wailed, desperately rubbing the blood off her face with the bedclothes. Jonathan rushed to her. The others could do nothing but witness the agony and the suffering.

"He drank my blood," sobbed Mina, "and stained me with his own!" The Professor stepped forward and lifted Mina's head with his hand.

"I will touch your forehead with the cross. In the name of the Father, the Son and the Holy –"

It seemed impossible that things could get worse. But as he pressed the cross on Mina's forehead she cried out in pain, and it seared into her flesh as if it were made from white-hot metal, to leave an ugly red welt. The Professor, for the first time in many years, began to cry.

"What else?" he shouted into the night. "What next?"

It was Jonathan who replied.

"Don't give up now, Professor," he said. "If you give up, we all will. And how can we do that, when Mina is in danger of. . . of being a. . ."

"Say it," Mina whispered.

But Jonathan couldn't, shaking his head miserably.

"Then I will instead," Mina said resolutely; "a vampire!" Her husband nodded, hatred for Dracula making him grind his teeth together.

"Tonight," Mina said, "there is no time for anything but grief and horror. But when the morning comes," she said bravely, "then we must start again."

The Vampire Vanishes

The house at Number Nine Piccadilly was not like Carfax, where they could enter at will without anyone seeing. It was at the very heart of a bustling city street where all manner of traders and hawkers were busily peddling their wares, and horses and carriages were clattering up and down.

"We'll have to break in," the Professor decided.

"But the street is *seething* with people," Jack said, "and I can see at least two policemen."

"Has anyone got a better idea?" A marked silence revealed that no one had. "Wait here," the Professor told them, walking away without explanation.

They found a bench to sit on opposite the house. It was a large town house, rather shabby, with shutters over the windows. It looked out of place among the elegant properties nearby, with their gleaming front doors and open windows.

"What is he *doing?*" Jonathan fumed after fifteen minutes had passed. The events of the previous evening had made him desperate to confront Dracula. Every wasted moment meant Mina became closer to being a vampire.

"I think something must have gone wrong,"

Arthur said eventually. "We'll have to –"

"Look!" Jack interrupted.

A carriage was pulling up outside the house. The Professor got out of the vehicle in a leisurely way and paid the driver. Another man got out of the carriage too, yawning wearily and scratching his not inconsiderable belly.

"Who's that?" Jonathan asked.

The old Professor laughed loudly at a joke made by the carriage driver. Then he turned to his companion, who was carrying a basket of tools, and said a few words.

"It's a locksmith," Arthur said. "They're going to break in, bold as you like, under everyone's noses!"

As the locksmith worked, the Professor sat on a wall and read about the cricket in *The Times*. No one took a scrap of notice of him until a policeman sauntered up and tapped him on the shoulder.

"Oh no," Jack muttered.

The constable and the Professor started to have a heated discussion.

"We're finished," Jonathan groaned. "Why didn't we stop him? Come on." He jumped up from the bench and walked over to the house. The others followed.

The policeman began to go red in the face, gesturing furiously as he explained something, and the Professor became equally animated in his response. While they were still arguing, the locksmith turned the handle of the front door and pushed it open.

"Ah, splendid!" the Professor declared, just as Arthur and the others came up to them.

"Well, it's been a great pleasure talking to you, sir," the policeman said, "even though you know less about cricket than just about any man I ever met. Why, W.G. Grace is the finest batsman in England!"

"The pleasure was all mine, constable, I assure you," the Professor replied with a smile, "although it pains me to say that your understanding of spin bowling seems to be less than adequate." He suddenly saw his friends watching them in bewilderment. "Arthur! Jonathan! And Jack! What a surprise! You can be the first to see my new house!"

"Er," said Arthur, "yes. How lovely."

"Well sir, good day to you," said the policeman as he walked away.

"And to you," said the Professor, waving cheerily. He paid the locksmith, led the others inside, and shut the heavy door.

"We thought you'd been caught," said Jonathan, amazed at his coolness.

"You underestimate me," the Professor answered. He sniffed the air, his brow puckering. "The next thing to do is find the source of that horrible smell."

They explored the house, sticking together in case Dracula was already there. It was a gloomy old place, damp and empty, and it looked like no one had lived in it for years. Upstairs there was no smell at all, but they searched each room anyway. Downstairs there was an awful stink, and when they went into the dining room, where the stench was so disgusting that it nearly knocked them over, they found what they were looking for. Numerous boxes were stacked up at one end of the room.

"It looks like they're all here!" Arthur exclaimed, quickly counting them: "fifteen, sixteen, seventeen, eighteen. . ."

"At last," Jonathan whispered.

". . . nineteen, twenty. . . Blast!"

There was one box missing. Jonathan and Arthur looked at the Professor in despair. He was carefully placing the contents of his bag on the floor.

"He has another hiding place," he said briskly, "but if we kill him today, what does it matter?"

"I hope he doesn't try that rat trick again," Jack said as they prepared to sterilize the boxes.

"He won't," the Professor said. "His vile powers can only work in darkness, although in the daylight he will still be strong and deadly."

Because it was daytime, it was far more likely that Dracula would be inside one of the boxes than had been the case at Carfax. They sterilized each box with great care, Jack and Jonathan levering off the lid, the Professor sprinkling in Holy Water, and

Arthur standing near, holding a stake and a hammer ready. The tension grew with every box they treated. After they had found that the nineteenth box had nothing but soil in it, they prepared themselves for the last one. It was at the very back of the room, slightly apart from the others. It somehow seemed more than likely that Dracula would be in it.

"Go on," Arthur urged, as Jack and Jonathan struggled to open it.

"This lid's a lot tighter than the others," Jack panted, pulling at it with all his strength.

"Get ready," the Professor whispered to Arthur. "Don't stop to think, just do it."

Arthur gripped the stake tightly in his left hand and raised the hammer in his right. There was the sound of wood splintering, then the lid burst open, and in his eagerness Arthur almost fell inside. The only thing in the box was earth.

"Well, well," the Professor mused solemnly.

"Now what?" Arthur asked, straightening up.

"Now we get our weapons ready, and we wait."

Jonathan clenched his hands into fists. His weary face seemed older than his years. How could he wait when Mina was facing a fate worse than death?

"What if he doesn't come?" he asked the Professor in a quiet voice.

"He will," the Professor said. "Although he may suspect we've sterilized the boxes, he won't know for sure until he actually sees for himself. Also," he continued, getting so wrapped up in his own explanation that he forgot about Jonathan's feelings, "he feasted well last night, so he will want to sleep."

He feasted well last night. . . the words tortured Jonathan, searing into his mind as painfully as the crucifix had seared into Mina's skin. Dracula had to be stopped! If they got the chance today, they had to succeed! Just as he was thinking this, he heard a noise. A key was slowly turning in the lock of the front door.

For a moment, they all stood stock-still, looking at each other. Then, without a sound, they positioned themselves around the room. They heard the front door being carefully opened, and the soft tread of Dracula in the hall. He was creeping nearer to them as slowly and as stealthily as a cat stalking a mouse. He seemed to stop just outside the door of the room.

Silence fell. It probably only lasted half a minute, but to the men inside the room, it felt like a week. Jonathan tightened his grip on the dagger he was holding. Every muscle in his body strained for action. He willed the dining room door to open, slowly, so that he could plunge the deadly blade into Dracula's chest. He had never felt more alert, more prepared, more –

BANG! The door burst open, and even as it slammed back into the wall Dracula was already in the middle of the room. He had sprung in with a single bound, so swift and agile that no one even had a chance to stop him. There had been something so panther-like in the vampire's movement, so inhuman, that they were all – even Jonathan – too shocked to move.

Dracula circled warily in the middle of the room. His hands were held out like claws, ready to swipe and slash. He snarled like a wild beast, savage and blood-thirsty. They knew he had none of his nocturnal powers, but he seemed more dangerous than ever, like a maddened animal in a trap.

The four men began to advance on him. Jack and the Professor were holding out their crucifixes, while Jonathan had his dagger raised above his head, and Arthur carried a hammer and a wooden stake, its tip sharpened to a deadly point. Dracula hissed and spat at them. The monstrous expression of loathing and fury on his face terrified his attackers, but they closed in on him relentlessly, so that there seemed to be no way he could escape.

Jonathan suddenly lunged forward, bringing his dagger down as hard as he could. He moved quickly and used all his strength, but Dracula was even quicker, side-stepping the blow so that the blade ripped through his clothes instead of his heart. From the rip in his cloak, dozens of gold coins came spilling out, bouncing on the floor and rolling into the corners of the room.

Jonathan stepped back, his eyes holding Dracula's gaze, his every thought intent on killing the vampire. The other three moved even closer in, trapping Dracula in a smaller circle. Jack's crucifix was so near the vampire's ghastly white face that he flinched with terror. Seeing his chance, Jonathan lunged again.

Dracula ducked with super-human speed to avoid the blow, then dived from beneath Jonathan's arm and out of the circle, rolling over once and springing to his feet. Arthur and Jack dived after him, but he was so fast that it was as if they were moving in slow motion. The vampire grabbed a handful of gold coins from the floor and then, with a single leap, threw himself at the window. There was an ear-splitting crash as the glass shattered into countless shards and splinters. He tumbled into the cobbled courtyard at the back of the house, springing up unharmed, then turned to face his attackers, who had run to the window.

"You think you can defeat me," he snarled, "but I am Dracula, Prince of Darkness, Lord of the Undead! I can never be defeated! I have time, more time than you can imagine. My reign will last for ten thousand years! I'll be sucking the blood of your children's children when each and every one of you is rotting in the grave!" Then he turned and fled, vaulting easily over a high brick wall.

The three younger men scrambled out of the window. Jack was first into the courtyard, and he ran to the wall and tried to climb it. Arthur ran up behind him and pushed him up. On top of the wall, Jack looked left and right onto a busy street. There was no sign of Dracula.

Jack slithered back down the wall, shaking his

head. The Professor joined them, having clambered down clumsily from the dining room window.

"Let us not despair," he said quietly. "He had fifty hiding places, and now he has only one."

"Yes," said Jonathan bitterly, "but he might choose to hide in it for a hundred years."

Back at the hospital Mina was waiting. She bowed her head when the Professor described how Dracula had escaped, knowing that her soul was still in peril. They decided to have a meeting, racking their brains about what to do next. But what could they do? They had nothing to go on. The house in Piccadilly had contained no clue, so Dracula's last box could be anywhere in London.

"As we can't hope to find him," Mina said after a long silence, "we have to hope he will find us again."

"What do you mean?" Jack asked.

"I mean that our only hope is that he will come back and. . . and try to. . . try to. . ."

"And try to what?" Jonathan asked gently.

"To suck my blood again," Mina answered flatly.

"What a terrible thing to hope for," Jack whispered.

"We have to make it easy for him," Mina said. "There must be no garlic rubbed around the windows. There must be no –"

"How can you suggest such a thing!" Jonathan cried. "How can you expect me to just let him waltz in and attack you?"

"But we have no choice!" Mina replied. "If he can't attack *me*, how can we attack *him*? And Jonathan, what have I got to lose?"

Jonathan looked at her. The red cross on her forehead, which looked so raw and painful, was the terrible proof that she was right.

It was a gloomy group of friends who prepared for the night ahead. Once Mina and Jonathan were in bed, Jack and the Professor hid themselves in the little boxroom which adjoined the bedroom, and Arthur positioned himself outside in the corridor.

The wait was long and fruitless. Each second crawled past like a minute, and each minute crawled past like an hour. No wind rustled the leaves of the trees; the night was silent, utterly silent. And when four o'clock became five o'clock, the Professor knew Dracula wouldn't come. Already the blackness of the night was beginning to lift. He led Jack out of the boxroom, and called for Arthur.

"I'm sorry," he said simply, "but he won't come now. Perhaps if we try again tomorrow night. And yet. . ." he sighed. "My fear, my great fear, is that Dracula will not come here again. As he boasted to us, time is on his side, and –"

"Professor," Mina interrupted him, sitting up in bed with a strange look in her eyes, "Professor, you must hypnotize me!"

Professor Van Helsing was so surprised by this sudden request that he didn't know what to say.

"Quickly!" Mina told him, "before the night has gone, but before the day is here. I don't know why, but you must hypnotize me!"

Doing as she said, he sat on the edge of the bed and started to swing his big old pocket watch slowly in front of her face. Mina's eyes followed the gentle motion. After a few minutes her breathing became slow regular and slow, and her eyes closed. She was in a trance. The four men watched her, fascinated, wondering what she was going to say.

"Who are you?" the Professor whispered.

"I am not me," Mina answered slowly in a low, dreamy voice.

"Where are you?"

"I do not know."

"What can you see?"

"Nothing."

"What are you doing?"

"Nothing."

The Professor sighed and looked up at the others, then turned back to Mina.

"What can you hear?" he asked, with little hope.

"I hear the sound of water. It is lapping at the hull."

"You are on a ship?"

"Yes."

"What else can you hear?"

"The shouting of orders. The flapping of the sails."

"What do you feel like?" the Professor asked.

"Like I am dead, but I am not."

"Then you are alive?"

"I am neither alive nor dead."

By this time the sun had almost risen. Mina became restless in her trance, her head moving from side to side and her eyelids quivering.

"Where are you?" the Professor asked again urgently.

Mina's eyes opened and she looked up at all of them.

"Was I talking in my sleep?" she asked.

"No," the Professor said gently, looking at her. "I'm afraid Dracula was."

After a stunned silence, they all started to bombard him with questions.

"I don't understand it myself," he said, raising a hand to silence them. "The dawn seems to be a critical time for vampires. Just as a vampire is neither alive nor dead, the dawn is neither the night nor the day. Somehow Mina has been able to access the monster's mind. Dawn has always been a time of mystery and fascination, a symbol of death and renewal, a subject for great art. The Ancient Greeks wrote poems about the dawn. And the Romans. In fact, if I'm not mistaken, I think you'll find that the Provençal poets of twelfth-century France had a category of poem called *Alba* – derived from the Latin for white, *albus* – in which they. . ."

While he talked, he started to polish his shoes

with his handkerchief, a sure sign that he was going to talk about something really boring for a very long time.

"Never mind all that now," Jonathan said brusquely. "This is our lucky break. He's on a ship. We've got to find him."

"That's why he picked up the money in the Piccadilly House!" Arthur exclaimed. "He needed it so that he could get home!"

"He is frightened of us!" the Professor declared with a broad grin. "He has taken his one box and he is trying to escape to Transylvania, and the safety of his castle!"

"He won't succeed," Jonathan vowed. "Even if we have to chase him right up to the front door of that miserable place, we'll stop him."

"That won't be necessary," the Professor said. "All we have to do is work out which ship he's on and which port it's going to. Then we can travel there by land, faster than he can, and wait for him."

After a quick breakfast, Arthur set off to visit Lloyds, the shipping organization. He had many contacts there, and was hoping that someone would be able to tell him about any recent sailings to Eastern Europe. The others stayed at home. Mina wanted to talk to Jonathan, and the Professor wanted to talk to Jack.

"What is it?" Jack asked, as his old friend led him into the study.

The Professor sighed, hesitating before he spoke.

"It's Mina," he said.

"What about her?"

"She's. . . changing."

A shiver ran down Jack's spine.

"I can see the fateful signs of the vampire coming into her face," the Professor continued. "It's very slight at the moment, but her eyes seem to be harder, and her teeth, if I'm not mistaken, appear to be sharper. And it seems to be a great effort for her to speak her mind. It's almost as if. . ."

"As if what?"

"As if there was a great battle going on within her, between good and bad, between what she was and what she will become. There will come a point," he said bluntly, "when she will be our enemy."

"Professor!" Jack whispered.

"It's the truth," his friend said, shrugging, "however unpalatable we may find it. But the thing is, I don't know what to do about it. If we take her with us she may, against her will, try to foil us. But if we leave her here, there'll be no one to. . ."

"To what?"

"To. . . release her," said the Professor tactfully, "from this curse – like Arthur did for Lucy."

Outside in the garden, Mina and Jonathan were pacing up and down.

"No!" Jonathan said, "I refuse to believe it!"

Mina put her fingers to her temples, as though speaking the truth actually hurt.

"Look at me Jonathan!" she implored him. "Look at my teeth!"

Jonathan could see only too well that her teeth were slightly longer and slightly sharper, but he didn't want to know.

"I am not a vampire yet," Mina whispered, "but I'm turning into one. And that's why I want you all to do something for me. . ."

At least when Arthur returned later that day, he brought some good news.

"Only one ship sailed to Eastern Europe yesterday," he informed them. "It's called the *Czarina Catherine*. It's going to Varna in Transylvania."

"Excellent!" Professor Van Helsing exclaimed.

"They're due to reach Varna in three weeks. If we cross the Channel tonight, then travel overland, we can be there in two."

They all began to discuss the best route, and what they would do when they arrived. All except Mina.

"Two weeks is a long time," she said quietly. She looked at each one of them in turn. "A lot can change in two weeks."

"I am glad you have raised this subject," the Professor said uneasily.

"I looked in the mirror today, Professor. Do you know what I saw?"

The Professor hesitated. Arthur put his arm around Jonathan, who had slumped against the wall.

"You saw that your teeth were longer," the

Professor said finally. Mina smiled at him sadly.

"Yes, I saw that my teeth were longer," she said, "but guess what else I saw?"

"I. . . I don't know," said the Professor. "It's true that your eyes can seem a little colder at times," he stammered, wincing as if it hurt him to say so.

"It's worse than that. I saw the clock on the wall."

"I don't understand," said the Professor flatly. "I could look in a mirror myself and see a clock on the wall. It all depends on the various physical laws of light and reflection. You see, the reflected ray of light lies in the same plane as the angle of incidence. Now, of course, some scientists think —"

"Professor, I saw the clock through my face."

"There was no reflection?" the Professor breathed in horror.

"No, I wasn't. . . I was there, but I wasn't there as well. I could see myself, but I could see through myself too." Her voice quavered a little, but she continued. "I know exactly what's happening to me, Professor, because I know what happened to dear Lucy. And it's my greatest fear that, as time passes, I will become a danger to the people I love."

"But —" Jonathan said.

"And it goes beyond just us," Mina continued. "God knows how much I love my husband and all of you, but the only thing that matters is the destruction of Dracula. That is why you have to make me a promise. You know what it is."

"Don't make me promise it," Jonathan begged.

"If the time comes," Mina said, "you must promise to kill me — to kill me in the way that we all know."

"You are a very, very brave woman," the Professor sighed. "And I. . . I solemnly swear to you that you have my promise."

"You have mine too," said Jack hoarsely.

"And mine," Arthur said.

Jonathan, blinking back his tears, could only nod.

The Deadly Chase

Mina, Jack, Arthur, Jonathan and the Professor left London in the morning, arriving in Paris the next night, where they reserved some seats on the Orient Express. The train sped through the night and reached Varna at five o'clock the next day. After they had found a hotel and unpacked, Arthur rushed off to the British Consulate. He had arranged for a telegram to be sent to Varna every day by Lloyds, telling him if the *Czarina Catherine* had been sighted. While he was gone, the others met in Mina and Jonathan's room. It was just before sunset.

"Are you ready?" the Professor asked Mina.

Mina nodded. He got out his old pocket watch and, holding it by the chain, he started to swing it to and fro in front of her eyes.

"What can you see?" he asked her, when she was fully hypnotized.

"Nothing. All is dark."

"What can you hear?"

"Waves lapping on the hull. . . Water rushing by, and the creaking of timbers."

"Where are you?"

Silence.

"At least we know he's still at sea," Jack said. "All we have to do now is wait."

"Wait!" Jonathan exclaimed bitterly. "I'm sick of waiting!"

"And Mina is sick *from* it," the Professor said sadly, scanning her sleeping face. The tips of two sharp teeth were protruding from her lips.

They had calculated that it would take up to two weeks for the ship to arrive, but in the end it took even longer. Every day Mina's teeth seemed fractionally larger, and her eyes slightly colder. She was starting to sleep in the day, and wake at night. And she spoke to them less and less.

"Seventeen days!" Jonathan groaned to Jack in the middle of the third week. "Seventeen days, when it should have taken fourteen, and not a word!"

"The ship must have hit bad weather," Jack suggested.

"That fiend can control the weather!" Jonathan exploded. But at that moment Arthur ran in with a telegram.

"The ship's arrived!" he cried. "But I'm afraid —"

"Thank God!" Jonathan said, and he snatched the piece of paper from Arthur's hand: *Czarina Catherine reported entering port of Galatz at nine o'clock today.*

"Galatz?" Jonathan groaned. "Galatz? In God's name, where on earth is Galatz?"

"That's what I wanted to tell you," Arthur said. "Somehow he's tricked us. Galatz is miles away."

They spent the whole day on a train, mentally urging it to go faster as it hurtled the hundreds of miles to Galatz. As soon as they arrived they went to the port and tracked down the *Czarina Catherina*. The Captain was only too pleased to meet some English people, and he took them aboard.

"The strangest passage I ever made in my life," he told them. "London to the Black Sea with a bloomin' force four on a bloomin' beam reach and barely a bloomin' jibe or ready-about to shake a stick at."

"Oh dear," said the Professor sympathetically.

"Oh dear?" repeated the Captain. "Oh dear? It was the best bloomin' wind I ever had!"

"In that case," Jonathan asked angrily, "why did you arrive so late?"

"And in the wrong port," Arthur couldn't help pointing out.

The captain gave them a long, withering look.

"Done a lot of sailing, have you?" he asked.

"Er. . ." said Arthur.

"Ever been battered from bow to bridge by a breaker in the Bay of Biscay?"

"Er. . ." said Arthur.

"Or faced freezing to death in the fo'c'sle in a frigorific fog off the Faroes?"

"Er. . ." said Arthur.

"As you know so much about sailing, you'd know what to do when a fog settles on a boat like a leech and won't shift for love nor money."

"A fog?" asked the Professor, his eyebrows rising.

"That's it," said the Captain, nodding. "Sat on the boat for six days solid, so we had to drop anchor, and yet the wind never let up. Now what do you make of that, sir?"

"Interesting," said the Professor.

"Never known a good blow to leave a fog alone like that. Meanwhile the crew gets the bloomin' heebie-jeebies, chattering about this blasted box we had below. Half of 'em wanted to chuck it overboard, and the other half wanted to open it up, throw in a couple of old crosses and a big bunch of garlic flowers, seal it, and *then* chuck it overboard. Bloomin' lunatics."

"Were they Transylvanians?" the Professor asked.

"Most of 'em," the Captain told him. "Well I says to them that I wasn't having any funny business on my ship, but I could see they might turn nasty, and as we were running low on food and water anyway, I decided to set sail."

"In the fog?"

"In the fog, using just the jib. Well that shut 'em up. Sailing in a fog is scarier than some old box, as our young sailing expert here will doubtless confirm."

Arthur nodded in agreement, his face turning red.

"And then what happened?" the Professor asked intently.

"After a bit I decided to belay avast, but a big bruiser blew midships and gave us a cringle, broaching the boat abaft, and that was that."

"I'm afraid I don't quite. . . follow you," the Professor admitted.

"Bloomin' landlubber," the Captain muttered. "We was blown into this 'ere port, miles from Varna where we was headed. And then, before I even knew where we were, a load of bloomin' gypsies came on board. They wanted that box."

"But surely you didn't give it to them?" Jonathan asked.

"Certainly not!" said the Captain in a hurt and offended tone. "I run a tidy ship, I do. You see, I'm a skipper of the old school, a seafaring gent with my good reputation to keep, and I don't allow any old landlubbers to march straight onto my bloomin' vessel and take whatever they bloomin' well want whenever they bloomin' well feel like it."

"Thank God!" Jonathan cried, seizing him by the hand and shaking it gratefully.

"Well, as I say, I'm a skipper of the old school, and I run my ship accordingly. So I charged them fifty quid, and. . ."

"You did what?"

". . . and off they went with it."

Jonathan dropped the man's hand as though it were a red hot poker. "You charged them fifty pounds?" he repeated. "You idiot!"

"I thought you said you were a skipper of the old school," Arthur said, "with your good reputation to keep. What sort of Captain sells his cargo off for fifty pounds?"

"You think it wasn't enough?" the Captain asked. "You might be right. They were flush with cash. Still, fifty quid is always fifty quid, no matter what you say. You can buy a lot with fifty quid," and, so saying, he rolled up his trouser leg to reveal a brand new, highly polished wooden leg.

"It's mahogany," he informed them proudly.

"I can't stand it any more," Jonathan said back at the hotel. "Every time we think we've got him, he gets away. And Mina. . . she. . . I. . ." He put his head in his hands and tried to regain his composure. It was easy to see why he was so distressed. Mina seemed to be ever more distant, and he couldn't bear to think about that dreadful promise.

Mina suddenly sighed, long and loud. They all looked at her. She had hardly said anything for two days. She was screwing up her face and clenching her fists, almost as if she were in pain.

"Don't. . . give. . . up," she said, grimacing. "Hypnotize. . . again," she managed, then sank back into her chair.

"Mina!" Jonathan exclaimed, rushing to her side.

"She's fighting an extraordinary battle," the Professor muttered as he fumbled for his watch. "It's sheer willpower that has stopped her from becoming a vampire already."

Once more the Professor put Mina under hypnosis and asked her what she could see.

"Darkness," she answered.

"What can you hear?"

"Water lapping on the hull, and the sound of –"

"He's still on the ship!" Arthur whispered in astonishment. "The Captain lied to us, he –"

"Silence!" the Professor ordered. Mina shifted uneasily.

"Where are you?" he asked. She groaned, and her hands gripped the sides of her chair.

"Where are you?" he said again.

Mina's mouth opened and closed. Her forehead was covered in sweat. Her breaths were coming in great, heaving gasps.

"Sereth!" she shouted, making them all jump. Then she fell into a deep sleep.

"There's no such place as Sereth," Arthur said, springing up, "but it doesn't matter because he's obviously still on that ship. The sooner we get back there, the better."

"It's true that there's no such place as Sereth," the Professor agreed. "But that's because Sereth is a river. It winds its way through deepest Transylvania, right to the Borgo Pass. He's on a riverboat."

They decided to pursue Dracula by horse.

"We'll never catch up in another boat," Arthur said, "but if we follow him up the riverbank, we're bound to get him."

"I'll travel directly to Castle Dracula," the Professor said, "and render it. . . uninhabitable for vampires, shall we say, just in case you don't succeed."

"And Mina?" Jonathan asked.

"She must come with me," the Professor said.

Jonathan's jaw dropped open.

"Do you mean to say that you would take Mina into the very jaws of that evil place?"

"But you don't understand –"

"No, *you* don't understand what that place is like, where every speck of dust is a monster, and even the moonlight is alive with vampires! Mina must not go there! She'll be safer with me."

The Professor shook his head. "I wish you were right," he said, "and I wish I didn't have to point out this simple fact."

"What simple fact?"

"That if you catch up with Dracula before he gets to the castle, and try to kill him, Mina would be a great hindrance."

"Why?"

The Professor took a deep breath before he answered.

"Because she may be on his side."

"Professor!" Arthur shouted, "Mina would never do such a thing."

"No," the Professor said, "Mina wouldn't. But who knows if she'll still be Mina tomorrow, or the day after?"

At first light next day, on the bank of the River Sereth, the two parties went their separate ways. The Professor helped Mina into their carriage. Jack, on a magnificent chestnut stallion, waved his hat to them, then galloped away. Jonathan remained motionless on his own horse. He was looking at Mina's face framed in the carriage window, and wondering if he would ever see her again. Then Arthur called to him, and together they chased after Jack.

All day long the Professor and Mina raced through the countryside, stopping only to change their horses. The next day, the country they rode through was noticeably wilder. The mountains enclosed them as though they were in a great rocky prison. The Professor expected to reach Castle Dracula by sunset. With every passing minute he could feel his anxiety building. It wasn't eased by the change coming over Mina, who seemed to be losing the awful battle raging within her. She was starting to smile in a disturbing way, looking eagerly to the most distant crags as though she were going home. And when he had tried to hypnotize her just before dawn, she had refused to answer.

It was at about four in the afternoon that the Professor halted the horses. There, ahead of them, was Castle Dracula, perched on the top of a mountain like an enormous raven ready to swoop, dark and ominous. A long, winding track led up to it, with dense forest encroaching on either side.

"We're here," he called loudly, jumping down and opening her door.

From inside, like a wolf in a cage, Mina watched him. A half-smile quivered on her lips, a smile of cunning and contempt. Her eyes flashed with sudden fury. The mark on her forehead was more lurid than ever, only now it seemed more like a badge of identity than a tragic scar.

"We're here," the Professor repeated in a quiet voice. "You must hang on, Mina, for one more day – please. Do you understand?"

Mina said nothing. Professor Van Helsing put his hands over his face in despair. The time had come. Mina herself had extracted the fateful promise from him – the promise to kill her. For the sake of her soul, and for all humanity, it had to be done. As he stared into her eyes, he tried not to remember how she had once been. He told himself that he was a scientist, a man of reason and logic, who had never shirked a plain fact in his life, no matter how painful. And the plain fact was this: she was a vampire.

"Forgive me," he whispered in a broken voice.

He shut the door and turned away to get the stake and hammer. There was a noise from inside the carriage and he looked back to see Mina pressing her face to the window, and sliding her hands down the glass. On her face was such an expression of anguish and turmoil that he cried out in alarm. She was mouthing something. He couldn't hear it, but he could tell what it was: "Jonathan."

He rushed back to her and opened the door.

"We'll risk another day," he whispered, holding the crucifix in his pocket with one hand and helping her down from the carriage with the other. He led her to a clearing where he intended to set up camp. The first thing he did, even before he fed and watered the horses, was to scratch a ring in the earth around Mina. Snow started to fall as he sprinkled it with Holy Water and pressed garlic flowers into the soil. Mina watched him listlessly, snowflakes spotting her clothes. At one point, when the circle was nearly complete, she seemed about to leap up and spring out, but that same expression of turmoil passed over her face again, and she sank to her knees. The Professor made a ring for himself too. His was to prevent a vampire from getting in. Mina's was to stop one from getting out.

Neither of them got much sleep that night. Mina had slept for most of the day, while the Professor was too scared, too cold, too racked with doubt to sleep. He had made a promise to Mina, the real Mina, the woman he had known and respected. And he had broken it. Only time would tell if it was the worst mistake he had ever made.

He was brought out of his contemplation by the sound of the horses. They were stamping at the ground. Then they began to whinny with fear, rearing up on their back legs, and before the Professor could do anything, they had snapped their ropes and bolted into the forest. At the edge of the trees, in a flurry of snowflakes, the Professor saw a great swirling shape begin to form. He shrank back, then glanced at Mina. The shape grew larger and more defined, then split into three figures. Although he had never seen them before, he recognized the figures only too well. They were the vampires that Jonathan had described in his journal. They were as terrible as he had thought with bright, cold eyes, sneering faces, and a chilling beauty.

"Mina!" the Professor shouted from within his circle, stretching his hands out to her.

"Do not fear for me," she said in a low, rasping voice. It was the first time she had spoken in days. "I am safe here. This is where I belong!"

As the Professor watched in horror, she threw back her head and laughed, the two long teeth glinting at each side of her mouth.

"Mina, resist this evil!" the Professor shouted, but Mina was no longer the Mina he knew.

"Come, sister," one of the vampires said softly. "Come to us, we are your friends!"

Mina moved closer to them, her arms outstretched. The vampires reached out to her. It seemed as though she would be enveloped in their arms.

"Mina!" he shouted once again.

Mina turned to him slowly.
"I'm thirsty!" she hissed.

The Professor felt his whole body shudder with disgust, but then, as Mina tried to step out of the ring, she gave an agonized shriek and was thrown back. It was as if some unseen force had picked her up and hurled her to the ground. She lay there whimpering, bewildered and dazed, as the three other vampires looked on.

"It was him," one of them snarled, pointing at the Professor with a long, pale arm. "He trapped her with – garlic," she spat, "and – Holy Water!"

With her two companions she began to advance upon the Professor.

"There won't be much blood in this old bag of bones!" the fair vampire said, laughing horribly.

The Professor shrank back, but then she too was thrown back when she tried to step into his circle.

The other two vampires hissed with anger, their fangs glistening. The Professor fumbled for his crucifix, then held it in front of him.

"Get back!" he commanded, raising himself from the ground, "get back to your foul lairs!"

The vampires moved away from him warily, powerless in the face of the cross. As they moved back into the forest they began to fade away, until finally they vanished completely. The Professor ran back to his circle and didn't stray from it again until daylight.

When he woke up after a few hours of uneasy rest, the Professor wasted no time. Leaving Mina in her circle, where he knew she would sleep all day, he set out for the castle. It took him over an hour to walk there. He shook his head in amazement at the height of the crumbling old walls. To think that Jonathan had climbed them! And there, in the courtyard, was the big door which had slowly creaked open, revealing Dracula. He wondered where the monster was now. Perhaps the others had already overtaken the boat and killed him. But perhaps not. . . Using a heavy hammer, the Professor forced the door open. Then, using Jonathan's journal as his guide, he searched for the chapel. He knew there were at least three coffins there, and he intended to find each one.

As he climbed down the spiral staircase that Jonathan had described, the air became putrid and rank, so he knew he was close. He entered the chapel cautiously, clinging tightly to the tools of his grisly task with one hand, and pressing a handkerchief to his nose with the other. He searched every nook and cranny, each room and chamber, determined to find Dracula's resting place. But when he finally stumbled into a dark, filthy vault it wasn't Dracula's grave he found. It belonged to the three vampires.

They lay in open coffins on the floor. The Professor stood over the fair-haired one. In her rest she was as beautiful as Lucy had been on that terrible night when Arthur had driven a stake through her heart. But then the Professor's eyes narrowed. This was no time for hesitation or doubt. Grasping the stake firmly in his hand, he placed its sharp tip over the vampire's heart.

As the hammer thudded down on the stake, a blood-curdling screech seemed to shake the castle to its very foundations. The body in the coffin shook and writhed. The Professor closed his eyes before he struck the stake a second time. When the shrieking stopped and all was still, he opened them again and stepped back in astonishment. In place of the body was just a small pile of dust. The vampire had crumbled away.

When he had dealt with the other two in the same way, he knew that he had rid the world of a great evil. But a greater evil still remained, and his next task was to destroy its sanctuary. Searching the rest of the chapel, he came across the crypt. It was a small chamber deep underground. Water dripped down the slimy stone walls and formed dirty, stinking pools on the uneven floor. The Professor had to step over them to get to the tomb in the middle of the room – a great casket, on a big stone plinth, the thousand-year old home of the most cunning and deadly vampire there had ever been. The one word carved into the plinth filled the Professor with dread:

DRACULA

The Professor opened the coffin and stared inside, thinking about the countless nights on which the monster must have taken refuge there, gorged with blood. Removing the stopper from his bottle of Holy Water, he slowly tipped its contents into the coffin. Dracula would never find sanctuary there again.

Back at the camp, Mina looked at him imploringly from inside her circle, almost as if she were trying to tell him something.

"What is it?" the Professor asked her quickly. "Tell me."

Mina seemed incapable of speech. She crouched on the ground with her head in her hands, as though engaged in a supreme struggle to conquer an unseen force.

"Go east. . ." she said finally.

"East!" Professor Van Helsing repeated with surprise. "If we go east we'll be going even farther into Transylvania, with no horses, few provisions, and no –"

"East. . ." Mina repeated, almost angrily.

The effort to speak at all, to resist the vampire in her, was now so great that she lost consciousness, sinking down into the snow. The Professor regarded her uneasily. In the night she had been a vampire, there was no doubt about that. Was it possible that she had managed to resist that evil force one last time so she could advise him where to go? And if so, why east? It was madness to go east. It was probably a trick, one of the cunning ploys that vampires use. The Professor knew what he ought to do – put this poor creature out of her misery, and head back west by himself. But. . .

The Professor went east. He didn't know why. It was something he couldn't explain even to himself as he helped Mina through the thick carpet of snow, always aware of her two sharp teeth near his neck. When she started to come to, he supported her with one hand, and kept a tight grip on his crucifix with the other. Never before had he felt so desperate or so lonely. The east-bound track seemed to wind on forever, with nothing certain at the end of it but his own death.

An hour or two before sunset, the exhausted Professor heard wolves howling. He couldn't see them, but he knew they were close and getting closer. He had to find somewhere safe to spend the night. Looking at the impenetrable trees on either side, he cursed himself for listening to Mina. But then the forest to the left petered out as the slope got steeper, becoming a crumbling rocky cliff over the valley below. Leaving Mina alone for a few minutes, the Professor clambered down and found a cave in the rock. It had a narrow entrance between two boulders, and was an ideal place to take refuge.

Some time later, contemplating death in the freezing cave, the Professor looked out over the Transylvanian valley. Far away he could see the huge range of the Carpathian mountains which pierced the sky like daggers. At the distant edge of the plain, a river snaked its way through the wilderness, twisting and curving into the middle of the valley where, half a mile away – suddenly the Professor jumped in surprise, banging his head on a rock.

"Mina! Mina, look!"

But Mina, lying motionless at the back of the cave, was incapable of looking. The Professor struggled to extract his binoculars from his bag. Thundering through the valley up to Castle Dracula was a group of mounted men. In their midst was a great wagon, pulled by eight horses and carrying a large box. The riders were swift and skilled, and looked very much like the gypsies Jonathan had described in his journal.

"My brave young friends have failed," the Professor whispered to himself in a halting voice. "They are probably dead."

Then he nearly dropped his binoculars. No wonder the gypsies were going so fast – behind them were three other horsemen! What they lacked in skill they made up for in guts and determination, and their horses were fairly flying over the snow-covered plain. It was Jonathan and the others. As the Professor watched, he could see that they were gradually catching up.

"Go on," he breathed, "go on!"

The wagon was on a course which would take it directly under the cliff. With his binoculars clamped to his eyes, the Professor saw Jack and Arthur, grim-faced and resolute, as they spurred their horses on and drew level with two fleeing gypsies. Shouting a quick word to each other, they leaped from their mounts onto the men. The four then tumbled to the ground, where the gypsies were quickly overpowered. The other gypsies slowed down in confusion. Their leader, a fiercesome looking man who was driving the wagon, issued a command. The wagon came to a halt, and the remaining horsemen surrounded it, each of them brandishing a weapon.

"Come on!" the Professor urged under his breath, glancing at his pocket watch. It was only a few minutes until sunset.

Arthur and Jack had now remounted and, led by Jonathan, were riding fearlessly at the gypsies. The look on their faces was so ferocious that, as they drew near, two of the gypsies suddenly panicked, broke away from the wagon and went galloping off. That left only five. They glanced nervously at each other, but held their ground.

Screaming like a banshee, Jonathan rode at them. Over his head he was swinging a huge wooden stake, and he knocked two of them clean over as he rode past, leaving them winded on the ground. He quickly wheeled his horse around. Jack and Arthur hadn't been very far behind, and they were engaged in one-to-one combat with the other gypsies. Jonathan dismounted and ran over to the wagon. The leader tried to block his path, but Jonathan couldn't be stopped. After a short struggle he pulled the man to the floor and held a pistol to his head. The man shouted a command to his followers. The battle was over. The gypsies surrendered, threw away their weapons and fled.

Letting go of the leader, Jonathan jumped onto the wagon. The Professor gasped at the sight of him. A wound in his stomach was bleeding, but he hardly seemed aware of it as he attacked the box. Arthur and Jack came to his aid, and between them, just as the sky began to darken, they wrestled the lid off.

There was Dracula, lying helpless in his coffin, but with that terrifying look of malevolence which they all knew only too well. For a split second, as the vampire saw the darkening sky, his red eyes flashed. It was only moments from sunset, when he would be able to change shape and escape. The Professor held his breath, expecting to see the monster transform into a huge wolf, or fade instantly into nothing. But this time there was no escape. The malevolent look turned to one of terror as Jonathan held a stake over his heart. Dracula frantically grasped it with both hands, but just as he did so Jonathan delivered a single mighty blow with a hammer.

Dracula didn't move, and made no sound. For several seconds his dying eyes glared in disbelief. Then, before Jonathan's triumphant gaze, the monster began to turn into liquid. The features on his face dissolved into a formless blob, which started to melt. Then his entire body oozed away, until there was nothing left of Dracula but a small, reeking pool of black sludge.

"We did it!" the Professor shouted triumphantly, turning to Mina, "we did it!"

"Did what?" Mina asked brightly, smiling at him as she woke up. Then she looked around at the cave. "Where am I?" she asked.

The Professor caught his breath as he looked at her. The hateful mark on her forehead had disappeared, and her vampire's teeth had gone.

"Back in the land of the living," was his reply.

It took them nearly an hour to clamber down the rockface. At the foot of the cliff, oblivious to the pain of his injury, Jonathan was waiting. Mina jumped from the last low rock, landing in the deep snow. Within seconds she was in his arms. They held each other tighter and tighter, speechless with relief.

Professor Van Helsing, still standing on the low rock, held out his lamp. He viewed the scene reflectively, then looked at Arthur and Jack holding the horses nearby. Jack put his arm around Arthur's shoulder, and he knew they were grieving for the woman they had loved. For a moment, the Professor closed his tired old eyes. He thought about Lucy, and how she died in Arthur's arms at Hillingham. He thought about the graveyard where they had seen her transformation. He thought about Carfax, where they had all but drowned in rats, and the house in Piccadilly where Dracula had eluded them. He thought about their desperate chase across the harsh landscapes of Transylvania to the very door of Dracula's castle. He contemplated wolves, bats, pain, suffering, fate and –

"Professor Van Helsing," Jack called, interrupting his meditations, "we owe you our thanks. We couldn't have defeated Dracula without you."

"We have all suffered so much," Arthur said quietly. "But without you we would have suffered even more."

"And I would have become a vampire," Mina said simply. The Professor sighed.

"We all played our part," he said. "I owe you my thanks for your courage and your endurance. We have had terrible moments, but we never gave up hope. That's why we succeeded. As for what you say, Mina, about becoming a vampire. . ." He paused, and his mind turned back to the dark deeds of the night, when she *had* been a vampire, when she had hissed those chilling words to him: *I'm thirsty. . .*

"Yes, Professor?" Mina asked. He hesitated, wondering how he could tell her. He looked at her and Jonathan, standing proudly together with their whole future ahead of them.

"I'm just more glad than I can say that you were spared that awful fate," he responded finally.

The truth was a secret he would take to his grave.

Other Versions of the Dracula Story

Dracula has been retold many times and it still inspires new versions in various forms, particularly films. Below are some examples of the best Dracula films, together with some other vampire tales too. All the films are readily available on video.

An early film version of the Dracula story was the silent *Nosferatu*, made in Germany in 1922 by F. W. Murnau. Though based on Stoker's novel, it does not follow the plot exactly, but it remains one of the most atmospheric films ever made. Tod Browning's *Dracula* (1931), starring Bela Lugosi, is the film that created the classic image of the vampire that most people think of today – a ghostly white figure in a formal dinner suit. It was the first in a long series of Dracula films made by Universal Studios in the 1930s, 1940s and 1950s. The original had dialogue, but very little music; in 1999 it was revived in a new version with music by the American composer Philip Glass.

Horror of Dracula (1958) was directed by Terence Fisher for the British company Hammer. An action-packed but quite accurate version of the Bram Stoker original, it starred Christopher Lee as Dracula and Peter Cushing as Dr. Van Helsing. The success of this film inspired Hammer to make many sequels.

Nosferatu (1979) was a remake by the German director Werner Herzog of Murmau's film of the same name. Starring Klaus Kinski as Dracula, it combines stunning photography with dark, brooding horror.

Bram Stoker's Dracula (1992), directed by Francis Ford Coppola, is probably Hollywood's most successful Dracula film. With a cast of stars that includes Keanu Reeves, Winona Ryder and Anthony Hopkins, and packed with special effects, it is a fairly faithful retelling of Stoker's novel.

Dr. Jekyll & Mr. Hyde

Retold by John Grant
With an introduction and notes by Anthony Marks

Illustrations by
Ron Tiner and Harvey Parker

CONTENTS

About Dr. Jekyll and Mr. Hyde   292

Inside the Cabinet   295

A Devil on our Streets   299

The Lawyer and the Will   313

The Door to the Dissecting Room   334

Horror on the Embankment   345

Dr. Lanyon's Terror   377

Back to the Cabinet   405

Jekyll's Last Letter   421

Novels and Movies about Jekyll and Hyde   426

About Dr. Jekyll and Mr. Hyde

The strange, thrilling story in this book is a shortened version of *The Strange Case of Dr. Jekyll and Mr. Hyde*, by Scottish novelist Robert Louis Stevenson. Stevenson was born in Scotland in 1850. He trained as a lawyer, but in 1873 he went to France to recover from a lung infection and it was then that his career as an author began. By the end of the decade he had written two travel books, including *Travels with a Donkey in the Cévennes* (1879), and published many articles and stories in magazines. Stevenson lived in several countries during his life, partly because he believed the cold, damp Scottish climate was bad for his health, and partly because he was adventurous and wanted to see the world. Apart from France, he spent time in the USA, Switzerland and Samoa, where he died in 1894. *Dr. Jekyll and Mr. Hyde* (1886), the book that brought Stevenson widespread popularity, was written while he was living in England. His other famous novels include *Treasure Island* (1883), *Prince Otto* (1885) and *Kidnapped* (1886).

Dr. Jekyll and Mr. Hyde charts the terrifying downfall of Henry Jekyll, a society doctor who invents a potion that alters his character. While under the influence of this drug, Jekyll becomes Edward Hyde, a man without any sense of good or evil who, acting like a wild animal, commits hideous crimes. Gradually Jekyll loses control over his evil counterpart, with dreadful consequences. This novel, like others by Stevenson, contains elements of mystery and suspense. However, compared to adventure stories such as *Treasure Island*, the ideas it explores are very different.

Much of *Dr. Jekyll and Mr. Hyde* is about hiding and concealing. Many people think Stevenson was commenting on Victorian society, pointing out that while rich and influential people pretended to be good, their lives often hid evil secrets. Some say he was also talking about hidden aspects of his own character. The story is set in Victorian London, where rich and poor, and good and evil, lived side by side. While London was one of the richest and most beautiful cities in Europe, it contained some of the poorest people, living in terrible conditions. The book tells us that cities, like people, can hide squalid, unpleasant parts behind impressive, elegant facades. It describes how the exteriors of buildings look different from their interiors, or the fronts look different from the backs. Additionally, many of the characters conceal things from each other. Jekyll hides his experiments from friends and colleagues (even Hyde's name is a pun); Richard Enfield at first hides Jekyll's identity from Utterson; and Utterson hides information from the police. The way the story is written uses concealment, too – many facts are hidden in scribbled notes, messages and letters, or letters within letters. Stevenson even hides some of the basic elements of a standard plot; for instance, the book has no real hero, and though there is an end to the story there is no real conclusion.

The 19th century was a period of great scientific development and many novels from the time, including *Dr. Jekyll and Mr. Hyde,* have science and the pursuit of knowledge as themes. Jekyll begins his experiments with good intentions. But he later admits to his friend, Hastie Lanyon, that he was driven to conduct more daring experiments by vanity, because he wanted the medical world to hail him as a great scientist. As his work progresses, he becomes addicted to the evil world of Mr. Hyde, finding it harder to shake him off, until in the end his quest for knowledge destroys him. In this way, Stevenson asks who is more wicked: the scientist's creation, with little sense of good and bad; or the scientist himself, who knows his experiments are wrong but prolongs them for personal gain. These problems still concern us today, which may well be why *Dr. Jekyll and Mr. Hyde* remains one of the most popular novels ever written.

Inside the Cabinet

If houses are faces, the house you're standing in front of is the stony face of a stern teacher who knows that the children are up to something but doesn't know exactly what. Yet behind this face is a household that is happy enough. The house is owned by a doctor, originally from somewhere on the Scottish borders. Dr. Jekyll came here to London some decades ago, after graduating from university. His household is managed by a staunch, rather silent man, the butler Poole, and by a cook and a handful of young servants. They regard him as a good, kind and considerate master and are loyal to him.

Coming around the side of the house you find a yard, partly covered in paving stones and partly cultivated as a vegetable garden. On the far side of the yard is an outhouse, built by the place's previous owner – a surgeon – as his dissecting room, a surgical theatre in which he used to give practical anatomy lessons to students. Nowadays this little building is called the Cabinet, and Dr. Jekyll often performs his experiments there.

He is doing so tonight. The rest of his household has gone to bed, but a light still burns in the window of the Cabinet. Wiping the greasy fog off the glass with the back of your hand, you can peer through the window to see Dr. Jekyll at work. He is leaning forward intently over his laboratory bench. A lock of his silvery-grey hair, which he wears rather long, has flopped down across his forehead, and he impatiently flicks it away with a toss of his head. In one hand he holds a glass beaker half-filled with a clear, blood-red liquid. In the other is a fold of paper containing a small heap of white powder. Sucking his lower lip in concentration, he slowly and carefully taps a little of the powder into the liquid. For a moment the surface of the liquid froths. As he gently shakes the beaker, the liquid changes, becoming a steely blue.

Cautiously he adds some more of the powder. And then some more. When at last all the powder has been used up, the potion in the beaker is dirty brown like a puddle.

He looks around him furtively, as if he senses you watching him through the window, and then for the first time in many minutes he dares to let out a deep breath. He twirls the beaker a few more times, and stands up. He climbs the few stairs that lead to the door of the Cabinet's smaller room. You can no longer see him, but through the open door you can watch the flickering candlelight make dancing shadows on the bare wall of the smaller room.

For a moment there is nothing else to see. Then a roar of anguish and despair – a roar you will never be able to forget – splits the silence of the deserted yard. There is a loud crash and the sound of breaking glass.

After a short while, a figure appears in the doorway at the top of the stairs – a small man, clutching at the door frame for support. He is younger than Dr. Jekyll, but he is wearing the doctor's clothes, which are several sizes too large for him; this should look comical, but it doesn't. The man's face, although not ugly, has a look of such malignance and cruelty that the breath catches in your throat. Although the fingers that hold onto the door frame are undoubtedly human, they make you think of a predatory bird's powerful claws.

Now strength is coming into the man, so he can push himself away from the door and stand upright. You can see the ferocious physical power coiled into the slight figure. It looks as if he is ready at any instant to explode into swift violence.

He raises that hateful face and you see his eyes, which are the worst of all. They are black and hard, and they seem to you like the openings to dark and perilous corridors.

And they are looking straight at you.

A Devil on our Streets

It had been a good dinner party.

Richard Enfield came to the corner of the street and leaned against the wall. Three o'clock in the morning and London was bitterly cold and seemingly deserted. Since leaving the Connaughts' house on the other side of the river he had seen only two other people, and once a hackney carriage had clopped by in the distance. For a moment, leaning there, he wished that he had hailed just such a carriage to take him home, but then he straightened his shoulders. He had decided that the cold night air was just what he needed to flush the effects of the evening's wine out of his brain, and indeed it had succeeded. The fog that had hung over the city earlier, making the air feel like thin, clammy glue, had lifted. The night was crisp and clear.

Pushing himself away from the wall, he turned the corner and came into a street that was unfamiliar to him. At least... The sign over a shop window jogged his memory. This was Mitre Street, and he knew it well enough in the daytime, when the gaudy contents of cheap shops spilled out onto the pavement and throngs of people in coarse, knitted clothing shouted and laughed and haggled. At night, when only the hiss of the gaslights and the echoes of his own footsteps were in the air, it seemed a different place altogether.

But then, when he was halfway down Mitre Street, he heard another sound – a voice.

"And mind you tell Dr. Strachan how much pain your Mam's in," said a man from a sidestreet off to the left. "Tell him to come quick, Mabel!"

"Yes, Da," said a child's voice, sounding resigned. Pausing, Richard could hear the girl's footsteps, and now he could see her in the distance, running towards him in the gaslight, her long nightdress tangling between her legs so that she kept half-tripping. He guessed she must be six or seven years old – very young to be out so late on a night as cold as this. He wondered if he ought to offer to help, to go with her to Dr. Strachan's house, wherever that might be.

Before he could decide, he heard another set of footsteps. Coming up Mitre Street at a fast walk was a small man dressed, like Richard himself, in a top hat, a dark tailcoat, a starched white shirt and a bow tie. Perhaps it was Dr. Strachan, already alerted to the crisis. Richard grinned. He might not have been sober at the start of his long walk home, but certainly he must look tidier than this gentleman. The bow tie had come almost undone, and there was a dark smudge of something on his shirt.

Richard twirled his cane and started to stroll onwards, but something made him look round to see what happened next. The child and the scruffy little man arrived at the corner at the same moment. The child, startled by the sudden encounter, made a move to dodge aside, but the man kept walking at that same rapid, determined pace; kept walking and trampled the girl underfoot.

Richard swore, and clenched his fist on his cane. "What the... ?"

The child's head hit the pavement with a loud *crack*. For an instant Richard thought she must have fractured her skull, but then she began to cry and then scream in pain and shock.

"Come back here, you swine!" yelled Richard.

The man paid him no attention, but continued to march ahead as if he were totally ignorant of what he had done to the child.

"Hey! You!" Gathering his coat tails around him and wielding his cane like a club, Richard began to chase him. He ran across the road, paused beside the screaming child to make sure she was not seriously injured, then sprinted after the swiftly receding man.

He caught up with him at the open mouth of a little side court, into which the small man was just turning. Dropping his own cane, Richard lunged forward and grabbed the other man by the collar.

"Hey! What the devil do you mean by... ?"

"Take your hands off me!"

It was a threatening snarl, and Richard almost obeyed. But then he tightened his grip. "No, sir!" he snapped. "You have something to account for before I let you go!"

His captive twisted around to look him in the eyes. Richard flinched. Then the man's fearful gaze dropped to look back along the street, where someone, presumably the girl's father, was cradling her in his arms, trying to calm her. Candlelight was beginning to appear in the windows on either side.

"A street child," sneered the man in Richard's grasp. "It is a matter of no consequence."

"Why, you..." Richard began, but then he saved his breath for the task of dragging the little man back to the scene of the incident. After struggling once or twice his captive came along easily enough, but Richard didn't loosen his hold.

Now there were several other people gathered around the child. "Mabel, Mabel," said the man holding her across his knees, her head clasped to his chest. "Hush your noise, Mabel, and tell your old Da what happened."

She gulped, drew breath and began to scream again when she saw the man standing beside Richard.

"I saw," said Richard. "This... this *gentleman*" – he filled his voice with sarcasm – "this devil on our

303

streets, this foul *creature* knocked your daughter to the ground and trampled her. He should be whipped. In fact, I've a good mind to... "

"Make room," said a voice from the far side of the little crowd.

Mabel's father, who had been fixing the scruffy man with a look of pure hatred, hesitantly turned his gaze away. "Dr. Strachan," he said quietly. "God must have sent you to where you are needed."

Strachan spared Richard and his prisoner hardly a glance but dropped down on one knee beside Mabel and her father. His presence seemed to calm the girl, because her screaming stuttered to a reluctant halt. He ran his fingers rapidly over Mabel's limbs, pressing gently here and there, then repeated the process with her chest and back. Finally he probed carefully beneath her hair.

"She'll have a lump the size of a goose egg on her head tomorrow, Sam," he said at last, "and she may have a greenstick fracture of her left forearm, but she'll live. I'll bandage up her arm and give her something to help her sleep tonight. Time enough in the morning to put her in splints."

"Dr. Strachan," said Mabel's father, "God bless you. But you know I have no money to..."

Strachan waved his hand impatiently. "Nonsense, Sam. You're an honest man, and I know you'll pay me when and if you can. And, even if you can't, your friendship is reward enough for me."

Richard had remained silent for several minutes, merely holding on to his captive's collar and trying not to look at the man's face. There was something terrifying about it that froze the blood. Now he intervened.

"Friendship doesn't fill many stomachs," he said. "Someone should settle your bill."

"Who might you be?" said Strachan sharply.

"I witnessed everything," Richard said, and quickly described what he'd seen.

"So I say," he concluded, "that either we can call a police constable and have this scoundrel thrown in prison for the night, or we can ask the rogue to pay young Mabel here sufficient compensation for her pain, with enough left over to settle all that Sam might owe you, Dr. Strachan. I'd say one hundred pounds should suffice."

"Or we could string him up from the nearest lamp post," muttered someone.

Strachan looked at the little man, his lip curling back with obvious distaste. "That may be a grand amount for Sam here," he said, "but the man who can afford those shoes would hardly notice it. A hundred pounds would scarcely seem enough… "

"I'll give you a hundred," said the small man unexpectedly, "if only you'll persuade this wretched thug to let go of my collar."

Strachan looked startled. "Do you mean that?"

"I said it, didn't I?"

"What's your name?" said Strachan, rising to his feet. "I seem to have seen you somewhere before." His look had turned to one of loathing.

"Well, I assure you that I've never laid eyes on *you*, sir!" said the small man. "Now, will you accept my offer or won't you? Speak, man, before I change my mind."

"There's always the lamp post," said Richard softly.

The little man stiffened, then relaxed. "Come with me to my house and I'll give you the money."

"I'll come too," said Richard flatly.

"What is your name?" hissed Strachan again to the little man.

"Hyde. My name is Hyde, as if it were any concern of yours, you backstreet sawbones."

Richard unobtrusively edged his body between the two men. "Your wife," he said to Sam. "You sent young Mabel to fetch Dr. Strachan for your wife."

Strachan eased his stance and turned away. "Sam," he said, "I'd better go and see Alice, if she's ill. Then I'll follow after you to this creature's lair."

"Mitre Court," said Hyde, suddenly seeming eager that the doctor should not abandon him. Richard was a tall man, and Mabel's father even taller. "Number Two, Mitre Court."

"I'll follow you," Strachan confirmed, and moved briskly away.

"One hundred pounds," said Hyde, fumbling with the key. Somehow, throughout the entire proceedings, he had managed to keep hold of his walking cane, which Richard noticed for the first time. The handle was silver, and cast in the form of a devil's head. "You gentlemen will wait here."

Richard looked around him. Mitre Court was set back a little from the street. It was covered with litter and smelled of decay. Light trickled unwillingly in from the gas lamps along Mitre Street. There were too many dark shadows for his liking. He shivered, not entirely because of the cold.

"What guarantee do we have that you won't dart out some back entrance?" he said.

"You have my word," Hyde said.

Richard snorted derisively.

"This place has no other street entrance," said Sam, his voice hoarse. Richard could see he was controlling his rage with difficulty. "There's no other way out."

Hyde looked at him gratefully as the door opened at last. "I'll be no more than a minute," he said, and disappeared inside.

To Richard's surprise, Hyde was as good as his word and returned to the door after a short while.

"I've only ten pounds in cash," he said, counting the sovereigns into Sam's outstretched hand. "You will have to accept a cheque for the remainder."

He produced the cheque with a flourish. Sam looked blank, and then began to growl quietly with disapproval.

"Our friend here does not patronize banks," said Richard. "He has no way to cash your cheque."

"Then you may cash it for him," said Hyde irritably, clearly wanting to shut the door on them. "I have made it payable to 'Bearer'." He pushed the piece of paper into Richard's hands.

Richard looked at it. The cheque seemed genuine enough. But then he saw the signature, *Henry Jekyll*, written in a large, elegant script. It was hard to imagine the claw-like, ever-twitching fingers of Hyde writing such a signature.

"Who's this Jekyll?" he said.

"A friend of mine. He was inside, and gave me the cheque to help me out of... my little difficulty."

"Where is he? Let us see him," said Richard.

"I'm afraid that would be... inconvenient." A sudden look of worry crossed Hyde's strangely repellent face.

"Then how do we know this cheque is worth the paper it's written on?"

"Because... because I will stay with you until the morning, when we can take it to my bank." The words were spoken impulsively, in a single blurt.

"And I will stay too," said Strachan, appearing out of the gloom.

"It is barely a mile to my rooms," said Richard, "and I have several bottles of fine port which I would willingly share with you."

"Then consider the matter settled," said the doctor, rubbing his hands together.

Sam looked uneasy. Strachan did his best to reassure him that his wife and daughter were in no immediate danger, but the man was obviously not entirely convinced. Politely declining Richard's offer of port, he arranged to meet them outside the bank the following morning and then strode off briskly in the direction of his home.

Some months later, Richard was out taking a Sunday walk with his cousin, Gabriel Utterson, when they happened to find themselves in Mitre Street. Pausing opposite Mitre Court, Richard was suddenly reminded of the strange events of that night, and he told his elderly cousin about the loathsome little man who had trampled down the child. He was careful not to mention Henry Jekyll, for in the meantime he'd heard that Jekyll was a highly respected doctor as well as a tireless worker for charity.

"To be sure," he concluded, "I counted my spoons in the morning, even though Strachan and I had taken turns through the night to stay awake watching the foul creature."

"And the cheque?" said Utterson. He was a lawyer and widely admired for his honesty and discretion. He had a craggy, severe-looking face and rarely smiled, though his eyes often twinkled with secret mirth or compassion. There was no twinkle in them now. His face was a mask of worry and bewilderment. "The cheque with another man's name on it – was it valid?"

310

"It was fine," said Richard. "Even though we had Hyde with us, I expected the bank to reject it out of hand as a forgery, but they accepted it immediately. When I pressed the cashier he said that he had met Hyde before; that this was not the first time the rogue had drawn money on that man's account."

Utterson drew a deep sigh. "What was the name on the cheque?" he said.

"The name is that of a good man," said Richard. "I have no wish to see that name tarnished. My conclusion is that the poor fellow is being blackmailed by this Hyde for some minor sin he committed in his youth. Whatever it might have been, it has surely been more than made up for by his good deeds since."

Utterson sighed again. "I fear," he said, "that I already know the name. I was only asking you to confirm the worst. This is sad news you have told me, Richard my friend. Very sad news indeed." He looked away, his eyes focused on something infinitely far away. "Sad news," he repeated under his breath.

"What's the matter?" said Richard. "Is he a friend of yours?"

"A friend and a client," replied Utterson. "I can't tell you any more than that. As a client he's entitled to my confidentiality."

Richard nodded. "Then why are you so certain that you... ?"

"I know that door," said Utterson brusquely.

"Your friend Sam was wrong when he said that there was no other street entrance. There is. Number Two Mitre Court is the outbuilding to another, greater house. The owner of that... No, I've said too much already."

"I don't want to pry," said Richard, "but is there any way we could help Jek... help your friend escape the clutches of this vile blackmailer? It is blackmail, I assume."

"No," said Utterson bleakly. "There's nothing you can do, and perhaps precious little that I can."

"But it's *blackmail!*" Richard exclaimed.

Utterson looked at him with eyes that were as cold and despairing as an arctic wind.

"Blackmail," he said. "It might be. Or it could be something far worse..."

The Lawyer and
the Will

Shortly after the discussion in Mitre Street, Gabriel
Utterson made some excuse to cut the walk short.
Leaving Richard on a street corner looking out for a
cab, he set off at a rapid pace for his own home. The
sunny sky of earlier in the day had disappeared
behind a thick carpet of grey cloud, and a brisk, cold
wind was blowing through the streets. But this was
not the reason why Utterson gripped his coat firmly
around him. The chill he was trying to shield himself
from was the chill of his own fears.

However, when he reached home the haste melted
from his movements. He called out to his
manservant, Molyneaux, that he had returned, then
carefully arranged his coat and hat on the stand in the
hall. There was a fire crackling in the upstairs drawing
room, and the lawyer settled himself on a leather-
covered chair in front of it, leaning forwards with his
hands out towards the flames.

Several minutes passed, and Utterson eased slowly
further and further back in the chair, his feet
stretched out in front of him. Anyone looking at him
would have thought that his gaze was fixed on the
fireplace, but he saw nothing of it. His mind was

focused on the scene in his office downstairs, when he had last seen his old friend Dr. Henry Jekyll.

Molyneaux glided in silently with a glass of dry sherry on a silver tray, and placed it on a little table by the arm of his master's chair.

Utterson muttered some acknowledgment, then raised the glass to his lips and drained it in a couple of gulps, barely conscious of what he was doing.

Molyneaux, seeing his master's mood, retreated from the room, then reappeared a few moments later with the decanter.

"Dinner will be served in fifteen minutes," said the servant, as if addressing the room in general. Again, Utterson mumbled something incomprehensible.

He ate dinner without tasting anything, his attention still far away, and after the meal took a glass of wine and a candle and went slowly down the stairs to the room that he used as an office. Molyneaux exchanged a glance with Annie, the maid. Always on a Sunday evening their master would sit in front of the drawing room fire reading a book until the clock chimed midnight. But not tonight. Something must have disturbed him greatly.

Not for the first time, Utterson thought that the flickering candlelight made his office feel haunted. The tall filing cabinet near the window seemed to be a plump, old lady leaning forward trying to hear any whisper that he might make. The shadows beneath the room's smaller desk, the one that was used during the day by his occasional clerk, Mr. Guest, appeared to be filled with dancing shapes, as if tonight were the night when the King of the Rats was holding his ghostly ball. The eyes in the oil portrait on the wall seemed alive, watching Utterson frostily.

The elderly lawyer seized the portrait by its imposing frame and lifted it clear of its hook. Set into the wall behind was a safe. Its face was dusty, but the dials of its combination lock shone brightly from frequent use. Putting the candlestick down on the larger of the two desks, Utterson reached up wearily to turn the dials.

A minute later he was seated at his desk, staring at the document he had pulled from the dark recesses of the safe. It had been folded in four, and at first he seemed reluctant to open it out. But at last he did so, and in the candle's uncertain yellow light he began to read it.

The document was a will; the will of Dr. Henry Jekyll. Utterson had read it several times before and knew its contents well; as he read it now his lips moved slightly, as if he were reciting a litany under his breath.

Jekyll had come to him several months before to discuss the making of this will. The lawyer had listened to him intently and then, when the doctor had finished explaining what he wanted to do, had thrown up his hands and begun to protest loudly.

"But this is nonsense, old friend!" Utterson had exclaimed. "Who is this man Hyde? I've known you for more years than I care to remember, Henry, and I've never heard you even mention his name. Does he have some sort of hold over you?"

But Jekyll had sat quietly on the edge of his chair, his hands folded primly in his lap. "My relationship to Edward Hyde is no concern of yours," he had said rather coldly. "You are my lawyer, Gabriel, not my confessor."

"But I'm also your friend, Henry. If you're in trouble, old man..."

"There is nothing more I wish to add," said Jekyll, closing the subject. "Will you make up my new will for me, Gabriel, or must I take my business to another lawyer after all these years?"

Utterson had breathed a heavy sigh.

"No, Henry. There's no need to find another lawyer. I'll hold your will for you, as I've always done.

But I can't bring myself to draw up this new will for you – that's something you'll have to do yourself."

So, with Utterson's help on the formal, legalistic wording, Jekyll had written out his new will. In it he left everything to his "friend and benefactor Edward Hyde". If this had been all, the lawyer would not have objected so strenuously. But there was an extra clause: Hyde was also to inherit everything Jekyll owned should the doctor "disappear or be absent without explanation for any period exceeding three months." This was what had offended Gabriel Utterson. To his sober and orderly mind, people in adventure stories might disappear mysteriously, but not well-established doctors with respectable positions in society. Besides, Utterson knew nothing at all about Hyde: if the man was a villain and knew the generous – the *over*-generous – provisions of the will, might he not be tempted to get rid of Jekyll? After the doctor's disappearance for three months, Hyde would be a rich man, and could flee abroad with the profits from his crime.

Now Utterson shuddered. Over the past few months, whenever he had worried about Jekyll's will, he'd been able to tell himself that he was just being a silly old fool, fretting over nothing: for all he had known Edward Hyde might have been a saint. But today, thanks to his conversation in the street with Richard, he knew otherwise. Some of the words Richard had used came back to him. Hyde had a "fearful gaze". There was something about the man's face that "froze the blood". And Richard said that he had small, hard, evil eyes...

Utterson shuddered again. The candle had burned low while he'd been lost in thought, and the flame was guttering. He picked up the will, handling it as if it were somehow unclean. "Henry must have sunk very low indeed to find himself in the clutches of such a villain," he muttered to himself as he slid the will back into its stiff, cardboard envelope. "I fear he must have done something awful. If it were only some minor indiscretion, surely he'd have braved the shame of exposure to rid himself of this parasite Hyde. No, it must be a *terrible* secret if he's so concerned to conceal it."

Molyneaux appeared in the hall just as Utterson was locking the door of his office behind him.

"What time is it, Molyneaux?"

"It is a quarter to ten," said the servant.

"A bit late," said Utterson, half to himself. "But Lanyon has never been one for an early night." More loudly, he said: "I'm going out to visit Dr. Lanyon. Bring my coat and stick. I may not be back before midnight, so there's no need to wait up for me."

Meanwhile, somewhere half-across London, in the middle of a network of narrow alleyways where the glow of the gas lamps seems to fight a losing battle against the darkness of human misery, a small man flits from shadow to shadow. It is Edward Hyde.

In one hand he carries a bottle, in the other a walking cane with a most distinctive silver handle, shaped in the form of a devil's head. Apart from the occasional glint of light on glass or silver, or on the teeth that show whitely between drawn-back lips, the small figure could be a shadow himself.

On the corner of Garter Lane and Langford Mews is a pub, the Groat and Sixpence. Light spills from its grimy windows; drunken shouting pours from its door. Inside, someone is playing loudly and badly on a cracked accordion while other voices are raised in discordant song. There is the sound of glass breaking. Hyde pauses at the door, enjoying the noise.

There is little pleasure to be found in this part of London, and what is available is normally paid for the next morning in the form of aching heads and broken limbs. The noise is the sound of people destroying their own lives. He likes it.

Dropping his bottle on the pavement, he throws open the door and steps into the thick, smelly air of the pub. Tobacco smoke greys the light of the lamps. The pungent stench of cheap gin is everywhere. More than one of the customers is stretched out on the floor, snoring, pockets presumably already ransacked. In the corner two old men – forty is an age that passes for old in these parts – are arm-wrestling, watched by a woman in scarlet lipstick and a too-broad smile.

The pub becomes briefly quiet as the new arrival picks his way to the bar.

"Champagne," says Hyde.

The landlord, a huge man with tattoos up both arms, gives a mirthless snort of laughter. "We don't

serve that kind of drink here," he says firmly. "I think you've wandered from your path, guv'nor. This is no place for a fine gentleman like you."

Hyde giggles. It is a strange, high sound that picks at the mind as if trying to uncover things that are best left covered. This time, when the racket of the pub grows quiet, it stays that way. Two or three hands stray towards hidden knives.

"In that case I'll have whatever wine you sell," insists Hyde.

The landlord glares at him, then abruptly glances away, looking oddly frightened.

"I told you before," he says in a low voice. "This isn't the place for the likes of you."

Hyde's cane comes whistling down to hammer the sticky wooden surface of the bar. Further along, a glass left perched on the bar's edge teeters and falls with a crash to the floor. The sharp sound fades away into complete silence.

"Then tell me what drink you do have that a gentleman might sample," snarls Hyde.

"We have gin," says the landlord nervously. "And ale. And cider. Nothing else." Clearly he feels that he should throw this stranger out into the street, and can't understand why he's not doing so.

"Gin, then!" says Hyde. "A bottle of it! But if you're forcing a gentleman to drink such muck you're surely not expecting him to pay for it. Are you?"

"No one drinks in the Groat and Sixpence that doesn't pay their way," says the landlord stolidly, mustering his resentment.

"And is that something you wish to argue about?" says Hyde quietly, leaning forward over the bar, his eyes steely.

The landlord holds his stare for a long moment, but then his gaze falters once more.

"No," he mumbles. "No. I don't want to argue with you."

When Utterson reached Hastie Lanyon's home in Cavendish Square, the doctor was indeed still up. Although he was visibly surprised to see Utterson this late at night, and glanced curiously at the lawyer's wind-blown clothing and perspiring face, he welcomed his old friend. Once they were settled in front of the fire, he looked over the top of his spectacles.

"It's been more than a year since last I saw you," he said.

"Old friends have a habit of not seeing each other for long stretches at a time," said Utterson. "And it's about old friends that I've come to see you, Hastie."

Lanyon continued to regard him steadily over his gold-rimmed glasses.

"It's about Jekyll," Utterson began.

"Jekyll!" The elderly doctor leaped to his feet and paced across the carpet to the window. There was nothing visible outside except the movement of skeletal trees against the lamplight. "The man's a fool!"

"Come now, old chap..."

"A fool, I tell you!" Lanyon turned from the window and stared earnestly at Utterson. "I used to count him as one of my closest friends, certainly my closest in the medical profession, yet he began to talk such drivel that I felt I had to estrange myself from him before I became associated with his lunatic ideas. And it wasn't just the opinions of my colleagues I was worried about, let me tell you. The unscientific, hare-brained theories he insisted on spouting were an insult to my intelligence! To our friendship! I told him more than once to keep his claptrap to himself, but he persisted. I had little choice but to stop seeing him! I run into him from time to time, of course. As doctors we occasionally find ourselves in the same company. But I can tell you, dear chap, that nowadays I take great care to make sure that my relationship with Henry Jekyll consists of no more than that!"

Utterson nodded, as if in sympathy. The thin old doctor's face was beginning to flush and threatened to become purple. The lawyer sensed that, if he defended Jekyll too well, he would find himself shown out to the street.

"I'm sorry to hear that," he murmured.

His soft words seemed to soothe Lanyon, for after a few more agitated paces the doctor sat down once more in the chair opposite Utterson. They talked of other matters for a while, as old acquaintances do.

At last the conversation turned back to Jekyll. Speaking carefully, not wanting to spark off another outburst, Utterson said: "There's a friend of his you may have come across – a fellow called Hyde. Do you know anything about him?"

"Hyde?" repeated Lanyon, taking off his spectacles and toying with them. "No, I can't say the name means anything to me. It's a common enough name, of course, but... No, I don't remember Jekyll ever saying anything about a Hyde. Why do you ask?"

"It's nothing important," said Utterson casually. He switched the subject swiftly. "Do you ever hear from old MacFinnon?"

It was well past midnight when he left the doctor's house. He had learned very little from Lanyon, but the old man's outburst about Jekyll had puzzled him and, if anything, made him even more uneasy than before. Crazy scientific theories? Even the phrase was enough to disconcert the lawyer, whose opinion of progress was that it had been an entirely undesirable invention.

When he finally reached home, the house was cold and dark. The servants had gone to bed. Utterson was grumpy because they had done so, and the knowledge that he himself had told them not to wait up only made him grumpier. He muttered crossly to himself as, candle in hand, he made his way up the long, curving staircase to his bedroom.

That night, sleep proved to be elusive. His bed seemed much lumpier than usual; his pillow might as well have been a block of wood for all the comfort it gave him, and the linen pillowcase seemed damp. He pulled the covers up over his head as the bell on the clock tower of St. Gregory's rang out for two o'clock.

He fell into a state halfway between sleeping and wakefulness. He knew that he was in his bed, but at the same time he seemed to be watching brightly-lit scenes that were happening somewhere else in London. Richard's description that afternoon of the little man trampling the girl underfoot came back to him, and he watched the incident play itself out again and again. Now it was as if he were soaring high over London, so that the whole city was laid out below him like a map; and on every corner, as far in the distance as he could see, there was an evil little man stamping a child to the ground.

He turned over, and as he did so the scene changed. Now he seemed to be in the darkened bedroom of a grand house. Just enough moonlight came in through the windows for him to see the form of his old friend, Henry Jekyll, stretched out on the bed. Jekyll appeared to be asleep, or was he... was he dead? Utterson tried to move from his position in the corner to see, but he found himself powerless: he was here only as a spectator, not as an actor in the scene.

Then the door of Jekyll's bedroom was thrown open, and a wedge of light from the passage fell across the floor. Silhouetted in the doorway was a small figure dressed in fine clothes – or clothes that had been fine, for the pocket on one side of the coat was torn, the white shirt was smudged, and the bow tie had been pulled around until it was nearly under the small figure's ear.

Somehow Utterson knew without question that the intruder was Hyde. And he knew Hyde was speaking, barking out instructions to the sleeping Jekyll, even though in his dream he could hear no voice. As Jekyll, moving like a sleepwalker, pulled himself up on the bed and got to his feet, Hyde came closer to the corner where Utterson stood, peering into the shadows as if he suspected that somebody was lurking there. In the dim light Utterson could see a malevolent gleam in the little man's eyes, but nothing more of his face.

And then, much worse, he could see that his vision of Hyde *had* no face.

The old lawyer sat up in bed with a jolt, clutching the blankets around him and staring at the grey dawn light of his bedroom. His mouth was open, but the scream he was about to give died before it had properly formed. In the distance, the bell of St. Gregory's rang, telling the world that it was six o'clock in the morning.

Although Gabriel Utterson still worked as a lawyer, he had allowed his business to run down over the past few years. He had earned enough money over the course of a long career to pick and choose whether he worked or not. Those few clients that still remained were either old friends or had become so. His duties consisted largely of the drawing up of wills or, increasingly frequently these days, the reading of them after the funeral.

As he ate his breakfast that morning, he realized that, unless one or other of his clients died, he had no especially pressing duties to attend to during the next few weeks. Mr. Guest, his clerk, could cope with day-to-day affairs. Utterson was free, if he wanted to, to indulge himself in a bit of detective work.

"Silly games," he mumbled to himself as Annie cleared his plate away. "Childish games. Highly unsuitable for an elderly gentleman like me. But..."

The "but" was enough to take him out onto the street, safely buttoned up in his overcoat, and to turn his steps in the direction of Mitre Street. He had no clear idea of what it was he was planning to do, except that he wanted to track down Hyde. From Richard's description, he knew that this was where the evil little man had trampled down the girl – and as he told himself, "if he can be Mr. Hyde, then I will be Mr. Seek."

He was an odd figure among the hawkers and traders of Mitre Street that first day, but most of the tradespeople were friendly. They soon started calling him "Your Lordship", a nickname he initially found irritating but soon came to accept as something of a compliment.

Accustomed to a cooked three-course lunch, he nevertheless found great satisfaction in making a meal out of apples and cheese from one of the stalls, and to wash it down he bought a bottle of beer, a drink he hadn't had since his student days.

Brushing the cheese crumbs from the front of his coat, he belched quietly and wondered what all his colleagues in the law and his servants would think of him if they could have seen him now.

That first day he was tired when he came home, but happy. The blood seemed to be coursing through his veins. When he went to bed – which was just after ten o'clock, and not around midnight as usual – he slept soundly the whole night through. Without dreaming.

In this way the lawyer passed the next fifteen days. They were a time of happiness for Gabriel Utterson as he began to feel more and more at home in Mitre Street. Gradually he became reluctant to leave at the end of the day, staying there later and later, until Molyneaux and Annie gave up having his dinner ready for him at seven o'clock each evening.

And at last he found his prey.

It was a little after ten o'clock on a frosty evening. For once, miraculously, there was no suspicion of fog in the air. The stallholders had long ago packed up their wares and retreated to their homes for the night. Utterson was just beginning to think that he should do likewise when he heard, clearly in the distance despite the hiss of the streetlamps, the sound of someone taking short and very rapid strides.

It was his man. It had to be. Cocking his head, Utterson listened intently as the footsteps grew closer and closer.

Instinctively he drew back to conceal himself, and clutched his stick more tightly. The footsteps suddenly became louder as the walker rounded the end of the street. Utterson peeped out, his breath steaming in front of him. There was the little man Richard had described. Utterson's dreams had shown him surprisingly accurately. Hyde obviously didn't notice the lawyer, for he kept walking at the same brisk pace, crossing the road and making straight for the door in Mitre Court, pulling a key from his pocket as he went.

Utterson moved without thinking. He reached the little man just as he was turning the key in the lock.

He touched him on the shoulder. "Mr. Hyde, I think?"

Hyde flinched from the touch, but didn't turn. "That's my name," he said. "What do you want? Who are you?"

"An old friend of Henry Jekyll's," said the lawyer. "He must surely have mentioned my name – Gabriel Utterson of Gaunt Street. Let me come in with you to see him."

"Jekyll's not here," said the little man, wriggling his shoulder away. "Go away." He shook his shoulder again, as if he were a dog shaking off water. Then he paused before adding: "And how did you know my name?"

"We have mutual friends," said Utterson, trying to sound casual. "They told me what you looked like."

"Mutual friends?" The little man sounded incredulous. Still he did not turn around. "Who?"

"Well, Henry Jekyll for one."

"Jekyll never spoke to you about me!" snapped Hyde. "You're lying."

Hyde spoke with such certainty that for a moment Utterson was completely flabbergasted. How could Hyde know? But the lawyer continued speaking, anxious not to lose his fish now that he at last had it on the hook.

"Please do one thing for me," he said.

"What?" said Hyde waspishly.

"Turn around, so that I can see your face."

Hyde shrugged and began to obey. For a moment Utterson thought in terror that Hyde would prove as faceless as in those half-waking nightmares. Then, when he was able to look full on the face that was revealed in the gaslight, he almost wished that his premonition had been correct. Those hard, staring, inhumanly wicked eyes were just as he had seen them. The rest of the face seemed unremarkable at first, but immediately afterwards a powerful sense of evil flowed through the lawyer.

He took a nervous step back. "Utterson's the name," he babbled. "Gabriel Utterson... of Gaunt Street. Jekyll's lawyer, as well as his friend. Here, take my business card."

Hyde took the card and looked at it briefly, then tucked it away in his jacket pocket.

"I may have need of you one day. One day soon." The voice was suddenly sinister and calculating.

He knows about the will, thought Utterson. *He knows about it, and he plans to kill Jekyll and...*

"So you had better have my address," continued Hyde. "In case you ever need to find me in a hurry. In case there's an emergency." Utterson's blood chilled at the way Hyde pronounced the word "emergency", deliberately, and with a sort of cloying fondness. "You'll find my lodgings at 43 Staplers' Gate. That is in Soho, off Greek Street. I would give you my address on a prettily engraved business card like your own but, you see, I am a man of only humble means."

He turned back to the door and twisted the key, then added two more words, as if as an afterthought.

"As yet."

And then he was gone, and the door slammed in Utterson's face.

The Door to the Dissecting Room

Poole wound the grandfather clock in the hall, as he always did before going to bed. It was nearly half past ten, and he was tired, yet he didn't feel sleepy. For the past few months, no one in Dr. Jekyll's house was finding it easy to sleep. Not since... not since things had *changed*.

He sighed deeply, the breath sounding like the wind sweeping autumn leaves along the pavement. He was old. He had been old when he had come into Dr. Jekyll's service twenty years ago. By all rights he should have long ago retired, spent his savings on a country cottage and devoted the rest of his life to his garden. But Dr. Jekyll had been insistent that he should stay on. "Good butlers are the very devil to find these days, Poole," he had said, "and there can be no one else like you. Do stay on, there's a good chap. I'd be lost without you."

That had been the *real* Dr. Jekyll speaking – the master whom Poole had grown, over the years, to admire and respect. In recent months, though, the *real* Dr. Jekyll seemed to have disappeared, his place being taken over by someone else who looked like him, sounded like him, but, in some strange, unfathomable way, wasn't him. Besides, Dr. Jekyll, even the false one, was hardly ever here any more. If he wasn't locked away in the Cabinet until all hours of the night, he was absent from the house entirely. And this new fellow was so often around – this new fellow for whom Poole could spare nothing but a sniff of disapproval. The fellow called...

There was a hammering at the front door.

Poole's right eyebrow rose. It was late for a guest. And guests were a rarity at Dr. Jekyll's house these days. The hammering continued as Poole made his slow way to the door.

He recognized the man on the doorstep. It was Mr. Utterson, the lawyer. He had come here often in the old days, when Dr. Jekyll still entertained a lot. But Poole hadn't seen him for months – and never in such a anxious state. The man's brow was creased with worry.

"Is he here?" gasped Mr. Utterson, as soon as the door was fully open.

"Dr. Jekyll?"

"Yes – Jekyll! Is he here?"

"I believe he is still at work in his dissecting room," said Poole gravely, "although he may have gone out. There is a back door, you see, sir, leading out onto Mitre Street."

"Yes!" cried Utterson, pushing past the butler. "I know all about that door, though I'm beginning to wish I'd never laid eyes on it! I was standing there only a minute ago."

"Perhaps you would take a seat by the fire," said Poole, opening the drawing-room door, "while I go to see if the master is available."

The fire had nearly burned out, but it still seemed welcoming after the cold night air. Utterson couldn't make himself sit down, though; instead he strode backward and forward across the room, rubbing his hands agitatedly together.

Poole was back in a minute. "Dr. Jekyll is not in the house," he said, "and he will not answer my knock at the door of the Cabinet."

"But is he there?" said Utterson urgently.

"I do not believe he is, sir. The place seems deserted."

"But I saw a man go in that door only a minute ago."

"That'll have been Mr. Hyde, sir. He has a key."

"Hyde! Yes, it was him! Your master seems to place a great deal of trust in him, Poole."

"That is true, sir." The butler looked sorrowful. "All of us servants have instructions from Dr. Jekyll to do whatever Mr. Hyde tells us, just as if he were our second master." It was obvious, from the expression on his face, that Poole found this a most lamentable state of affairs.

"You don't like that much, do you, Poole?" said Utterson more gently.

"Dr. Jekyll is an excellent employer," said Poole.

There was a pause.

"I don't believe I have ever met Mr. Hyde myself," said Utterson at last. "It seems strange that Jekyll should not have introduced me to such a close associate."

"Mr. Hyde never dines with us," said Poole. "Dr. Jekyll does not choose to have him around when there are guests here. Indeed, even we servants rarely see Mr. Hyde. He spends most of his time, when he is here, in the Cabinet with Dr. Jekyll working on their experiments together. We are not allowed to disturb them when they are at work. Even the meals the maid leaves on a tray by the door are generally left untouched."

Utterson was thoughtful. "He's an odd fellow, this Mr. Hyde of yours," he said.

"More... more *frightening* than odd, sir," confided Poole, and then realized that he had said too much. "Dr. Jekyll is an excellent employer," he repeated, and Utterson realized he would get no more from the loyal old butler.

On his way home it struck Utterson for the first time that his days as a detective were over: he had found his quarry, so there was no further need for him to haunt the stalls of Mitre Street. He stopped walking for a moment, somewhat saddened by the thought. Then his mind turned back to the problem of Jekyll – and Hyde. He knew his friend had been rather wild in his youth, but that had been decades ago. Surely something he had done then could not be held against him now; no blackmailer could hope to extract money from him by threatening to expose it to the world.

"Yet," he breathed to himself, "while society may forgive deeds done nearly a third of a century ago, God doesn't forget so easily, not God, and perhaps not... other beings." He shook his head. He didn't like where his train of thought was leading. He was a sensible man, an educated nineteenth-century man, not some medieval peasant to be terrified by fears of the dead.

And yet – and yet, there had been that dreadful face, the very sight of which had been enough to freeze his blood. He could believe anything of that face, and of the evil that glowed so visibly behind it. He could believe that... Utterson shook his head again. He was ashamed to admit it, even to himself, but he found it quite easy to believe that Hyde might be a vengeful ghost.

Or even the Devil in person...

Two weeks later, Utterson was surprised to receive a dinner invitation from Jekyll. It had been over a year since Jekyll had shown any signs of wishing to entertain guests. Driven by curiosity as much as anything else, Utterson promptly accepted. The evening passed pleasantly, with a few old friends (Hastie Lanyon was not among them) dining well on the cook's unimaginative but plentiful food, and drinking perhaps too much wine. Jekyll seemed relaxed, cracking jokes and telling tall tales; yet occasionally Utterson thought he saw a look of quiet, rapidly-concealed despair in his friend's eyes.

When the others left, Utterson stayed behind for a final brandy. He and Jekyll chatted lightly for a while and then, when Poole had withdrawn, Utterson got to the point.

"I've been wanting to speak to you for some while, Henry," he said. "It's that will of yours. I don't like it. The thought of it keeps nagging away at me."

"I thought we'd agreed not to talk about that subject any more." Jekyll spoke firmly, yet he was obviously ill at ease. He was a big man with a broad face. Utterson knew he was in his early fifties, and yet he could easily have been mistaken for a man in his mid-thirties had it not been for the silvery greyness of his hair.

Jekyll eventually gave a nervous laugh. "I felt so guilty after I'd left you that day. You were very obviously distressed by the way I had drawn up my will, and I hated to give pain to such an old and dear friend. Yet that is the way it has to be."

"I've learned more about Hyde since then," said Utterson doggedly. "More than I would have wished to, had I known beforehand that –"

"I do not wish to talk about Mr. Hyde," said Jekyll. "Nor about my will. Please can we consider the subject closed."

"I would be a bad friend if I didn't persist." Utterson stared at the brandy swirling in the glass he held. "Has that ghastly man got some hold over you? Does he know some dreadful secret of your past? If that's the case, old chap, you know you can tell me all about it – I can keep a confidence as well as the next man, if not better. If you tell me, I can help you plan how to rid yourself of him."

"You always were the very best of friends, Gabriel," said Jekyll, "and I thank you for wanting to help me. But this is a matter in which you can be of no help at all."

"Is it something *very* dreadful?" said Utterson gravely. Jekyll laughed. There was an edge of hysteria to the laugh. "No," he said. "Oh, no, dear Gabriel.

There's nothing so bad as that. I'm an old fuddy-duddy doctor with no secrets that aren't as fuddy-duddy as I am myself."

"Hyde is not so blameless," said Utterson. "There is one thing that I've been told about him... well, it was abominable."

"Hyde is my associate," said Jekyll crisply. "I am not his master. What he chooses to do outside the walls of my home is no concern of mine."

"But –" began Utterson.

Jekyll held up a hand to silence him. "No, Gabriel. I won't talk about this any longer. The position I'm in is a very difficult one. But I'm not being blackmailed – by Hyde, or by anyone else for that matter. And if it makes you feel happier I can tell you one thing: I can get rid of Mr. Hyde at any moment I choose."

"Then I wish to blazes you would!" said Utterson. "I've met the blighter, you know, and he was –"

"He was horribly rude to you," interrupted Jekyll. "I know. He has a terrible manner and I can only apologize for him."

"These really must be exceptionally important experiments you're conducting," muttered Utterson, "and Hyde must be vital to them if you find it's worth putting up with him."

Jekyll smiled, and this time the smile was genuine. "They're indeed important experiments," he said. "Far more important than I could possibly explain to you, Gabriel."

"Try me."

"No fear," said Jekyll with another broad smile. "I tried to tell Hastie Lanyon about them, and even he – a medical man – failed completely to understand the importance of what Hyde and I are doing. He called me a crackpot. Suggested I should try to gain admittance to a lunatic asylum. And, when I refused, he swept out of the house – and, even though he had been my friend almost as long as you have, dear Gabriel, I have to confess that I was glad to see him go. There is nothing more destructive to scientific progress than a hidebound mind."

Jekyll seemed please with this turn of phrase, for he repeated it softly, rolling the words around his mouth, appreciating them.

"Then it shall be as you say," said Utterson, draining the last of his brandy. "I can't pretend that I like your Mr. Hyde, or that I will ever be able to like him, but your wishes will be obeyed. The terms of your will shall be respected. You have my word."

"Please do that," said Jekyll. "I trust you, Gabriel. If anything should happen to me, I know that you'll see Hyde gets his rights. I beg you, in the name of our friendship, to see that he receives justice."

"I swear to that," said Utterson, thinking: *If anything happens to you, Jekyll old chap, I'll make sure Hyde receives justice all right!*

After Utterson had departed into the night – amid much clapping of shoulders and loud promises to get together again soon – and after Poole and the other servants had gone to bed, Jekyll returned to the drawing room to linger in front of the fire a while longer. If Utterson could have seen the expression that was now on the doctor's face, he might not have agreed so readily to let matters lie. For in place of the earlier calmness, agonized doubt was written clearly across Jekyll's broad features.

"I wish I could be so sure," he said quietly to the dull red embers. "I told Gabriel that I could get rid of Hyde at any moment. I wish I felt as certain as I sounded."

He shuddered. "I might as well wish I could get rid of myself," he continued to himself, letting out a little snort of mirthless laughter. "And that," he added after a pause, "might well be the best way of finishing all this..."

He mused on. "Yet I'm a scientist," he said suddenly, as if trying to justify himself to the dying fire, "and it is my duty to seek out knowledge." The corners of his mouth twitched, but only for a moment.

"Yet if, ten years ago, I had known what I know now..."

Horror on the Embankment

Kate Stewart was in love with William, the footman at Number 27. She knew that it was love because no other emotion in the whole of human experience could possibly compare with what she felt. And that, surely, was the test of love. Sitting by the window of her room, high above the Embankment, overlooking the Thames, Kate played a game with her fingers. Her right hand was to count off the fingers of her left hand, counting "He loves me" for one finger, "He loves me not" for the next, "He loves me" for the one after that, and so on. But the fingers of her left hand kept dodging away from her right, so that she could never tell – *really* she could never tell – how many fingers she would count before the game came to an end. Of course, she was the person who decided when the game *did* come to that end, so perhaps it wasn't so surprising that the last finger to be counted was always "He loves me".

She was seventeen years old, and lucky to have such a secure position: maid to a rich widow. Of course, Mrs. Farquharson could be terribly tiresome at times, but she was a good-hearted old soul and she'd told Kate that her job was secure for as long as she wished it to be. Mrs. Farquharson didn't yet know about William, and might not take kindly to her maid becoming a married woman, but that was a problem Kate would face when she came to it.

Tired of her game for the moment, Kate looked out of the window. There was a bright full moon high in the sky, and the air was frosty clear. The surface of the river was black except where it shone silver with reflections of the streetlamps on the South Bank, and the water seemed almost still.

The Embankment was deserted. It was too cold a night for anyone to venture out who didn't have to.

She was vaguely aware that a hansom cab had passed by a few minutes ago, but otherwise there had been nobody on the street this past half-hour or more.

No – there was someone coming. Pausing from time to time to lean on the parapet by the riverbank, an elderly gentleman was ambling along. He had a dark greatcoat reaching almost to the ground, and around his neck he had a long white woolly scarf. His mane of hair was as silvery as the moonlight. In one hand he carried a light walking stick; with the other he occasionally plucked his pipe from his mouth. Watching him, Kate began to smile: he seemed so very content with the world, even though it was freezing cold, that it made her feel warm inside just to look at him.

And now someone else was approaching from the other direction. Kate frowned. This person didn't give her the same feeling of comfort as the old man with the greatcoat and silvery hair. It was a little man, walking very quickly and busily, so that his body seemed to be all elbows. He didn't have an overcoat on; he was dressed in trousers and tails and a flowing cloak, as if he'd been to a party. He carried a thick walking stick. She couldn't see his face, but she felt certain she wouldn't like it. There was something unsettling about the scuttling figure.

She turned her attention back to the old man leaning on the parapet. He, too, had noticed the fast-moving pedestrian, and had raised his head, removing his pipe from his mouth and smiling in greeting. She could see him speaking, probably saying that it was a fine, fresh night to be out and about.

The little man came up to the older one and stopped abruptly. From the movements of his head she could tell he was saying something very forcefully, perhaps even shouting. From this distance, through the glass of her window, she could hear nothing. The smile was gone from the silver-haired man's face now, replaced by a frown. He put up a hand towards the other, as if to calm him down. Perhaps the little man was a lunatic, walking the streets in that industrious way and stopping to rant at anyone he passed.

Kate was beginning to feel scared. She leaned forward, her breath coming in sharp little panting noises. The glass in front of her steamed up, and she hurriedly wiped the mist away. She gasped when the moonlight revealed the little man's face. But what she saw next was enough to make her faint dead away.

The little man had taken a step back, and now he was raising his heavy walking stick high above his shoulders, and he was bringing it down in a great swooping arc on the head of the silver-haired man, and...

In the distance, leaning against the parapet, Edward Hyde sees an old man, rather too fat for his own good. The first thing he notices about him, though, is not his plumpness but the impressive mane of thick silver hair that covers his head and flows down almost to his shoulders. He is puffing comfortably on a big, curved pipe.

Hyde approaches him swiftly. He has spent the evening drinking and brawling in one of the seedy areas down by the docks, and by all rights he should be exhausted by now. Instead, the deeds he has done this evening have made the blood sing in his veins, so that every part of his body seems to be twitching with life. He feels he needn't rest or sleep for the next century or more; that he's as strong as the world itself. He wishes there were more men to fight, more dogs to set against each other, more mugs of frothing ale to drink, more opium to smoke...

He wants *more* of everything – more, more, more of this glorious exhilaration, this gratification of all the senses, that is called "life".

As he comes close, the fool with the silver hair leers idiotically at him.

"A fine night, my friend!" says the man.

"Finer than you might think!" snaps Hyde. "Too fine to waste time talking about it!"

"I didn't mean to offend," says the old man in a placatory fashion, half-turning away.

But then the man turns back again, wrinkling up his eyes as he peers at Hyde's face. "Good lord! I didn't recognize you for a moment. You're... But no, now I look again I see you're not. You're much too young to be him. It was just a trick of the light. I'm so sorry." He smiles again, and lifts a hand in apology.

All of a sudden Hyde is full of contempt for this fat, complacent old buffoon. Seven decades this fool must have occupied space on earth, and through all of that time he cannot have felt even a breath of the *life* that Hyde has come to expect every second to bring him.

Somewhere in a far corner of his mind a small voice is telling him that this is no smug, idle old fool but Sir Danvers Carew M.P., one of the few respected politicians in the land – the man who single-handedly forced the government to give greater help to the poor and the homeless. But Hyde ignores that little voice in the shouting rush of his uncontrollable contempt and anger.

Besides, Carew has half-recognized him...

"Get out of my way!" snarls Hyde.

Carew frowns perplexedly.

"But I'm not *in* your way, dear fellow," he says. "This pavement is wide enough for a dozen to walk side by side." Then his face relaxes into the artificial smile of someone who thinks he's dealing with a madman. "But if it would make you happier, my friend, I'll press myself a little closer to the parapet..."

He leans forward to touch Hyde reassuringly on the shoulder.

That's the last straw!

Feeling a curious vitality surging through every part of him, Hyde swings up his heavy walking stick, faster than the speed of thought, and brings it crashing down on Sir Danvers Carew's silver-haired head. The sound of that terrible blow seems to echo along the fronts of the blank-faced houses on the other side of the street.

Carew drops to his knees, letting his cane fall to one side. He lifts his hands up to his head, where the silver hair is already blotted dark with blood in the moonlight. A wheezing groan comes from his mouth. Hyde brings his stick down again. This second blow, even more forceful than the first, kills Carew instantly, and he slumps over to one side.

Hyde cannot stop himself. His mind seems to be filled with an angry mob chanting: "Kill! Kill! *Kill!*" He thrashes downwards with the stick, this time reversed so that its heavy silver handle sinks into the dead man's face. He knows he is making little yipping noises of glee as he carries on raining blows down on the motionless body. He almost wishes that his yelps would attract attention, and that someone would come running to the scene, for his appetite for blood suddenly seems greater than any appetite he has ever known...

Kate came around to find herself stretched across the floor. She pulled herself to her knees, shaking her head muzzily. She must have fallen asleep sitting at the window and dreaming of William, she concluded. It had been a long, hard day – Mrs. Farquharson had been particularly demanding because of her asthma – and Kate must have been more tired than she thought.

Her candle had burned away completely. Moving clumsily, she undressed in the dark and put on her nightgown, then climbed into her narrow bed.

Images spun through her head – vivid pictures drawn from the dreadful nightmare she had had while lying on the floor. An old man with silver hair suddenly turning dark...

She shivered, and not just from the cold of the sheets. That nightmare had been very... realistic.

Telling herself she was being silly, she slipped out of bed again and tiptoed to the window.

There was a dark form spread across the pavement on the far side of the street. Even from here the shape looked broken.

That was when she began to scream.

Gabriel Utterson was eating his breakfast when the message came. Molyneaux gave him the hand-delivered letter, and Utterson scanned it as he crunched on a slice of toast and ginger marmalade. As his eye drifted downwards, his body stiffened, and he laid the rest of the toast on his plate.

There was a second letter tucked inside the first. Although the envelope had been stamped, the letter had not been posted. The envelope was addressed to Utterson, and he quickly opened it. The letter was from Sir Danvers Carew, whom he had known casually for years and whom he occasionally served as lawyer. It was an invitation to come to the Houses of Parliament for coffee the following Tuesday. Utterson turned it over in his hands, looking for anything else, but there was nothing except, on the envelope, a tiny smear of blood.

The policeman who had brought the message was waiting with Molyneaux in the hall.

"We must go immediately," said Utterson. "Do you have a carriage ready?"

"It's waiting outside," said the young policeman. "Inspector Newcomen did say as it was urgent that you, er..."

"Quite, quite!" said Utterson hurriedly. "Molyneaux, my coat, my hat and my gloves!"

The butler had them ready, and Utterson swiftly put them on. A moment later he was rattling along Gaunt Street in the police carriage, with the young constable sitting beside him.

"Is it really Sir Danvers Carew?" said the lawyer.

"We're not certain," said the constable uneasily. "The head was so badly beaten that it's hard to distinguish the face. We thought that you, as a friend of his might..."

The constable broke off. Utterson glanced sideways and saw that the young man was looking sick.

They were soon at Strand Police Station, and Newcomen was shaking Utterson's hand. "Thank you so much for coming, sir," said the detective. He and the lawyer had met each other several times before in the course of their duties. "This is a ghastly business."

Utterson was shown downstairs to the mortuary. The air smelled of damp and death. He felt his half-

eaten breakfast shifting unsteadily in his stomach. An attendant pulled back a bloodstained sheet from a body laid out on a low table.

The lawyer had seen death before, but never like this. He turned away, his eyes stinging sharply. Newcomen put an arm around his shoulders.

"I'll be all right in a moment," Utterson gasped.

It took longer than a moment, but at last he was able to turn and look at the corpse again. The head was a mess of blood and silver hair. Only the nose had survived intact, and Utterson recognized the prominent aquiline beak of Sir Danvers. Gesturing to the attendant to pull the sheet down further, Utterson saw the broad gold wedding ring the politician had always worn.

"That's Sir Danvers Carew, all right," he said in a choked voice.

"He had a birthmark on the back of his right hand. Would you be so kind as to... ?"

The attendant turned the hand over, and there among the bruises was the cherry-red blob that Utterson remembered.

"It's him," he said. "But who could have done this? The man didn't have an enemy in the..."

He paused. Carew's campaigns on behalf of the poor had earned him enemies among the rich, who begrudged the increased taxes they had to pay. But this was surely not enough to drive anyone to murder.

"Come upstairs," said the detective gently. "There's something else we want to show you."

Newcomen's office was tiny, barely more than a cubicle, and full of books. The detective showed Utterson to an upright chair, then shifted piles of paper to clear a space on his desk. He sat down himself.

"There was an eyewitness," he said once the two men had settled. "A maid in one of the nearby houses was at her window, and saw the whole thing."

"Then..."

"She knew the attacker. She'd seen him before when he'd come calling on her mistress, a Mrs. Farquharson. She says she didn't recognize him at all until the very last moment, and then she fainted."

"She's certain?" said Utterson. "If she fainted right afterwards she might be confused."

"She's an intelligent lass, is young Kate," said Newcomen, his weaselly face cracking into a smile. "And an observant one, although she seems not to have noticed the kind of activities her mistress engaged in. The man that she saw was probably a customer for Mrs. Farquharson's opium. And it's an old rule that where there's opium there's likely to be murder, sooner or later."

"Where there's opium there's likely *not* to be Gabriel Utterson," said the older man primly. "There should be a law against the stuff. Presumably this was some rogue from the docks?"

"No," said Newcomen. "Mrs. Farquharson's customers come from among what society chooses to call 'the gentry'. The attacker was what passes for a gentleman. A Mr. Hyde."

Suddenly Utterson's mind was thrown back a full year, to the conversation he had had with Jekyll in which the doctor had said he could rid himself of Hyde at any moment. Could it be the same Hyde?

"Is he a small man, all elbows and motion?" he said. "With a face that... a face that you don't much like to look at?" he ended lamely.

"You could have taken the words right out of Kate's mouth," said Newcomen, leaning forward earnestly. "What do you know of Mr. Hyde? And do you recognize this?"

He pulled the upper half of a walking stick from beneath his desk and laid it on the surface. The thick stick was splintered where it had broken in the middle. There was still some blood on its heavy handle, which was made of silver and shaped in the form of a devil's head.

"I do indeed," said Utterson slowly. "I bought it myself, ten, maybe twelve, years ago. It was a present to a friend of mine."

"To Mr. Hyde?"

"No. Someone else. I don't want to drag his name into this unless I must."

"You may have to."

"Yes, but not yet."

Newcomen was visibly dissatisfied.

"But," said Utterson, "I have Hyde's address – at least, the address where he was living a year ago. I have it written down in my notebook."

"I must go there at once," said Newcomen. He leapt to his feet.

"I'll come with you," said Utterson, remembering his promise to Jekyll. "Although I've met the swine only once, I seem accidentally to have become his lawyer."

Newcomen raised his eyebrows in curiosity, but made no comment.

Twenty minutes later, the police carriage drew up in front of the shabby house at Number 43 Staplers' Gate, Soho. Utterson looked around as he climbed down from the carriage. There were heaps of windblown litter wherever he looked. The window of the café on the corner had been broken during the night, probably by one of the empty bottles rolling around on the pavement. This was not a part of London he came to often, and every time he did so he was reminded why his visits were so rare. Although it was nine o'clock in the morning, it seemed as if it were twilight, for there was already a heavy brown fog crouching over London. Utterson shuddered.

Newcomen moved rapidly ahead of him to the door of Number 43, gesturing to a constable to position himself at the side of the door. Clearly the detective wasn't taking any chances. Utterson had seen Newcomen issuing revolvers to two of his men before they left Strand Police Station. Briefly he wondered if he himself might be in any danger but, dismissing the thought as fanciful, he joined Newcomen at the door.

It was opened by an elderly woman. She peered up at them through bloodshot eyes.

"Is this the residence of one Mr. Edward Hyde?" said Newcomen pompously.

"It is," she said. Utterson had the feeling that she was looking them both over to see if either showed signs of being profitable. "He's been a lodger here these past two years. Are you friends of his?"

"Perhaps, if he's an honest man," said the detective.

Utterson broke in. "This is Inspector Newcomen of Scotland Yard," he explained. "You must tell him as much as you know, about Mr. Hyde."

"I don't see as there's much I can tell," she said, wringing her hands together. Her eyes were now evasive, darting here and there, looking everywhere except at the faces of the two men. "He keeps himself to himself, does Mr. Hyde. Not that we see him all that often. Sometimes months go by when he's not here, then he just suddenly turns up, like he did last night."

"Last night?" said Newcomen eagerly. "What time was this?"

The woman looked at him as if wondering whether he would pay her a sovereign for the information.

"I'm a police officer, madam," Newcomen reminded her, and her face fell.

"He came in very late," she said. "And very noisy. He woke me up. He ran up the stairs and slammed his door shut, and then he was busy there doing something. But I gets back to sleep somehow. Only to be woke up by him again a bit later when he goes out again, every bit as loud as the last time."

"What hour was this?" said Utterson.

She shrugged her thin shoulders under her grimy wool shawl. "Can't say. Never been much of a one for clocks, myself."

"We must see his rooms," said Utterson, turning to Newcomen.

"Can't be allowed, it can't," said the landlady. "Those rooms is Mr. Hyde's, and he's always told me most special that no one but him's allowed in there."

"This is a police matter," the detective said. "I insist."

All at once her face was wreathed in a gloating grin. "He's in bad trouble, then, is he?"

"He might be," said Utterson, coughing into his hand. "We don't know for certain yet."

The house seemed almost derelict. The old woman led them up the uncarpeted stairs to the first-floor landing. "Mr. Hyde has the two rooms on this floor," she explained, fumbling a large key from the pocket of her flannel skirt. "They connects," she added. "And the bathroom on the floor above is his as well."

Newcomen let out a slight whistle of astonishment as the woman pushed the door open, but Utterson found himself curiously unsurprised. There could have been no greater contrast with the unpainted landing. The room was shelved on three sides with books, while the fourth had a long mahogany table set beneath the window and an easy chair beside it. The men's feet were silent as they ventured across the thick-pile carpet towards the inner door, which they soon discovered led into an untidy bedroom. The walls of this second room were covered in pictures. Some were of the sort that Utterson would not have permitted into his own home, but all were of the finest quality; although he was no expert, he was willing to swear that one of them was a Rembrandt.

"He's not short of a quid or two, our Mr. Hyde," muttered Newcomen.

"There's a fortune in paintings here," Utterson confirmed.

"And a fortune in wine, too," said Newcomen, pointing at the open door of a closet; through the door, Utterson saw dozens of neatly stacked bottles. Moving his gaze, he saw that all the drawers of the chest had been pulled out onto the floor; a few socks and a dirty shirt lay on the crumpled bedclothes. It looked as if Hyde had hurriedly packed and fled.

The Inspector moved back into the main room and went to examine the fireplace. This was built into one of the walls of bookshelves, and Utterson wondered about the risk of accident. Newcomen was crouched down, sifting with his fingers through the ashes in the hearth.

"What have we here?" Newcomen asked. Shaking off cinders, he held up the remains of a chequebook. "Looks like he was trying to make part of his life disappear altogether," he said, "but was in too much of a hurry to do the job properly."

He opened the chequebook and blew on it. Soot rose. "Gilvey's Bank," he read. "My officers will pay a call there and see what they can find out. Too early for the banks to be open yet, so maybe my boys will get a nice surprise when Mr. Hyde drops in to clear out his account." His smile transformed his thin features. "If we're in luck."

"I shouldn't think you will be," said Utterson sourly. "Mr. Hyde may be many things, but I don't think he's stupid. That's certainly not the impression I've gained of him."

"You may be right," said the Inspector, "but he doesn't seem to have been clever enough to take the other half of the murder weapon away with him."

Utterson followed the detective's gaze and saw, propped up against the books behind the door, the broken-off lower part of the walking stick he had given Jekyll so many years before.

"Ah," he said thoughtfully. "I imagine this creates enough of a case against Hyde – my client – for you to be able to issue a warrant for his arrest."

"Yes, indeed," said Newcomen, grinning. "I should think this discovery just about wraps up the case. We'll launch a manhunt for Hyde" – Utterson noticed that the detective had stopped calling him Mr. Hyde – "and have him in the cells before nightfall."

"Assuming he hasn't left London," said the lawyer.

Newcomen's grin slipped a little, but he tried to conceal it. "Yes, sir," he said. "Assuming that's the case. But that would have meant leaving behind all the money in his bank account, which according to this chequebook is nearly seven hundred pounds. No, I should think we'll nail him at the bank, sir."

"We'll see," breathed Utterson.

It was late in the afternoon before Utterson could rid himself of the police, and all the time he was worried that Newcomen would suddenly remember to ask him about the friend to whom he had admitted having given the walking-stick. But the detective had plenty on his mind, and as the day progressed his face grew steadily gloomier. No one of Hyde's description had turned up at Gilvey's Bank, and, although police were combing the streets of London in an ever-widening circle around Staplers' Gate, they were hampered by the lack of any picture – or even a clear description – of the man they were hunting. All anyone could say, including Utterson himself and the keen-eyed Kate Stewart, was that Hyde's face had no particularly distinguishing features except for the fact that even to glance at it was enough to make you feel you were in the presence of a very great evil. Everything else paled beside that: it was impossible to remember what Hyde actually looked like.

When Utterson finally asked if he were free to go, Newcomen dismissed him rudely, as if glad to see the back of him.

The fog had lifted. The lawyer went straight to Jekyll's house and beat impatiently with his cane on the heavy wooden door. Poole appeared almost immediately.

"I must see your master," growled Utterson. "At once. I don't care a fig if he's up to his eyes in another of those blasted experiments of his – I need to see him right now."

"He is indeed in the Cabinet," said Poole.

"Then take me there!"

"At once, sir. If you will follow me."

Utterson had seen the back yard many times from the upstairs windows, but this was the first time he had been in it. He was dimly aware of orderly vegetable beds, but his attention was focused on the smaller building on the other side of the yard. A few worn steps led up to a green-painted door. The walls of the little building were of plain brick, blackened by the years. There was a single small window covered in grey grime; by comparison with the rest, one part shone where someone had been wiping at the glass.

"So that's the famous Cabinet," said Utterson.

"It is," said Poole. The old butler climbed the wooden stairs and knocked timidly at the door.

There was a mumble from inside.

"It is Mr. Utterson," said Poole in response to the mumble. "He says he must see you right away."

Another mumble.

"He insists that it is urgent."

"Tell him I won't go away until I've seen him," said Utterson.

Poole repeated something of this to the door. At last there was the sound of a bolt being drawn back. Henry Jekyll appeared in the doorway.

Utterson was aghast. His friend looked as if he had aged twenty years. The wrinkles of his broad face (surely there hadn't been nearly so many of them before?) showed the marks of recent tears. His eyes were wide and flickering. He was jacketless and tieless, and his shirt was torn at the collar. If Utterson had seen him in the street he might not have recognized him, but hurried on by.

"Good heavens, Henry!" the lawyer exclaimed. "What on earth has happened to you?"

"It's not what's happened to me," said the doctor hoarsely. "It's what's happened to poor old Danvers Carew. I heard the newsboys calling it in the square."

"Then you must know that the police are seeking Edw..." began Utterson, then remembered that Poole was still with them.

"Yes," said Jekyll. "I heard the rest of it. Poole, perhaps you should go indoors now."

The butler bowed slightly and left them.

"Come into the dissecting room," said Jekyll wearily.

Utterson followed him into the Cabinet and found himself in a fully equipped laboratory. He was not a man of science – indeed, he carefully cultivated as much ignorance as possible of scientific matters – but the place seemed to him to represent a considerable amount of money. There were two or three gleaming machines, the function of which Utterson could not even begin to guess. Over in the corner was a cumbersome device made of metal and coils of wire, and Utterson deduced this must be one of those electricity-generating machines he had read about in the newspapers, for further wires led in a tangle from it to the other gadgets that crowded at one end of the laboratory bench.

The table was covered with numerous flasks, stands, jars and bottles, as well as leather-bound books and notepads. Two walls of the dissecting room were lined with glass-fronted dressers containing countless little corked bottles of powders and liquids. A fire-axe hung from a hook behind the door, and a bucket of sand was on the floor beneath it.

At the far end of the room, three steps rose to a door covered in red fabric. It was partly open, and Utterson could see that on the other side of it was a smaller room where a fire crackled brightly in the hearth. The vigorous flames seemed out of place: the dissecting room was otherwise filled with the air of bleak despair.

Jekyll led him up to the smaller room. "This is the Cabinet proper, although we've adopted the habit of using that name for the whole building," he said, warming his hands as Utterson sat in an armchair.

"My predecessor in this house, a doctor like myself, had this outhouse built so that he could teach his students the principles of anatomy. He lectured downstairs in the dissecting room, cutting up the cadavers, and retreated here to the Cabinet when he wanted to do his own private reading and research. Unlike him, I do no dissection, so I have turned the surgical theatre into a chemical laboratory. But still I like to read and relax in this room where no one will disturb me."

"No one except Edward Hyde," said Utterson heavily. "Stop beating about the bush, Henry. You know why I've come."

"I do indeed," said Jekyll sadly.

"Is he here?"

Jekyll took a moment to reply. "No," he said eventually.

"I didn't like that pause," said Utterson. "Let me make myself plain, Henry. You're a long-established client of mine, and have been a friend for even longer than that. But Carew was my friend and client as well, and I am determined to see his murderer brought to justice. Even if I had loathed the very sight of Carew I'd want to see the killer seized. No man should die the way that Carew did. I've seen the body! Hyde must have gone berserk!"

"Hyde isn't here," said Jekyll. "I swear to that. And I swear that I shall never set eyes on him again. You have my word. The world shall never be troubled by him again." He spoke bitterly.

"How can you know this?" demanded Utterson.

"I've had a letter from him. It came this morning. I've spent all day wondering whether I should burn it or hand it over to the police. I was just on the verge of deciding that the wisest course would be to give it to you, as my lawyer, when you arrived." Jekyll took a folded sheet of paper from the mantel and passed it to Utterson.

The letter was short, and written in spidery handwriting that, without his glasses, Utterson found hard to decipher:

My dear Jekyll,

By the time you read this I shall be far away. For these past two years I have repaid your constant generosity with nothing but selfishness. But this time I have gone too far. I have done something despicable and vile. The police would hang me if they caught me, and would be right to do so, but I have a powerful affection for this miserable life of mine and so will not give them the chance. The place where I am going is far from the reach of the law, and I shall be safe among friends there. All that I regret is that I shall never again look upon the face of the best friend I ever had: Dr. Henry Jekyll.

Your unworthy associate and sorry friend,

Edward Hyde

"Do you have the envelope?" said Utterson when he had finished reading.

Jekyll shrugged unhappily.

"I threw it on the fire before I realized what the letter was about," he said. "But there was no postmark, I do remember that much. Hyde must have shoved it through the letterbox himself before the household awoke this morning."

"And you don't know whether you should give it to the police or burn it," said Utterson. "To tell you the truth, Henry," he continued, rubbing his eyes with the back of his hand, "I don't know either. If you haven't any objections, I'll hang on to the letter and decide tomorrow what would be best."

"I would be very grateful if you did that, Gabriel," said Jekyll. "I... I seem to have lost all confidence in my own judgment."

"Tell me one more thing," said Utterson as he rose to his feet, putting the folded letter carefully into his breast pocket. "That confounded will of yours – it was Hyde who dictated its terms to you, wasn't it?"

Jekyll looked pale. "Yes. It was."

"I knew it!" exclaimed Utterson. "It was what I was afraid of! The scoundrel meant to murder you, in due course, and inherit everything you had. What on earth was the hold he had over you, Henry, that you agreed to draw up that infernal document?"

"That is behind me now," said Jekyll firmly. Although the voice was quiet, Utterson could see in the set of the doctor's jaw that there was no point in asking him anything more. The secret was one that Jekyll would take to his grave.

"I shall call on you tomorrow," Utterson said stiffly. "I'll tell you of any decision I make about this letter before I do anything else."

"Thank you, Gabriel," said Jekyll, sinking into the armchair and burying his face in his hands. "Thank you for... for everything."

That night Utterson asked Mr. Guest, his clerk, to come and have a drink with him before going home. Guest was a man whom Utterson trusted completely, and he didn't feel he was betraying any faith with Jekyll in asking the clerk to take a look at the letter.

Guest made a hobby out of studying handwriting, and it was possible he might notice something which Utterson had missed.

Briefly he recounted to Guest the circumstances that had brought the letter into his possession.

"There was one odd thing," he concluded. "As I was leaving Dr. Jekyll's house I asked Poole, the butler, if he had seen the person who left the letter, and he told me there had been no post for the house at all today. I pressed him about it, but he was quite insistent: there had been nothing."

"The letter could have been delivered through the door in Mitre Court," Guest observed.

"Yes," said Utterson slowly.

"I suppose that's probably the case. But the thought nags at the back of my mind that the letter might even have been written in the Cabinet itself. Hyde had a key to the place. Chances are he still does. Perhaps Jekyll made him write the letter before he fled – maybe my old friend was lying to me. A couple of years ago I would have trusted my life to the word of Henry Jekyll. It's a sad thing to admit that I'm no longer so certain." He sighed.

Guest took the letter and looked at it closely. "This writing is very distinctive," he said. "Rather *too* distinctive, if you see what I mean."

Utterson looked blank.

"As if it had been forged by someone who was trying to make the handwriting look as different as possible from his own," explained Guest. "It's something you can't do. If you want to produce handwriting that isn't like your own, the best thing is to change just a few things – the way you cross your 't's or dot your 'i's, for example. If you try to make it look entirely different, you almost certainly retain certain distinguishing marks that anyone interested in the subject will be able to recognize."

"Does that handwriting make you think of anyone in particular?" said Utterson, suddenly gripped by dread.

"I mightn't have noticed if we hadn't been talking about Jekyll," said Guest. "If I could perhaps make a comparison, to satisfy myself?"

Utterson went downstairs to his office and fetched a note that Jekyll had sent him some months earlier.

"Yes," said Guest slowly, carefully examining the two sheets side by side. "It's as I thought. Look here at the swash of the 's'. And the capital 'B' is almost identical."

He went on to point out some more similarities, but Utterson had already heard enough.

"This is an interesting exercise," he said. "But of course it cannot prove anything."

Guest, glancing up, saw the expression on the old lawyer's face and hurried to agree. "No proof that any court of law would accept," he said. "Yes, of course it wouldn't be sensible to spread my ideas on the subject around as I might all too easily be wrong. I suggest that we keep these... these suppositions to ourselves, Mr. Utterson."

"I had come to precisely the same conclusion myself," said the lawyer. "If we spoke about this to anyone else, an innocent man's name might well be brought into disrepute! That would be terrible!"

"Too, too terrible," murmured Guest. "Too terrible to contemplate."

But both men knew that they weren't deceiving themselves, and after the clerk had left, Utterson remained up for a long time, worrying and chewing at his nails.

"Henry Jekyll forging for a murderer!" he said over and over to himself. "What ghastliness would force him to do that?" And his mind conjured up images of frightful crimes.

What had Jekyll done?

The question dogged him for the next eight weeks.

Dr. Lanyon's Terror

Hyde looks around the dissecting room with a gleam of satisfaction in his eyes. It is so long since he has been here – how long, he cannot tell, but it seems to him as if it has been almost forever. He swears savagely, cursing the name of the man who has for so long kept him imprisoned in the cell of nonexistence: Dr. Henry Jekyll.

Then his mood changes abruptly, and there is a skip in his step as he goes up the stairs to the Cabinet. The wallpaper hides the door of a cupboard in the corner. He opens it and pulls out a gentleman's black dress suit, a dusty black top hat, a pair of scuffed black shoes, a dirty white shirt and a dilapidated black bow-tie. He fumbles a bit longer in the cupboard, seeking the walking stick that always used to be there, and then dimly recalls breaking it. He cackles as the memory becomes clearer. Who would have thought the old man to have so much blood in him?

Soon he is dressed. He looks at himself in the mirror over the fireplace, and is evidently very satisfied with what he sees. He feels so full of life. He finds some money – fifty or more pounds in notes – in his trouser pocket, and riffles through it gleefully. One of the very first things he must do tonight is buy himself a new walking stick; something a little stronger than the last one.

Coming back down into the dissecting room, he looks around him, and then giggles. There's the very thing! He picks up the metal stand from Jekyll's laboratory bench and hefts it in his hand. Its lead base is suitably heavy. He strips the clamps quickly off the upright shaft, and tests the stand for balance again. It won't be much use as a walking stick, of course, but in case he should feel a sudden, uncontrollable desire to *hit* someone...

He pauses a second, puzzled. Always before he has awoken to find an emptied beaker on the laboratory bench, but today there isn't one. It's not a matter of any importance, of course, but it's a variation from the routine and, as such, unsettling. He frowns a moment, then decides to forget the whole thing.

Hyde lets himself out into Mitre Court. It's very late at night and there doesn't seem to be anyone else around; even so, he shuts the door quietly behind him, for fear of attracting the attention of the servants in the main building.

As he finishes locking the door, a small tabby cat comes up and starts rubbing itself against his leg. He bends down to tickle it behind one ear, and it arches its neck backwards in pleasure, purring loudly. Putting down the laboratory stand carefully, he picks the cat up in both hands and holds it so that its yellow eyes are level with his own. He giggles again.

Then he clutches the cat to his face and bites out its throat.

"The master is not home," said Poole.

"But he *must* be home!" cried Utterson. "I have his invitation here in my hand!"

The butler abandoned his loftiness. "Dr. Jekyll has not been entirely himself recently, Mr. Utterson," he confided.

"He seemed healthy enough last Thursday, when I dined here with Lanyon," said Utterson. "At least let me in out of the rain, man!"

Poole stepped aside so that Utterson could come into the hall. "It's been just these past few days," said the butler. "He's hardly been in the house, day or night, and when we've seen him he's looked like he's kissed Death itself, he has. Most of his time he spends in the Cabinet, and how often he comes and goes from there through the Mitre Court door we have no idea. But I knocked at the Cabinet door just five minutes ago and there was no reply."

Utterson thought rapidly. Poole hadn't said the name, but it was clear he was thinking it: *Edward Hyde*. For the past two months Jekyll had seemed to be free of the loathsome man's malevolent influence, and had rejoined the social circle he had so long deserted, dining with friends, throwing parties, going to the theatre. But, from what Poole had just said, it sounded terribly as if Hyde were back, despite Jekyll's promise.

"Have you seen Mr. Hyde?" said Utterson.

"No, sir. Not a trace of him."

"Well, that's a relief." Utterson drew a hand across his brow.

"Although," he continued, "that's no guarantee he hasn't returned. He could just be taking more care to conceal himself."

"I'm afraid so, sir."

Utterson grunted. During these past two months, while the police had been searching for Hyde, the newspapers had been full of details about the evil little man's career of crime. No, "crime" wasn't really the right word. The things that he had done were characterized not so much by lawbreaking as by malice. He had enjoyed the creation of pain and misery. He was like a child who had never grown out of pulling the wings off flies, but had become an adult who liked pulling the limbs off cats and dogs – and even people. The police now thought he was responsible for at least six other murders in addition to that of Sir Danvers Carew; two of his victims had been hideously mutilated after death. Elsewhere there were broken lives, and people who would wear the scars inflicted by Edward Hyde for the rest of their days.

At nights, Utterson prayed to be forgiven for wishing for the news that Hyde was dead.

Utterson's mind went back to the forged letter. It still lay in his safe. After much thought, he had decided not to hand it over to the police. Now he wondered if he had been wise.

"Let's hope that Hyde hasn't come back to haunt us, eh, Poole?" he said, trying to sound cheerful.

"I hope not indeed, sir."

"Tell Dr. Jekyll I've called," added Utterson, turning to the door.

"I shall indeed, sir."

On the pavement Utterson mused for a moment or two. For the sake of his friendship with Jekyll, he had kept matters from the police for too long. It was time he confessed everything. It was his civic duty. If Jekyll had renewed his association with Hyde, then he had deliberately set himself outside the boundaries of friendship. If Jekyll were innocent, then the intervention of the police would be at worst an embarrassment. Utterson felt as if he had been wandering aimlessly around a maze these last few months, and that now a door had opened to show him the correct route to the heart of the problem.

Yes, he must go and see Inspector Newcomen. At the very least the detective would surely put some men around the house, with instructions to keep a specially close watch on the door in Mitre Court, in case Hyde did choose to come back. Utterson hailed a cab and asked the driver to take him to Strand Police Station.

Two hours later, Dr. Hastie Lanyon was deep in a book when his butler disturbed him.

"A hand-delivered letter, sir," said the man.

"At this time of night?" said Lanyon, taking it.

"I heard it land on the mat just a few moments ago," said the butler.

Lanyon tore open the letter and read it:

Dear Hastie,

I need to ask you to help me. I want you to do as I wish without asking any questions. Believe me, my reputation and probably my very life depend on your prompt assistance.

There are some drugs I need urgently from my house, but for reasons I cannot explain I cannot fetch them myself. By means of a message delivered not long before this one, I have instructed my butler, Poole, to call a locksmith to my house. I want you to go there and, with Poole and the locksmith, break open the door of my Cabinet. But you alone must go inside.

You will find a glass-fronted cabinet just to the left of the door. I think it is unlocked but, if it isn't, please break into it. The drugs I require are all in the fourth drawer from the top. Please bring away with you the entire drawer and its contents, and take them back to your house in Cavendish Square. If you act as soon as you receive this note, you should be home by eleven o'clock.

At midnight, a man will come to your house. Please be alone in your consulting room by that time. Give him the drawer and he will go. Your part in this whole miserable business will be over.

I know these requests will seem bizarre to you, but please be reassured that I have not lost my senses — or, at least, not in this respect. Should you decide you cannot agree to my requests, however, then, my dear Hastie, madness will be the very least of the things that I have to fear.

Your good friend, a man in need —

Henry Jekyll

"Jekyll must be crazy," muttered Lanyon under his breath. "I've never heard of such a..."

Yet Jekyll had been his old self of late — and Lanyon had known him for so many years.

He looked up at his butler. "Call me a cab," he said. "I have to go out for a while."

Barely a quarter of an hour later he was at Jekyll's house. He found that Poole and the locksmith, a burly fellow named Baldwin, were waiting for him, just as Jekyll's letter had said they would be. As the butler let him in, Lanyon had the uncomfortable sensation that someone was watching him, but when he turned around to look there was no one there except a uniformed constable strolling past on the other side of the street.

The door to the Cabinet was stronger than it looked. Lanyon had wondered why Jekyll should have gone to the trouble of hiring a locksmith when it would have been just as easy to break the door down, but as soon as he examined it he realized that the door was built so as to be virtually indestructible: two men with pickaxes might have been able to force a way in, but only by reducing the door to matchwood.

It took nearly an hour for Baldwin to open the lock, which was as well-made as the door. Lanyon kept glancing at his pocket-watch, fretting over the delay. At this rate he would be lucky to get home by eleven o'clock, and he began to worry about being in time for his mysterious midnight appointment with Jekyll's nameless associate.

Once the door was open, however, everything went very quickly. The glass-fronted chest that Jekyll had mentioned stood open, and it took Lanyon only moments to pull out the fourth drawer and wrap it up carefully in a sheet supplied by Poole. The cab, which he had kept waiting all this time, rattled him home briskly to Cavendish Square, and he was inside with the doors closed behind him just as the church clock began to toll eleven.

Once he had taken off his coat and gloves, he instructed the servants to go to bed and carried the drawer, still wrapped up, into his consulting room. Jekyll's letter hadn't actually forbidden him to look at the stuff in the drawer, and his curiosity was aroused.

He was disappointed. There were several bottles of different powders. He sniffed at these, hoping to be able to identify them, but, apart from guessing that one of them contained bicarbonate of soda among its ingredients, he had no idea what the chemicals could be. There was also a corked jar containing a clear, blood-red liquid, which moved sludgily as he turned the container around. He pulled out the cork and then instantly rammed it tightly back into place as the liquid's eye-watering fumes reached him. Once he could focus clearly again, he peered at the liquid warily through the glass of the jar. That single whiff of powerful fumes told him that the mixture probably contained phosphorus and ether, but obviously there were other a number of other substances in there as well.

Without subjecting the stuff to a full chemical analysis, he had no way of finding out what these were, but there could be no doubt that the mixture was poisonous.

The drawer also contained papers and a leather notebook. Lanyon opened it eagerly, recognizing it as Jekyll's notes of his experiments. Perhaps here he would find an explanation for his friend's frequently odd conduct over the past couple of years.

But he was disappointed once again. Page after page was filled with nothing but columns of dates, most of which had some cryptic comment beside them. "Double," said one. "Total failure!!!" said another. The first date was for nearly ten years ago; the last, with another "Total failure!!!" recorded beside it, was for just under a year ago.

After that the pages of the notebook were blank. It looked as if Jekyll had wasted nine years of his time on a series of experiments that had come to nothing.

Lanyon had learned very little from the contents of the drawer. But the fact that they seemed innocent disturbed him: why should Jekyll set up this cloak-and-dagger arrangement with him? He could just as easily have sent his nameless messenger to his own home to fetch the materials he needed. Come to that, why hadn't Jekyll done it himself?

After worrying away at these questions for a few minutes, Lanyon rummaged through a cabinet until he found his old army revolver and a few rounds of ammunition. As he loaded the gun he realized he didn't know whether it would still fire, or even whether it would blow up in his face. But, he reasoned, anyone threatening him wouldn't know that either.

Lanyon settled himself in the chair usually reserved for his patients. The drawer and its contents were hidden under the sheet on the table in front of him. The revolver was stuffed behind the chair's cushion.

He didn't have long to wait. As St. Gregory's sounded out midnight, there was a timid knock on the front door. Lanyon hauled himself to his feet and went to let Jekyll's messenger in.

He had hardly opened the door when a little man sprang in and slammed it shut behind him.

"Where is it?"

"In my consulting room, as Jekyll demanded," said Lanyon. "Why all the urgency?"

"Where is it? Where is it?"

The man shoved him aside and scampered through the door to the consulting room.

"Now just wait a minute!" said Lanyon angrily, as he followed. "I deserve some sort of an explanation! What the devil's going on?"

Coming into the light of the consulting room, he saw the visitor's face clearly for the first time, and before he could stop himself he recoiled. He had often seen faces twisted by the final stages of disease,

but he could not recall ever having seen anyone quite so... quite so *loathsome* before.

The man, who had been pacing agitatedly around the consulting room, paused mid-stride.

"You're quite right," he said. His rasping voice was sinister, but it was obvious he was doing his best to be polite.

"You're certainly owed that explanation, Hastie. But first – where is the drawer Dr. Jekyll asked you to fetch?"

Lanyon's eyes narrowed. He had never met this person before, yet the stranger had the impertinence to address him by his first name, as if they were close friends. Jekyll kept some odd company. Utterson had let slip, a few weeks ago, that old Henry had even been acquainted with that villain Hyde...

That villain Hyde! Who, according to all the newspaper reports, was a little man with an evil light in his eyes! Who moved quickly and jerkily, and who spoke in an unpleasant, rasping voice! *Who had slaughtered Sir Danvers Carew and had probably butchered six other people!*

"The drawer is here," said Lanyon, feeling his heart thumping inside his chest. He tugged the sheet back and, the moment Hyde's attention was distracted, plunged his hand down behind the cushion, grabbing his revolver. He yanked it up to point it at the little man, wishing his hand didn't shake so much.

Hyde froze. "What is this?"

"You can have the drawer once you tell me what's going on."

The man's face suddenly twisted with pain. There was a savage grinding noise, and Lanyon realized with horror that it came from Hyde's mouth: his jaw was gnashing in anguish. Hyde's hand went to his heart, and now his face was turning purple, his eyes wet with tears.

"F-f-for God's sake, Hastie!" he sobbed, his other hand clutching at the edge of the table.

Lanyon didn't know what to do. He could hardly just stand here and watch the wretched man die. At the same time, he didn't trust him: he wasn't going to lower the revolver.

"What do you need?" he said at last. "How can I help you?"

"A beaker!" screamed Hyde. "A moment to mix the compound!"

Still holding the revolver pointed at the visitor, Lanyon reached behind him to take an empty beaker from the shelf.

"Here," he said, putting it down on the table. Hyde grabbed it and, hands trembling feverishly, ripped the cork out of the jar containing the vile-smelling blood-red liquid. Lanyon took a step backward as a plume of white fumes rose, but they didn't seem to affect Hyde, who was already unscrewing the top of one of the bottles of powder.

The little man dribbled some of the liquid into the beaker Lanyon had given him. Even though his whole body was shaking with urgency, he poured carefully, watching the level of the liquid rise against the gradations etched into the beaker's side. Once he was satisfied that he had exactly the right amount, he recorked the jar and put it to one side. Lanyon could see he was having to exert an almost superhuman effort to keep his twitching limbs under control.

"Hastie," said Hyde. "I'll give you one warning. You can go out and close the door and see nothing of what happens next. I'll let myself out the back way, and no one will ever be any the wiser."

Hyde's teeth were clenched and his face was contorting with the effort of forming each tortuous word, but Lanyon could see he was determined to finish his speech.

"Or, if you insist," Hyde hissed, "you can stay in here and witness what happens next. You'll solve a mystery that has been troubling much of London... but it won't bring you much contentment. I cannot be held responsible for the consequences should you stay. I would advise you against it. But it's your own choice."

"I'll stay," said Lanyon, his voice quivering. "I don't trust you out of my sight."

Hyde put his head to one side. "Fair enough," he said. "But you've been warned."

As Lanyon watched, Hyde, working as carefully as before, tapped some of the powder into the beaker of red liquid. He swirled the beaker around, and the liquid turned blue. Again Lanyon sensed that Hyde was having to strain to maintain control of his body; that his limbs wanted to burst into explosive motion, but that his mind was keeping them in check. Hyde added a little more powder and swirled the beaker again; now the liquid was losing its sheen of blue and becoming a muddy brown. The little man grunted in satisfaction.

"A final warning, Hastie," he said. His face was now a truly alarming shade of purple, almost black. He was obviously in excruciating agony. Lanyon was rooted to the spot.

"Can't bear to tear yourself away, eh?" added Hyde with an attempt at a laugh. "Well, be it on your own head."

He gave the beaker one last shake and, before Lanyon could move to stop him, threw his head back and drained the liquid in a single gulp.

Then he shrieked as if his insides were being wrenched out. He clutched his throat and staggered backward, tripping over a stool and crashing to the floor. Lanyon stared in amazement. Hyde's eyes rolled up in their sockets and his head jerked from side to side as if an unseen hand were trying to twist it off his neck. His heels drummed on the thin consulting-room carpet.

How long this went on Lanyon couldn't guess. It could have been half a minute or half an hour. He turned away, unable to watch what he assumed was a ghastly and prolonged death agony. But, when at last the high screeching stopped, he could hear the man's ragged breathing. Then a voice, slightly hoarse but quite calm, as if merely remarking on the weather, said to him: "So now you know my little secret, eh, Hastie?"

Lanyon looked round. "Henry!"

"None other." Jekyll was picking himself up off the floor, moving warily and grimacing as if his joints were hurting him. "Dr. Henry Jekyll, until two years ago a respectable member of the medical profession, and now... this!"

Lanyon sank into the chair. "This is impossible!"

"Not impossible." Jekyll moved to sit down behind the desk, as if he were Dr. Lanyon and Lanyon his patient. "Just improbable."

"But..."

Jekyll held up a hand. "Now you know the truth, Hastie, and yet you know none of it. Let me explain. It's about time I was able to talk to someone about all that I've done. And who better to talk to than an old and dear friend?" He grimaced again. "Although we've had our ups and downs, hmm? Still... still, let me have my say."

Lanyon felt a cold sweat on his brow. He was not a young man, and in recent years his health had not been good. His heart was still pounding violently from the shock of what had happened. And what *had* happened? How had Jekyll substituted himself for the evil-faced man who had been here until moments ago?

Then he looked down at Jekyll's hands and recognized the cuff-links – the same ones Hyde had been wearing when he raised the beaker to his lips – and at last he had some glimmer of understanding.

"Hyde," he croaked. "Jekyll. You're both one and the same man!"

"Yes," said Jekyll sadly. "That's the truth of it."

"But... how?"

A rueful smile appeared on Jekyll's lips.

"A few years ago," he said, "you told me that my theories were insane. Well, you were right – and wrong. You were wrong because my theories were perfectly correct, *dreadfully* correct! You were right because, now, I can see that it was insane to follow

them as far as I did. Oh, I have done dreadful things in the name of science, Hastie!"

He put his hands to his face and began to weep.

Lanyon, his chest tight, said: "Tell me everything, Henry."

So, composing himself, Jekyll told him.

"Years ago, when I was still a young man and not long established as a doctor," said Jekyll, "I led a merry life. I had inherited enough money to keep me in comfort for the rest of my days, and I was also earning a fair income from my practice. When the last patient left each evening, I could either stay at home and read or I could go out on the town. What choice would any young man have made?

"So by day I was the sober, steady Dr. Jekyll, trusted by his patients and respected by his peers in the medical profession. And by night – ah, by night I was wild Henry, known in all the music halls and drinking dens of Whitechapel and Soho. My private life was one of wine, women and song. Nothing could have been more unlike the personality I presented to the world during surgery hours!

"The strain of leading this double life eventually became too much for me. I had to abandon either staid Dr. Jekyll or wild Henry, and of course it was my loose-living self that I dropped, throwing all my energies into the pursuit of science and into doing various charitable works, helping the poor where I could, and making gifts of money to several hospitals.

"But I couldn't just *forget* the way I'd been. And you see, Hastie, the whole business began to strike me as most peculiar. During those years I had been, in effect, *two quite different people*. If you'd seen prim Dr. Jekyll in the street, his umbrella neatly furled, beside wild Henry, with a drunken woman on each arm, you wouldn't have thought the two men were related, let alone the same person. I don't even know if the pair of them, if you'd introduced them to one another, would have had anything much to say to each other.

"So I began to ask myself some questions. Now that I was, or so it seemed, entirely Dr. Jekyll, where had wild Henry gone? Had he just been destroyed entirely, this other human being? I couldn't believe it. Or was he still living inside me, biding his time? That seemed altogether more likely. He was the other side of my coin. He was the rascally hell-raiser, while I was the pillar of society. While the pillar of society lived his life out as Dr. Jekyll, the hell-raiser slumbered.

"But I soon came to see that this picture wasn't completely correct. There were bits of wild Henry that showed in the character of Dr. Jekyll, and there had always been bits of Dr. Jekyll evident in wild Henry's personality – for wild Henry had never done anything vicious or spiteful... anything truly *wrong*, even if society might have strongly disapproved of his activities. Wild Henry had even done deeds of kindness, helping people with one hand while lifting a bottle to his lips with the other. So it wasn't a simple case of Jekyll being good and wild Henry being evil.

"Yet there was certainly more good than evil in Jekyll, and certainly more evil than good in wild Henry. They were, like the whole of me, a mixture. Although I appeared to the world at large to be just one person, in fact I was two: an evil person and a good one. It struck me that, if I could isolate the evil person from the good in some way, I might be able to eject the evil person from myself entirely. And I wasn't just thinking of myself.

"*Everyone*, unless they are a perfect saint (and I don't accept there are such paragons any more than you do, Hastie) *everyone*, I say, is made up of these two individuals: a good person and an evil one. How much happier would the world be if it were filled only with good persons! *Then* there might be perfect saints whom you and I could believe in!

"It was at about this time that I began to question the nature of the body. (This was the question I was asking, if you recall, when you broke off our friendship, Hastie. But I had been asking it of myself for years before then.) Our bodies seem to us firm and solid and, except as we age, unchanging. Our souls live in our bodies but, we think, do not affect them in any way. This struck me as implausible. If we come to live in a new house, we soon change it one way or the other, so that it better expresses our own character: Dr. Jekyll, for example, put grey, drab curtains in his windows, but wild Henry, if he had ever been allowed to have his way, would have replaced them with gaudy cloth. Why, then, should the soul be satisfied with the house – the body – in which it lived? Wouldn't it want to... change the curtains, as it were. And the paintwork. And perhaps even build a new bay window?

"In short, the soul would remodel the body in order to express itself more suitably.

"I can see you wanting to object, Hastie, and you are quite right to do so. We've all known beautiful women and handsome men with devils' hearts. But those lovely exteriors are, surely, part of their souls' treachery! And we've known hideous-looking people, ugly people, who are the kindest and finest human beings imaginable. But, in those instances, isn't it the case that their souls are splendid enough not to contain pride, not to need any outward display of prettiness?

"I began to experiment with various chemicals. Of course, I used those drugs only on myself – I knew how dangerous my research was becoming. And I discovered that, yes, I could alter my body. Just a little, and not for very long. If I'd published my results at that stage, Hastie, can you imagine how the scientific world would have hailed me? My name would have gone down in history as the greatest medical theorist of all time!

"But... but even the sober Dr. Jekyll was no saint. I kept the results to myself. Vanity drove me. I wanted to announce something much more spectacular to the world! All this time I had been continuing my parallel experimentation into the possibility of divorcing the evil person inside me from the good, and now it seemed that I would soon be able to bring together the two strands of research.

"It was a lot more difficult than I'd thought it would be. I was so close, and yet it took me several years of cautious, patient experimentation, changing the dosages by the tiniest of fractions here and the merest grain there. But at last, at last I triumphed!

"That was the foulest triumph a man has ever achieved, as I now know.

"I sat down one night – late, after the servants had gone to bed – and I mixed up the precise concoction

I required. I said a prayer, Hastie, if you can believe this, that I would use my knowledge wisely and for the benefit of humanity. I believed I was on the verge of saving the world.

"And then I drank the potion.

"Nothing happened for a minute or two, and I began to think that, in my excitement, I must have measured the ingredients wrongly. But then, all of a sudden, the changes were upon me.

"It was agony, Hastie – agony! That first time was the worst, and even the memory of it makes a scream of pain begin to rise in my throat. My teeth ground together as if they were going to wear each other away. The plates of my skull grew and shrank, their edges wrenching and tearing. My jaw seemed about to leap from its sockets. Every joint in my body seemed to be aflame. I really thought I was going to die. I prayed to be *allowed* to die.

"And then, slowly, the pain receded. I began to see the world clearly again – more clearly than I had ever seen it before. My senses were heightened extraordinarily. The air of the dissecting room, which if I'd noticed it at all before I'd have said was stuffy and rank, was now filled with all kinds of delightful scents: even the slight tang of decay from the sink's drain seemed to me to be a delicious, bracing smell. The tiniest sound sang to me. I felt I could have heard a sparrow in a distant, deserted glade... just like God Himself.

"And, most of all, I felt *life*, Hastie. I was a young man again! I could sense the throb of existence in every last cell of my body. My blood was no longer just blood – it was *wine*! The wine that the gods on Olympus drank!

"But what I had never known before was that life was not virtuous. It was not self-sacrificing. It did not believe in the merits of performing charitable works.

"In the terms that you and I – conscious human beings – use, *life was evil!*

"I wallowed in it! I danced in it! I was the wickedest person that ever lived! There wasn't a scrap of goodness in me! I was the master of the world, because I wasn't hampered by even the slightest trace of morality! I could do anything I liked, and already my mind was brimming with evil deeds!

"I grabbed a mirror and took a look at myself. I was smaller than Dr. Jekyll – poor, ineffectual Jekyll, whom I now despised. And I looked half his age. I was also, I persuaded myself, twice as handsome – and, even if I weren't, what did it matter when I had the undiluted power to make sure that everybody thought me so?

"But then I paused. The man I had become was far from lacking in cunning. Lesser creatures the rest of the world might be, but they could still, because of their numbers, overpower and hang me. I couldn't just commit all the acts of gleeful wickedness I wanted to in the full gaze of the world!

"I needed somewhere to hide. In a moment I saw the answer: where better to hide myself than behind

the mask of that respected, boring, hideously dreary pillar of society, Dr. Henry Jekyll?

"I mixed up a beakerful of potion again. It had worked one way. Would it work the other? I drank it down before I could have a chance to think. And it did work! The pains were almost as bad as before, but this time I luxuriated in them. For isn't pain one of the purest expressions of *life* there is? Long moments passed before the sweet agony ebbed away...

"And when I looked in the mirror again, there was Henry Jekyll."

Jekyll stopped speaking.

There was a long silence before Dr. Lanyon coughed. The noise seemed to startle Jekyll out of a trance.

"That was the first time I encountered Edward Hyde," he said. "I called him 'Hyde' because, of course..."

"Yes," said Lanyon. "I understood that. Because he had to hide. Jekyll," he continued, shifting in his seat.

"I think you've told me quite enough – far more than I ever wished to hear. I'd be grateful if you went now; if you left this house and never returned again." Lanyon picked up his spectacles from where they had fallen, unnoticed, into his lap, and settled them back on his nose.

"Do you know 'The Rime of the Ancient Mariner', Hastie?" said Jekyll quietly. "The poem by Coleridge? Once the Ancient Mariner had started to tell his story, there was no way it could be stopped until it was finished. I'm like the Ancient Mariner, Hastie... but my story is a longer one, and far more frightful than his."

And, as Lanyon sat powerless to move, Jekyll proceeded to tell him all the hideous things that Hyde had done.

Back to the Cabinet

Several days later, Lanyon accepted the fact that he was dying. He had not been a well man before that dreadful night when Edward Hyde had come to his house. What Henry Jekyll had told him of Hyde's doings had been so ghastly, so inconceivably vile, that it had sounded his death-knell. His body no longer wished to live, if human life could encompass such loathsomeness. All the police estimates of Hyde's crimes were woefully inadequate: the man had murdered dozens of times. And the things he had done to his victims before they died...

Hastie Lanyon wanted no further part of this world. He looked forward to dying. He didn't care if Heaven awaited him or emptiness: even emptiness would be better than this existence. And anyway, what Jekyll had told him had shaken his faith that there might be a heaven.

But, before he could depart this life, he had certain responsibilities to the living. He had promised Jekyll, before the man had slipped away into the pink-orange light of dawn, that he would never reveal his secret as long as they both should live. He felt that the circumstances were such that he really should break

his promise immediately, but he couldn't bring himself to do so. What he *could* do, however, was to leave an account to be read by others after they had both died.

He summoned his failing energies one evening and wrote everything down. Reliving it was almost as painful as listening to it the first time had been, but he persevered. How much worse must it be, he thought, for Jekyll, knowing not just that these repulsive deeds had been done, but that it was his own flesh and blood, his own other self, that had done them? Hastie Lanyon was not an especially forgiving man, but he forgave Henry Jekyll mostly because of the mental torture he knew the man must be suffering every moment of every day.

For Jekyll had told him one more thing, just before vanishing into the dawn. Just over two months before, he had sworn to himself never to touch the potion again; to let Edward Hyde be dead forever.

And, for nearly eight weeks, his restraint had been enough. Edward Hyde had, apparently, disappeared, and Henry Jekyll was free to live his own life.

But Hyde, like wild Henry before him, had only been sleeping. One night, without any need for the potion, he had broken through again, throwing off Jekyll like someone throwing off an overcoat. It had taken all the efforts of the tiny piece of Jekyll that survived with Hyde to drag the little man back to the Cabinet and force him to mix another dose of potion, and drink it. Since then, at any moment, Hyde could suddenly reappear.

It could happen in the street, when Jekyll was out walking. It might happen at the theatre, if Jekyll were fool enough to go there. It might happen *anywhere*. So Jekyll kept himself locked away in his Cabinet, conserving his energies so that, whenever Hyde thrust himself back into existence, the doctor might force him to drink more potion. But the night before Jekyll had come to Lanyon's house in Cavendish Square, the doctor hadn't been able to restrain his other self. Hyde had gone drinking and carousing all over Whitechapel in a binge that had lasted through the next day. When at last Jekyll had been able to exercise some command over his other self, he had found the police secretly guarding his home. He knew that he couldn't go there without being arrested on sight, so he wrote two letters, one to Lanyon and one to Poole, and gave an urchin a halfpenny to deliver them both.

But Jekyll was uncertain he would be able to bring even this much control to bear another time. And it could be no more than a matter of days, surely, until Hyde battled his way into existence again, perhaps, this time, for good. Especially since, during the two months that Hyde had been banished from the world, the pharmacist who had supplied Jekyll with the drugs he needed for the potion had gone out of business. Other pharmacies supplied what seemed to be exactly the same, but the mixture was not absolutely identical. And the potion made from these drugs didn't work.

Jekyll no longer had the means to banish Hyde.

The envelope was among the rest of the morning's letters, and at first Gabriel Utterson paid it no special attention. It was only when he was about to slit it open that he noticed the envelope was unusually bulky. Inside was a note and another sealed envelope. The note said:

Gabriel,

The enclosed letter is for you, but do not read it yet. I have given my word to Dr. Henry Jekyll — and how I curse the day I ever heard that name! — that what it contains shall not be revealed to the world until he and I are dead.

I have issued instructions to my butler to send this to you after my death, which, as I write, I do not expect to be more than a few days away. I hope and pray that the death of Dr. Henry Jekyll will not be much longer postponed than my own.

Harsh words to use of an old friend? I trust you will understand and share my views when you have read my letter.

Yours,
Hastie Lanyon

Utterson put the sealed envelope away in his safe before he allowed his grief to flood over him; grief over Lanyon's death, and over the way in which, as he thought, scientific rivalry between two of his friends had descended so suddenly into such bitter hatred.

He cried like an infant.

After Lanyon's funeral, held on a bleak day a week later, Utterson hurried home to his dinner. Sleet had tormented the mourners as they stood around the graveside, and steam rose from his damp trouser-legs as he ate. Usually after a funeral Utterson felt his heart lighten, as if his soul recognized that the burial marked some official end to mourning, but this time he remained heavy-spirited. The matter of Jekyll was still nagging away at the back of his mind.

He was startled, though in a way only half-surprised, when Molyneaux interrupted to tell him that Dr. Jekyll's butler, Poole, had called, and was waiting for him in the hall. Utterson put his knife and fork to one side and, still wiping his lips with his napkin, hurried downstairs to meet the elderly servant.

"What's the matter?" he said at once. "What's happened to Jekyll? It must be something serious for him to have sent you out on a vile night like this."

"He didn't send me, Mr. Utterson," said Poole nervously. "I came of my own accord." Now this *did* surprise the lawyer. "But it is about the master," continued Poole. "You see, sir, I'm frightened for him. I'm frightened *of* him, as well. We all are — all us servants. We've taken as much as we can, and then a bit more, and now we've just had enough. So, as you're the only friend the master has left, I thought I should come to you."

Utterson groaned. "Tell me what's wrong this time, Poole."

"He's locked himself away in his Cabinet these past eight days, and he won't come out for all our pleadings. We leave food outside on a tray by the door, and sometimes it's taken though most often it's not, but we never see him. And sometimes the voice that shouts back at us doesn't sound like his voice at all, but like the other gentleman's. And once or twice I swear I've heard them both in there, arguing as if the whole world's at stake. And sometimes..."

"Enough," said Utterson, raising a palm to stem the flow of words. "Can't you see what's going on through the window?"

"He's put a cloth over it," replied Poole, his hands twitching anxiously. "We can't see anything. All we can do is hear, and that's bad enough."

"It might just be a difficult experiment," began Utterson.

"That's what we thought at first. He's had us scouring all the chemists in London for some compound he needs – we must have brought it to him a hundred times or more. But each time it seems it isn't good enough. For minutes after it's gone from where we leave it outside the door, we hear him moaning and yelling, as if Satan himself were teasing his soul. We're at our wits' end!"

Looking into Poole's eyes, Utterson believed it. "I'd better come to the house," he said.

Poole's face lit up. "Would you, sir?" he said. "We were hoping you would say that. Perhaps he might come out for you, his dearest friend, where he's ignored all our appeals."

"Let's hope so," said Utterson glumly. But in his heart he wasn't optimistic. He sensed that the end of the strange story of Dr. Henry Jekyll was in sight.

"Molyneaux!" he called. "My coat!"

It was a wild night. A pale moon lay on her back as though the wind had tilted her. The wind made talking difficult, and seemed to have swept the streets bare of pedestrians, for Utterson thought he had never seen this part of London so deserted. He wished it weren't so, for he felt a desperate need for the presence of other human beings; his mind was full of a crushing presentiment of calamity.

When he and Poole reached the door of Jekyll's house, they paused a moment, as if to gather strengh for what they might find inside. Across the street, the howling wind was forcing the thin trees of the garden in the middle of the square to lash themselves against the railings. It was not a reassuring sight.

"Here goes, then," said Utterson dourly.

"Here goes, indeed," said Poole. "May God be with us."

"Amen."

The other servants had chained the door, and opened it only when Poole shouted his name through the letterbox. Inside, Utterson found all of Jekyll's staff huddled together. When they saw him, a housemaid began to weep shrilly, and the cook came running forward as if to take him in her arms.

"Stop this at once!" the laywer snapped. "What would your master say if he could see you like this?"

"You must forgive them, sir" said Poole quietly. "They're terrified." Then, not aware of any contradiction, he bellowed at the housemaid to shut up, threatening to fire her that very night if she didn't control herself.

"Let's get this over with as quickly as possible," said Utterson when the butler had calmed down. It was obvious to him that Poole was not far short of cracking. *And you could say the same about me*, thought Utterson grimly.

The two men, with some of the servants trailing behind them, went through the house and across the back yard to the dissecting room door. In the enclosed space of the yard the wind seemed like a living thing, dancing and capering and pulling at the men's coats. Utterson looked up and saw thin, shredded clouds chasing each other across the crooked smile of the moon.

"Let's get this over with," he said again. "Knock at the door, man."

Poole obeyed.

The door of the dissecting room swung open. Inside was blackness. Poole, clearly terrified, would have fallen down the steps if Utterson had not caught his arm to steady him.

"It's the first time in over a week it's been unlocked," whispered the butler. "He had a brand-new lock fitted after Dr. Lanyon was here, and he kept the only key." He hesitated, then added: "I... I dread to go in there, sir."

Utterson found himself stuttering with fear. "T-t-to tell you the truth," he said, "so do I."

"But we must," said Poole. Gesturing to the others to keep their distance, he held out a candle. The lawyer cupped his hands around the wick, and Poole lit it. Then the two men advanced, step by trembling step, into the dissecting room.

As soon as they were inside, a blanket of silence descended on them. It was as if the windswept night outside were a hundred miles away. The dim light of the candle seemed pitifully weak. The surgical theatre seemed huge, and somehow its shadows seemed all the wrong shape.

Poole lifted the candle high above him. Utterson could make out the laboratory bench, cluttered with equipment. Boxes and papers lay everywhere on the floor. In the corner he could see the bulk of the electricity-generating machine: to his seething mind it looked as it were crouching, waiting to pounce on the intruders.

"I can't see him," he said at last. His voice sounded hoarse, and he cleared his throat self-consciously. "Can you?"

Before Poole could answer there was a low moan, and both men started.

"What was that?" whispered Utterson.

Poole swallowed loudly. "It came from the Cabinet, sir," he said. "I think." He nodded towards the steps and the door at the far end of the theatre. "In there."

Picking their way with difficulty through the darkness across the littered floor, the men crept to the foot of the Cabinet's steps. They shrugged at each other. What next?

"It's my duty, sir," whispered Poole. He climbed the steps reluctantly, clearly ready to bolt at any instant, and quietly knocked.

Once. Twice.

Again that moan from within, then a low voice. "Go away."

"It's Mr. Utterson here to see you," said Poole loudly. "Mr. Utterson the lawyer."

"Tell him to go away as well," shouted the voice. "I cannot see anyone." And then it began to sob.

Poole tugged the lawyer away from the door to the far side of the theatre. Through the open door to the yard, Utterson could see the servants' anxious faces, but again there was that feeling that they were a great distance away.

"Tell me," demanded Poole urgently, "was that my master's voice?"

"It seemed... very much changed," answered Utterson slowly. He felt his face grow pale.

"*Changed!*" said Poole, with a snort. "I've been twenty years in my master's service. Do you think I wouldn't know his voice? Sir, that was not him!"

"Then who was it?" hissed Utterson, though in his heart of hearts he knew the answer. Even so, he tried to find some other explanation. "Perhaps he's suffering from one of those terrible diseases that punish the body so dreadfully that the voice is changed entirely. No wonder he sends you and the others out to scour the local pharmacies for the drug he needs to cure himself! He recognizes his own illness, and seeks to..."

"That was not his voice," said Poole, flatly.

"Then," said Utterson after a long pause, "then we must find out whose voice it was. We must break down the door."

"There's a fire-axe on the wall, sir," said Poole. He turned to the servants outside. "One of you go and fetch the poker from the kitchen for Mr. Utterson," he called.

Utterson should have felt more confident with the heavy poker in his hand, but he didn't. He was aware of Poole instructing a footman to go around to the door in Mitre Court and guard it, but his thoughts were elsewhere. Behind the Cabinet's red door, he

416

was certain, he and Poole would find Henry Jekyll, but whether the doctor was dead or alive was something he couldn't guess. And what of the other voice that had replied to them? The voice that Poole insisted was not his master's was one that Utterson was certain he recognized from another cold night, long ago, when he had laid his hand on the shoulder of a little man at the dissecting room's rear door.

"Hyde," he breathed.

Poole heard him. "I think so too, sir," he said.

The two men stood looking at each other. "I've sent the knife-boy to fetch the police, but I think my master would prefer it if we were the ones who..."

His voice trailed away, but Utterson knew what the butler was thinking. A police siege would be splashed all over the newspapers tomorrow and Jekyll would not wish it. Better, even if they found the man dead, not to let his name be dragged through the gutter like that.

"I agree," he said. "I wish I didn't."

Poole fetched the fire-axe from its hook on the wall. The two men once again stole across the floor to the base of the steps leading up to the Cabinet.

Utterson touched Poole's arm, and nodded to the man to keep silent.

"Jekyll!" he shouted. "It's me! Utterson! I demand to see you at once!"

"Go away!" shrieked the voice from behind the door.

Hyde's voice. The lawyer was sure of it now, but he tried one last time.

"I warn you, Jekyll, that if you do not open this door we will break it down! Let us in!" He took the candle from the butler's shaking hand.

"Utterson!" cried the voice. "For God's sake have mercy."

The lawyer could bear it no longer. "That's Hyde," he shouted. "Smash the lock, Poole! Hurry!"

The butler swung the axe. The crash sounded like thunder in the dissecting room. The door jumped on its hinges. Wood splintered. From beyond the door there was a piercing scream of raw animal terror.

"Again!" yelled Utterson.

Another crash. Another scream. The door held. Poole cursed.

"Again!" bellowed the lawyer. The head of the axe caught in the wood of the door, just above the lock, and Poole tugged to work it free.

"No! No! No!" came Hyde's voice.

And then there was a dreadful silence except for Poole's gasps and the squeak as the axe pulled clear.

"Wait," said Utterson. He didn't know why.

They stayed motionless, both of them breathing heavily. From the other side of the door there was a terrible, strained, agonized sigh and the noise of something heavy falling to the floor.

Utterson found there were tears in his eyes. "I think it's over," he said quietly. "One more blow of your axe should let us in, Poole."

"I don't like to think of what we shall find, sir," said the butler, hefting the axe uneasily as if reluctant to use it.

"Nevertheless," said Utterson, "we must go in."

"We must," agreed Poole, and once again he swung the axe.

The lock broke and the door fell askew. Jumping ahead of the butler, Utterson pushed it open with his shoulder.

At first glance there seemed nothing wrong. A fire was burning in the hearth, and tables and chairs were placed neatly around. Two of the drawers of the desk were open and some papers had fallen to the floor, as if someone had been searching through them, hopelessly, time after time, hunting for something that wasn't there – but otherwise, apart from a picture hanging crooked on the wall, the room was as tidy as if it had been prepared for a tea party.

Except for the body that lay face down and horribly twisted in the middle of the floor.

Utterson, with Poole at his shoulder, ran to it. As he knelt down beside the body, the limbs gave one final convulsion and were still. Utterson clutched at the wrist, trying to feel a pulse, but there was nothing.

"Dead," he said bitterly.

"Yes, sir," said Poole, seemingly calm again now that the worst had been revealed. "But *who's* dead?"

Jekyll's Last Letter

Utterson never forgot what happened next. Still kneeling, he looked up at Poole, then looked down again. *I don't want to do this!* his mind screamed at him. Ignoring it, he reached out and gently rolled the body over.

The face staring glassily towards the ceiling was contorted as if in fear of the very Devil himself. There was purple froth around its lips, and the eyes seemed almost to have leaped from their sockets.

But it was unmistakably the face of Edward Hyde. *Then where was Henry Jekyll?*

Much, much later Gabriel Utterson sat behind his desk in his own office, looking in horror at the three letters that lay in front of him. The first was very short. Poole had found it on the doctor's desk, and wordlessly passed it to the lawyer. It read:

My dear Gabriel,

When you have this in your hands, I will have disappeared — in one way or another. I do not know exactly what is going to happen to me, but all my instincts tell me

that the end is sure and that it cannot be far away.
Although my body may, in terribly different form, still
walk this earth, you may be certain, Gabriel, that your old
and undeserving friend Henry Jekyll will be dead.

Hastie Lanyon told me he had sent you a letter detailing
all that happened between him and myself the other night.
Read it, and then read the narrative you will find in the
bottom left-hand drawer of my desk in the Cabinet. I fear
I am asking you to do a lot of reading, dear friend! Yet I
hope you will come to understand that this sorry individual
is no demon wallowing in wickedness, but instead a man who,
though blinded perhaps by vanity, sought only to bring
benefit to the world. That it should have come to this is, I
believe you will agree, a matter for all of our griefs.

But you yourself must judge your most respectful and
admiring of acquaintances,

Henry Jekyll

422

Utterson turned over the two other documents on the desk yet again. He had read both of them twice, and had no wish to do so again. The whole terrible truth about Dr. Jekyll and Mr. Hyde was set out in them. Of how the doctor, seeking glory where he could have sought only knowledge, had kept everything to himself until it was too catastrophically late. And of how he had become addicted to the *life* he gained whenever he walked the world in the guise of Hyde – the other person, the one made up from the evil that dwelled within Jekyll. Yes, Jekyll had become *addicted*, there was no other word for it, to the sense of freedom he had when he threw off the shackles of responsiblity towards others and allowed himself to do exactly what he wanted.

Utterson mused sadly. The trouble was that no one could do exactly what they wanted, and only a fool would try. People had to live with each other. They had to discover the much greater pleasures that came from helping one another. Sir Danvers Carew had had it right: he had devoted much of himself to improving the lives of the poor, and even as he died on that cold pavement down by the river, with the cruel blows of Hyde's heavy stick raining down on his head, he must have known the true happiness of having spent his life well.

The lawyer looked back over his own actions of the past months, and found much to criticize. He had been too much concerned with public appearances, too little with the good of his fellow human beings. He should have told the police at once of the connection between Dr. Jekyll and Mr. Hyde, not held back hoping that the whole affair could be swept under the carpet and forgotten about; had he done so, perhaps Jekyll and several murdered innocents would still be alive. Their lost lives were, in part, Utterson's own fault. Evils didn't just go away because you wanted them to. You had to work to get rid of them.

For Jekyll, he was surprised to discover, he felt nothing at all – no compassion, no grief, not even any hatred. Just nothing. For a time he had thought that Jekyll was a good man lured into wickedness by circumstances. Then he had thought him a fool.

But Jekyll could have stopped everything before it had properly begun. He could have asked his friends for help. Instead, fascinated by his creation, he had played with it, heedless of the consequences, until it had become too great for him. Until *it* was playing with *him*.

It wasn't just the body of Edward Hyde – or Henry Jekyll – that had died last night, Utterson realized, but Jekyll himself and everything that Utterson had ever liked or admired about him. For the man was dead in Utterson's heart.

Grunting at the pains in his stiff old joints, the lawyer heaved himself to his feet. He picked up the three letters, glanced at them one last time, then very deliberately fed them to the fire. It took some time before the last of the pages crumbled to ash, but Utterson was patient.

Then, dusting his hands, he went upstairs to bed.

Novels and Movies about Jekyll and Hyde

The book you have just read is a complete retelling of Robert Louis Stevenson's original story. To make the story easier to read, there have been a few minor changes, though these do not affect the overall plot. This is not the first time another writer has sought a new approach to the story or investigated similar themes. Several novels and movies have put their own interpretations on the story. Here are some of them.

Novels and stories

The Picture of Dorian Gray (1891) by Oscar Wilde, tells a story different from Stevenson's, but the basic idea is rather similar. Dorian Gray is a man who stays looking youthful and innocent while leading a life of excess and cruelty. But many people are taken in by his good looks and charm because he never appears to grow any older and remains physically unaffected by his lifestyle. Instead, all these changes appear on a portrait of him painted years before, which he keeps locked away. When people finally discover the portrait, they realize that the smiling face of Dorian Gray in fact conceals a despicably evil man.

The Man who Saw the Devil (1934), by James Corbett, returns to Stevenson's idea of one man living a double life, but in this case neither of the two personalities knows about the existence of the other.

Methinks the Lady (1945), by S. Guy Endore, concerns a woman who has Jekyll-and-Hyde characteristics. It gives a psychoanalytical explanation for this sort of situation, looking at the mind of the victim and what causes her behaviour.

The Dark Other (1950), by the U.S. science-fiction writer Stanley G. Weinbau, once again explores the situation in terms of people's understanding of psychology in the 1940s.

In *The Trial of John and Henry Norton* (1973), by Roland Puccetti, surgeons cut the link between the two lobes of a man's brain, and each lobe becomes in effect a separate person. One of the Nortons commits murder but, because the two share the same body, they have to be tried together.

Dr. Jekyll and Mr. Holmes (1979), by Loren D. Estleman, features Sherlock Holmes investigating the case of Dr. Jekyll.

Jekyll, Alias Hyde (1988), by Donald Thomas, is a detective story. Inspector Swain and Sergeant Lumley pursue the killer of Sir Danvers Carew and in the end find a perfectly rational explanation for how two men might seem to share a single body.

Two Women of London: The Strange Case of Ms. Jekyll and Mrs. Hyde (1989), by Emma Tennant, is a feminized version of the story.

The Jekyll Legacy (1990), by Robert Bloch and Andre Norton, is a continuation of Stevenson's story.

Mary Reilly (1990), by Valerie Martin, tells the whole story from the point of view of a maid working in Dr. Jekyll's house, and coming to love him.

If you want to find out more about all these different retellings of the story, you could try *The Definitive Dr. Jekyll and Mr. Hyde Companion* (1983), by H.M. Geduld.

Movies

The earliest surviving movie of the story was made in 1910 by the Danish director August Blom, though some film historians claim that there was an earlier film, made in America in 1908, which is now lost. The first really successful version was made in 1920 and starred John Barrymore as both Jekyll and Hyde: some critics say this silent film, with its special effects and fine acting, is the best film version of the story. Another lost version is *Der Januskopf* (1920) by the German director F. W. Murnau, who made the great Dracula movie *Nosferatu*.

However, the version usually regarded as the classic is *Dr. Jekyll and Mr. Hyde,* released in 1931. Directed by Rouben Mamoulian, it stars Fredric March (in an award-winning performance) as the two characters. It is available on video and is still sometimes shown on television even today.

Another movie of the story was made in 1941, again called *Dr. Jekyll and Mr. Hyde*, and directed by Victor Fleming. This had a star-filled cast, including Spencer Tracy, Ingrid Bergman and Lana Turner, but it was not a great success. After this, more and more film-makers began to deviate from the original plot, using the names Jekyll and Hyde more as a shorthand for a horror plot about a villain with a hidden life than as a reference to Stevenson's book. Further spin-offs included *Son of Dr. Jekyll* (1951) and *Daughter of Dr. Jekyll* (1957). In 1960 the Hammer studio released *The Two Faces of Dr. Jekyll* (also called *House of Fright* and *Jekyll's Inferno*). Directed by Terence Fisher and starring Christopher Lee and David Kossoff, it is probably the first modern horror film to use the story – though again, much changed from Stevenson's original.

The story was also the source of a number of film comedies. One of the earliest is the Tom and Jerry cartoon *Dr. Jekyll and Mr. Mouse* (1948), which was nominated for an Oscar. *Abbott and Costello Meet Dr. Jekyll and Mr. Hyde* (1954) takes the comedy duo to London, where they hunt down the "monster", who is played by Boris Karloff. *The Nutty Professor* (1963) updates the story to set it on a U.S. university campus. Jerry Lewis plays both Professor Kelp and Buddy Love – the Jekyll and Hyde figures.

Another movie version of the original story appeared in 1968, followed in 1971 by a slightly gory version called *I, Monster*. Strangely, in this later movie, some of the characters' names were changed: Dr. Jekyll becomes Dr. Marlowe and Edward Hyde becomes Edward Blake (both roles are played by Christopher Lee); yet Utterson, Lanyon and the young Richard Enfield appear under their own names.

Dr. Jekyll and Sister Hyde (1971) has the additional twist that Jekyll, on swallowing the potion, turns not into another man but into an evil woman. The two starring actors, Ralph Bates and Martine Beswick, look just like male and female counterparts of a single person, without looking exactly the same.

A French version of the story, *The Strange Case of Dr. Jekyll and Miss Osbourne* (1981), starts with a girl being murdered when she arrives at Dr. Jekyll's house, and proceeds from there. This film has been released under a number of different titles, including *Bloodbath of Dr. Jekyll* and *The Blood of Dr. Jekyll*.

Jekyll and Hyde – Together Again (1982) updates the story, setting it in a modern U.S. hospital. Like *The Nutty Professor,* this is a comedy.

More traditional are *The Jekyll Experiment* (1983) and *Dr. Jekyll and Mr. Hyde* (1986), the latter an Australian animated movie made for television. *Edge of Sanity* (1988), a French movie starring Anthony Perkins (star of Hitchcock's *Psycho*), mixes up Jekyll, Hyde and Jack the Ripper. It's a scary film, but again the plot is rather different from the original. *Mary Reilly* (1995) is a film version of the book by Valerie Martin (see page 140). A remake of *The Nutty*

Professor (1996), based on Jerry Lewis's original screenplay and starring Eddie Murphy, was followed by a sequel, *The Nutty Professor II*, in 2000.